BAD DAY ON THE BEACH

At last, the sheriff's Suburban plowed up the beach, leaving a thick tread in the sa̶ ̶ ̶ ̶ed frantically and pulled my hoodie closer ̶ ̶ ̶ ̶ ̶ morning seemed to have somehow ̶ ̶ ̶ ̶

Th̶ ̶ ̶ ̶ ̶ ̶ ̶ut, and a man in his ̶ ̶ ̶ ̶ ̶ ̶ ̶ ̶ d at the temples and ̶ ̶ ̶ ̶ ̶ ̶ ̶ ̶ ̶ ̶ ̶ m, approached. The star-s̶ ̶ ̶ ̶ ̶ ̶ ̶ ̶ ̶ki shirt flashed in the morning lig̶ ̶ ̶ ̶ ̶ ̶ s clouds covered the sun.

"̶ ̶ ̶ ̶ ck Koppen," he said.

"He s over there." I pointed to the rocks, the tide now far enough out to have exposed the body fully. The sheriff stepped on the rocks, then without changing his expression, muttered a few words into his radio before turning to me.

"Help me turn him over," he said.

"Me? I—"

He'd already leapt down from the rocks and knelt at the body's side. "If there's a chance he's alive, I'll need your help."

I gulped and crawled over the rocks but kept a few feet away from the body. Instinct told me there was no reviving him. The sheriff laid a hand on the body's neck, then shook his head. Gently, with one hand on a shoulder and another on a hip, he rolled the body faceup.

My breath froze in my throat, but I couldn't look away. The blood in my ears roared like the surf. The dead man couldn't have been much older than I—late twenties or maybe thirty. He wore a sand-incrusted T-shirt and jeans, but his feet were bare. His curly brown hair stuck to his skull, and tattoos formed sleeves on his arms. What seared me deepest were his eyes. Wide open and blue. That, and the three-inch gash in his chest . . .

Blown Away

clover tate

BERKLEY PRIME CRIME
New York

BERKLEY PRIME CRIME
Published by Berkley
An imprint of Penguin Random House LLC
375 Hudson Street, New York, New York 10014

ISBN: 9780425283547

First Edition: FEBRUARY 2017

Printed in the United States of America
1   3   5   7   9   10   8   6   4   2

Cover art and design by Sandra Chiu.
Book design by Kristin del Rosario.

For my father,
whom I can always count on for encouragement
and good advice no matter what crazy scheme I attempt.

acknowledgments

Thank you to editors Julie Mianecki and Allison Janice for their expertise and good natures. To my agent, John Talbot, thank you for your insight and advice. I owe cozy author extraordinaire Kate Dyer-Seeley a big thanks, too, for her encouragement.

My critique group—Cindy Brown, Christine Finlayson, Doug Levin, Dave Lewis, Ann Littlewood, and Marilyn McFarlane—were instrumental hand-holders and plot sharpeners during the writing process. As always, I'm grateful.

Finally, Rich Durant generously showed me around his workshop and walked me through the kite-making process, coming up with at least a dozen ways to kill someone with the tools at hand. Thanks, Rich. You'll recognize the inspiration you provided, especially toward the book's end.

chapter one

THE FIRST RULE ABOUT FLYING KITES IS THAT WHEN THE wind lifts them skyward, you give them line, not reel them in.

That's why I winced when I heard the familiar rattle of my parents' VW bus in the driveway. I'd moved from Portland to Rock Point, on Oregon's coast, to open a kite shop, and, yes, escape their overbearing attention. At twenty-eight, I'd had enough parenting.

My best friend—and, as of that day, roommate— Avery left the box of art supplies she was helping me unpack and crossed to the living room window. "Emmy, it's your mom and dad," she said. "Looks like they brought the dog, too."

I moaned. "Can't they give me at least a week before they start interfering again?"

But Avery was already at the door, letting in my mother,

whose enthusiastic greetings competed with noise of the crashing surf from the beach below.

"Oh, Avery, it's so nice to see you again. I can't believe we haven't been out to your place since your parents passed away. Emmy *would* have to move when Mercury is in retrograde. That can never go well. But, did she—"

"Mom," I said, and stepped up for a hug mostly to slow her down but also because, well, she was my mother, and despite her smothering, I did love her. "Let me take that bag." I relieved her of a grocery sack undoubtedly loaded with her idea of a housewarming gift, which could be anything from a raw-food casserole to a Chinese fountain meant to improve feng shui.

Bear, the family Australian shepherd, wedged his way in the front door with my father. He squirmed at my feet, wanting to jump up, and I had to laugh. "Come here, boy." I scratched him between the ears before he darted to the bedroom, where Avery's friend, Dave, was putting together my bed frame.

My mother lifted something from the bag—yep, a casserole—and set it down when Dave emerged from the bedroom. She dropped the bag immediately and swept toward him, hand extended. "You must be Avery's boyfriend. I'm Deb, Emmy's mom."

Avery's boyfriend, huh? My gaze passed from Avery, who was nonplussed, to Dave, who'd colored a bit, although it was hard to tell under his close-cut beard. It seemed to be common knowledge that Dave had a thing for Avery. Common knowledge to everyone except Avery, that is. Dave owned a kayak shop in town, but most days at lunch you could find him at Avery's coffee shop, the Brew House, or at the glorious, if run-down, beach house we lived in, finding something to help her fix.

"Deb, I'd like you to meet my friend Dave," Avery said. "He's helping get Emmy settled in."

"Have a seat," I said to my parents, and gestured to the sofa. I took an armchair, and Bear trotted over to put his head on my knee. His ice blue eyes stared from his merled face. How I loved that dog. Leaving Portland had been long overdue, but I'd miss my regular visits with Bear. "I see you brought food."

"Gluten-free, vegan casserole," Mom said. "And I made you a few herbal remedies. Moving is stressful, so I put together some Lassitude Tea to help you relax. Plus, a sweater. Alpaca. Loomed by blind Guatemalan girls." She lifted a lumpy gray pullover from the bag.

"Thanks, Mom." She sure knew how to enhance a girl's sex appeal. That sweater could turn Marilyn Monroe into Grandma Moses.

"How's the kite shop coming along?" Dad asked.

I'd been driving to Rock Point every other weekend for months to find a space for Strings Attached and get the store ready for business. Tomorrow was its grand opening. My stomach twinged with anxiety and excitement. Maybe a cup of mom's Lassitude Tea wouldn't be such a bad idea.

"The store looks great. Everything's ready. Tomorrow's the sand-castle competition, so, fingers crossed, I should be getting a lot of business." I smiled in a way I hoped said "confident businesswoman."

"Rock Point has changed so much since we rented that cabin when you and your sister were kids." Mom sighed. "Avery's coffee shop, the condos up on the bluff, that new gastropub. What's it called?"

"The Tidal Basin," Dave said, and Avery looked away for a second. She'd briefly dated its chef.

"I hear they're even thinking of building a resort," Mom said.

"Been down to old man Sullivan's kite shop yet?" Dad asked.

Dave and Avery exchanged glances. Dave was about to say something, but Avery shot him a look, and he closed his mouth.

The visit to Sullivan's Kites—Rock Point's other kite store—was the one chore I hadn't yet accomplished. Old man Sullivan was a bit of a grouch, as I remembered. Avery and I used to visit his shop when we were kids. I'd done a solid business plan, though, and I was sure the tourist town could sustain two kite shops. Plus, old man Sullivan's kites were practical, conventional kites. Mine were innovative and artistic and would appeal to a different crowd. I'd spent four years in art school plus the six years since dreaming them up and testing prototypes.

"Not yet." I cast around for an excuse. "Tomorrow. Thought I'd wait until the store was, you know, up and running."

Mom rose. "Well, we'd best be getting home and let you kids finish unpacking. Your father has his Watergate-reenactment-club meeting tonight, and we don't want to be late."

"Watergate reenactment?" Avery said.

"We thought about a Lewis-and-Clark-expedition re-enactment group—" Dad began.

"But you know I don't approve of firearms, and your father's knee isn't up to all that canoeing," Mom said. "They've even chosen Tom to play President Nixon." She beamed at him.

"There's no end of Watergate scripts, at least," Dave said.

Great. Now my father was Tricky Dick. Tricky Dick with a VW bus and a bent for composting.

"Anyway, we have one more housewarming gift." She looked to my father. "Tom?"

"We're leaving Bear with you," Dad said. At his name, Bear perked his ears. "His things are in the car."

"But—" I started. "Who will play Checkers?" I asked, referring to the Nixon family's dog. The truth was, I adored that dog and would love to keep him.

"If it's all right with Avery, of course," Mom said. "Girls living alone should have a dog for protection. Besides, I know you love Bear."

"It's fine by me," Avery said.

"We don't need protection," I said, secretly hoping that my protests weren't too convincing.

"You keep him," Mom said. "You'll need him. I told you it wasn't a good idea to move while Mercury is in retrograde. Not a good idea at all. Anything could happen."

I ROLLED OVER AND LOOKED AT THE CLOCK. SIX IN THE morning. It had been a late night, thanks to the bonfire on the beach and a long talk with Dave, who was surprisingly chatty once he relaxed. He was especially interested in my stories of art school with Avery. But late night or not, I was too worked up to stay in bed. Today was my big day—Strings Attached's grand opening.

I fluffed a pillow and sat up. I'd managed an outdoor

store in Portland for five years, but it would be different running my own shop. If my business plan worked out, I'd make a modest but perfectly respectable living. Plus, I'd see my kites—all those beautiful designs in yellows and spruce greens and rich plums—sailing above the beach. Either that, or I'd go bankrupt, as my parents had warned me too many times.

I pushed back the covers, and Bear, on his cushion near the foot of my bed, popped up and trotted after me to the kitchen. When you live with the owner of a coffeehouse, you can count on a good cup of joe in the morning. As the coffee machine filled the room with its rich scent and Bear snarfed his breakfast, I washed out a cup and tea ball Avery had left in the sink. I sniffed it and smiled. Lassitude Tea. Avery hadn't been feeling well and had left the bonfire early in the evening.

Mom would be happy to know her herbal remedies were put to good use, although at the same time I wished she would let me come up with my own remedies to life once in a while. I hoped that by living a few hours away, I'd prove I was perfectly capable of living a happy, productive life without her unbidden casserole deliveries. It had been a long time since I was an asthmatic kid who needed her protection, and I was determined to prove it to both of us.

Cup of coffee in hand and Bear trotting behind me, I pushed Avery's bedroom door open a crack, but she was still in full-lassitude mode. One thing I'll say for Mom's teas, they work as advertised. I pulled on an old hoodie and some fingerless gloves to ward off the spring morning's chill and headed for the beach.

Avery's house was in an enviable location, just at the edge of town and up on a bluff. Her family had owned it for generations, and while its joists moaned during storms, and Avery had become proficient at blocking drafty windows and coaxing the chimney to draw, I knew the house and the land it occupied were worth a mint. Not that Avery would ever sell. Why should she? The sunsets from the front porch alone were worth every one of the old house's ailments, and Avery's talent at interior design meant that each room soothed and comforted.

Bear was overjoyed to be out. He dashed ahead of me down the trail and set off after some sandpipers. Where the trail joined the beach, I stood a moment, sipping coffee and looking out at the ocean. Clouds thickened in the horizon, but a shaft of early-morning sun cracked the sky and met the surf where a house-sized cluster of rocks—the rocks the town was named after—jutted from the water. The tide was high now, and waves sprayed against the smaller formations rising here and there along the otherwise sandy beach. A salty tang infused the brisk air. For the millionth time since I'd arrived, I thanked my lucky stars to be living here.

Mom would have said the stars weren't nearly so propitiously aligned, what with her talk of "Mercury in retrograde." She couldn't have been more wrong. I had a stunning view of the ocean and Oregon's wild coast, my dream career starting in a few hours, a gorgeous old home with my best friend, and a good cup of coffee. And my dog. I inhaled the morning's fresh, cool air. What did Mom know, anyway?

Bear ran back toward me, then quickly circled away toward a clump of jagged rocks with surf swirling around them. Up to his knees in water, Bear sniffed around the rocks. Then stopped. And began to bark.

"Bear!" I yelled. "Quiet." Not that I was worried about

disturbing anyone. At this time of the morning, this early in the season, the beach was deserted.

Bear stopped barking but began whining at the rock. What did he see? I drained the rest of my coffee and walked toward him. Probably a dead gull or a fish that had washed in with the tide. At my approach, Bear began to bark again.

"Hush. What's wrong? If it's dead, you'd better not roll in it. Avery is patient, but not that patient. You don't want to be sent back to Mom and Dad, do you?"

Bear's whine intensified, and he skittered in place in a nervous prance.

"All right, all right." I picked up a driftwood branch, still wet, to poke whatever it was—probably a jellyfish or a rotting crab—back into the surf. I stepped up to the rocky outcropping and peered over the edge where Bear had been barking. He yipped again.

Facedown, legs licked by the surf, lay a dead man.

chapter two

I RAN BACK TO THE HOUSE AND ARRIVED, GASPING, IN my bedroom, where I fumbled in my purse for my cell phone. Cell coverage was spotty here, so I took the phone to the porch and punched 9-1-1, screwing it up once and having to take a deep breath and try again. At last the emergency dispatcher answered.

"I found a body. Rock Point. On the beach below the Cook house."

The dispatcher took my information and said she'd send the county sheriff.

I shut Bear in the house, ignoring his whining, and hurried back to the beach. Would the body still be there? The tide was going out, so the body should have less of a chance of washing away. I scrambled up the rock, peeked down, and jerked my head away. Still there. I descended to the beach and turned my back toward the body.

"Come on, come on, come on," I said under my breath, willing the sheriff to hurry. A raft of seagulls cawed to a landing farther up the shore.

At last, the sheriff's Suburban plowed up the beach, leaving a thick tread in the sand. I waved frantically and pulled my hoodie closer around me. The morning seemed to have somehow grown colder.

The Suburban's door clunked shut, and a man in his midforties, with jet black hair grayed at the temples and pulled back into a neat ponytail, approached. The star-shaped badge on his khaki shirt flashed in the morning light, then dulled as clouds covered the sun.

"Sheriff Nick Koppen," he said.

"He's over there." I pointed to the rocks, the tide now far enough out to have exposed the body fully. The sheriff stepped on the rocks, then without changing his expression, muttered a few words into his radio before turning to me.

"Help me turn him over," he said.

"Me? I—"

He'd already leapt down from the rocks and knelt at the body's side. "If there's a chance he's alive, I'll need your help."

I gulped and crawled over the rocks but kept a few feet away from the body. Instinct told me there was no reviving him. The sheriff laid a hand on the body's neck, then shook his head. Gently, with one hand on a shoulder and another on a hip, he rolled the body faceup.

My breath froze in my throat, but I couldn't look away. The blood in my ears roared like the surf. The dead man couldn't have been much older than I—late twenties or maybe thirty. He wore a sand-incrusted T-shirt and jeans, but his feet were bare. His curly brown hair stuck to his

skull, and tattoos formed sleeves on his arms. What seared
me deepest were his eyes. Wide open and blue. That, and
the three-inch gash in his chest.

"Oh my God," I gasped.

Sheriff Koppen studied the body dispassionately. He
murmured a benediction in a language I didn't understand,
then said, "Miles Logan."

Miles Logan. Miles. Where had I heard that name before? My brain had turned to sludge.

"Looks recent." The sheriff squinted toward the ocean.
"With the tides, this must have happened last night. The
medical examiner will say for sure."

Still unable to speak, I shivered as I thought of the man's
body buffeted all night in the sea. While Dave and I had
laughed and talked by the bonfire and Avery slept off a
headache, this man's life was taken, and he was dumped
off a boat to wash up here.

The sheriff stood. "You called this in?" Behind him,
another Suburban, this one red and topped with a siren,
rumbled up.

"Yes," I managed. "I'm Emmy. Emmy Adler. I live up
there." I pointed up the bluff to the house.

"The Cook house," he said. "You're the owner of the
new kite shop, right?"

I nodded, still breathing erratically.

"I'll come see you soon. Right now I have other things
to attend to." He turned back toward the body.

WHILE THE SHERIFF AND PARAMEDICS WORKED ON THE
beach, I climbed back to the house, my breath coming
faster than it should. A dead body. I'd found a body.

Inside, Avery still slept. Not surprising, considering it was barely seven o'clock and a Saturday, at that. I considered waking her but decided against it. After all, she hadn't been feeling well, and she had an efficient morning crew at the coffee shop. I'd fill her in on the drama later.

I wandered the house, Bear at my heels. Breakfast didn't sound good, and there was no way I could settle down and read the newspaper. I left a brief note for Avery, then grabbed the first thing I could find—the sweater my mother had given me—and left the house. I'd go to Strings Attached and get ready. With the annual sand-castle competition and the unofficial opening of tourist season, it was sure to be a big day. Besides, anything would be better than staying at home while the sheriff worked on the beach below.

It was barely half a mile to the center of town on quiet roads, so I rode my bike. The clouds had dispersed, and it was shaping up to be an unseasonably fine day for June. Anyone else—say, a visitor staying in one of Rock Point's guesthouses, or one of the year-round residents readying a fishing boat—would breathe the fresh, piney-salty air and proclaim the day downright beautiful. But none of them had started the morning with a corpse.

I pushed my bike up the steps of the shop and leaned it on the porch while I unlocked the door. Strings Attached was in the lower level of a Victorian house just a block from the beach. The building's owner, Frank Hopkins, had an apartment upstairs he used from time to time during the summer, as well as plenty of other real estate in town. He'd leased me the whole ground floor, with a retail space in front and space for a kite workshop in the old kitchen in the rear. I wheeled my bike to the workshop and leaned it out of the way against the entrance to the stairwell that used to connect the building's floors.

I surveyed the front of the shop with pride. Vibrant rows of kites dangled from the ceiling. Extra line, kite parts, and kits waited on shelves that lined the room. One of the glories of renting a storefront in an old house was that I had hardwood floors and panes of stained glass in the front door.

I sighed. Two hours until opening and nothing to do but obsess about the dead body. I needed something else to pass the time. Maybe I'd brainstorm kite designs. With a pencil in my hand, I could lose hours completely absorbed. Plus, I had an idea for an asymmetrical kite that would be tricky to keep airborne, and I wanted to flesh it out.

As I turned to the workshop to get my sketchbook, I heard a sharp rap on the front door. Curious, I threw the bolt and cracked the door open, then opened it wider. A jeans-clad woman with long gray hair and an elegant figure stood on the porch.

"Good morning," she said. "I couldn't help but see you come in." Her smile was warm, welcoming. "I've been eyeing those gorgeous kites through the window for the past few weeks, and I simply must meet you." She stuck out her hand. "Stella Hart."

"Oh," I said abruptly. After the morning's shock, I wasn't feeling overly friendly. The woman's smile amped a few watts, and I relented. "Emmy Adler," I said. "This is my shop."

She waited. She glanced up at the kites, then back at me.

"Would you like to come in?" I asked.

"Why, thank you." Stella stepped over the threshold and audibly drew in her breath. "Astonishing! Those, there on the left. Inspired by Matisse cutouts, are they?"

"Yes, they are." I was surprised. Most people think my kites are simply "artsy," and they never expect they'll fly. "I adapted his dove design, so the tail is aerodynamic. It was one of my first appliquéd designs."

"And this one could be drawn from a midcentury Picasso." The woman touched the edge of a sky-blue, rounded rectangle with a lily on it.

"I hesitated to make it blue since the sky is blue—"

"But the sky is mostly gray here."

"Exactly what I thought," I said. The woman's cheekbones were strong, and the skin drawn taut over them was nearly translucent. A pink glow—not makeup, because she clearly didn't wear much—infused her complexion.

"Ms. Hart, would you like a cup of tea? It's still early, but today is Strings Attached's first day, and I was too excited to wait at home." I let it rest at that.

"Call me Stella. Please," she said. "And yes, I'd love a cup of tea, if you don't mind. I see that you're an artist, and I'm an artist myself. I'd love to see more of what you've done."

I invited her to my workshop, and we christened my first day with a hot cup of Darjeeling and a discussion of kites and art. It turned out that Stella had been a schoolteacher during the day but had painted at night. After she retired, she'd turned to painting full time, and now her work was shown in galleries along the coast and in Portland and Seattle. Her husband died a few years ago, and she'd moved to Rock Point not long after to "be near beauty," as she put it. Now she was painting during the day and greeting guests at the Tidal Basin at night "for stimulation." I felt entirely comfortable with her. Before the pot of tea was finished, I was telling her about the body I'd found that morning.

"Sheriff Koppen, huh?" she said. "A good man. Part Clatsop Indian, you know. Catches a lot of flak because of it among some of the less open-minded. But I don't know anyone who complains about how he's done his job."

She was sensitive enough not to ask me a lot of questions about the body, and I was reluctant to talk too much about it yet. "I couldn't really get a read on him."

She seemed not to hear me and turned to stare out the window. "Something's changed in town lately. Bad feeling is going around. I can't quite figure it out." She tapped a finger absently on the table. "Not that I ever expected this. A body . . ."

A body. I pushed the teapot away and took a deep breath. "I know."

"I'm sorry, darling." Stella reached across the table and laid a thin hand on mine. "Don't let this ruin a special day for you. Congratulations on Strings Attached."

"Thank you." I tried to appear composed. At some point the sheriff would show up and start asking questions. His emotionless face flitted across my mind.

"One more thing. It's a small town here. There are sure to be a lot of wagging tongues. Don't pay them any mind." With a smile, she was gone. I watched her trim figure head up the street and disappear around a corner.

Strange. She hadn't even asked who the dead man was.

ALONE IN MY SHOP ONCE AGAIN, I GLANCED AT THE clock, an old hand-wound mantel clock Avery had found at a rummage sale and insisted would be perfect in the room. As usual, she was right. The serious lines of the clock set off the front room's antique molding and complemented the more frivolous waves of kites. It was still barely nine thirty, and the shop wouldn't open until ten. I drew a deep breath. What the heck. It wasn't like the morning could get any worse. Why not go see old man Sullivan and his kite shop and get it over with?

I grabbed my keys, and, on second thought, the lumpy sweater my mom had given me, and set out up the street. Rock Point teemed with tourists during the summer, but now, early in the season, the town felt cozy and small. Sullivan's Kites was only two blocks away, in a stand-alone storefront on the town's main drag, past Martino's Pizza and the tiny sheriff's office—was he there now, or still on the beach?—and a block below the street where Avery's café, the Brew House, stood. I took a chance that someone would be readying Sullivan's Kites before opening. This was a big day, and people would be driving in from up and down the coast to build sand castles and, hopefully, fly kites on the beach.

I rapped on the glass front door.

"Come in," I heard from within the store.

I pushed open the door and passed into the place I remembered so well from my childhood, the store that had inspired my love of kites. Above me, rows of kites—many more than I had at Strings Attached—danced in the faint breeze I had stirred. Unlike my fanciful kites with chiffon tails and unusual shapes, these were practical sport kites and traditional designs. I moved toward the back, where I remembered the counter being.

Behind the counter stood a man I'd never seen. Believe me, I'd remember if I had. He was tall with thick brown hair brushed behind his ears. He swept it back with one hand. His eyes were gray and velvety as a tabby cat. On the customer's side of the counter was a woman, her back to me.

"Can I help you?" he asked.

"Yes. I, uh—" I started. The woman turned to me now. She was probably originally a mousy brunette, but she'd dyed her hair blond and hyped the effect with a prairie-style sundress with the top two buttons undone. "I'm looking for—" I bit off "old man" and simply said "Mr. Sullivan."

"I'm Mr. Sullivan," the man said.

The blond gave a shuddering sigh. "Jack. I just don't know what to do . . ."

Flustered, I backed up a step. "I'm sorry. I seem to have arrived at a bad time. I just wanted to say that I'm Emmy Adler, and I'm opening a new kite store today, Strings—"

"Attached," he finished. "I'm Jack Sullivan. Pleased to meet you."

He proffered a hand, and it took me a second to snap out of my daze and shake it. "But I thought—"

"My grandfather started the shop. I've been running it for a few years now, since he died." He nodded toward the blond. "This is Annabelle Black. I'm afraid she's just had some bad news."

This was old man Sullivan? No wonder Avery and Dave had been smirking when my dad called him that. They'd pay for this, one way or another. They were probably yucking it up even now.

"My—my friend is dead." Annabelle hitched her breath. "They found his body this morning." She broke into sobs. Jack kept his distance.

My stomach dropped. She had to be talking about the body I found. "I'm sorry to hear that," I ventured.

"Murdered," she added.

"Oh," I said. Inadequate, but it was all I could muster. "I'm so sorry."

"You couldn't possibly understand," she said. "Don't even try."

Harsh. I took a step back and reminded myself that she was still in shock. "I'm so sorry," I repeated.

"Do I know you?" Annabelle asked when her sobs subsided. Her eyes were surprisingly dry. She let her gaze pass over me. "Nice sweater."

I looked at the lumps of gray wool. "It was knitted by blind Guatemalans."

"Blind, huh?" Annabelle said.

"I've seen your kites through the window," Jack said. "They sure are, uh, colorful."

What was that supposed to mean? "I studied art, but I assure you they're—"

"I didn't mean that," Jack said. "I'm sure they fly fine, especially if you're more interested in how a kite looks than in performance."

Good grief. I'd just dropped in to say hello, not be double-teamed with animosity. "Maybe I'd better go now. I'm interrupting your talk."

"I loved Miles," Annabelle cut in, apparently eager to get back to her tragedy. "We were meant to be together. Sure, he took up with that coffeehouse woman, but that was only a fling, a reaction before he came back to me. Sometimes you just know. I knew."

And at last I knew, too. Miles Logan. The chef at the Tidal Basin. Avery's last boyfriend, and the man whose body I'd found that morning.

chapter three

THE MORNING AT STRINGS ATTACHED PASSED SURPRIS-
ingly quickly. It seemed that only moments after I flipped
the sign to "Open," customers appeared. Many, lattes in
hand, were simply window-shopping, but I appreciated
their compliments on my kites, especially the kites I'd
designed myself. Among these wanderers were also a few
serious customers.

A Matisse kite sold to an out-of-towner who also made
kites. We talked about the difficulty of appliquéing ripstop
nylon as I carefully rolled the kite and slipped it into its
protective canvas bag. I sold a few of my more practical
beginner kites, too. Maybe one of them would spark a love
of kites like my own.

Mostly, though, I feigned an upbeat attitude and thought
about Avery and Miles, her ex-boyfriend. They'd broken

up a while ago—not long after the new year, if I remembered right. Avery had never seemed too serious about him, but she'd be shocked, all the same.

I was picking up my cell phone to call her when the front door's bell rang to let in Frank Hopkins, my landlord, carrying a grocery sack.

"I hear you found a body," Frank said.

It had started. Stella had warned me that I'd be getting curious visitors, but most of my customers this morning had been tourists in town for the sand-castle competition. They either didn't know or didn't care about the dead chef. Frank Hopkins was the first local—if you wanted to call him that. He owned enough property in town to be important, but rumor had it he spent his winters in Palm Springs. If his brand-spanking-new Land Rover in the garage was any indication, he was doing pretty well.

"Unfortunately," I said, and turned to the cash register, hoping he would get the hint.

"I heard it down at the market. I was out of town for a few days, wanted to restock the fridge." Frank truly did look sympathetic. "I'm sorry. It's a rough way to kick off your grand opening. I brought you some flowers." He drew from the grocery sack a dozen tulips in white and lipstick pink. "Congratulations on the store, and don't let it get you down. All the hullaballoo about the body will be over soon, so don't get too caught up in any of the gossip about your roommate."

"Gossip about Avery? What does she have to do with it?"

"I shouldn't have said anything. You know how people talk. In any case, I'm sure it was just an accident."

It could hardly have been an accident, not with a gash

that size on the chef's chest. My throat tightened at the memory. "It's only been a few hours since I—" I paused. "You know. What are people saying about Avery? Tell me."

He set the sack on the counter. "You're new here, so you may have never met him, but the body you found was Miles Logan. He was kind of a minor celebrity around here—a tremendous chef, too, the Tidal Basin won't be the same—and, well, you know about him and Avery."

"Sure. They dated. A long time ago."

"Like I said, people talk. I wouldn't listen, if I were you."

I forced a smile. I'd been planning to order a sandwich from next door and keep the shop open, but this was an emergency. "Thank you so much for the flowers. I'll just clean up here and close for lunch. A bowl of soup at the Brew House would be perfect about now."

STILL SHAKEN BY FRANK'S HINTS ABOUT "GOSSIP," I pushed open the Brew House's oak front door and took a moment's comfort in the warm scent of coffee and hiss of the espresso machine. Like Strings Attached, the Brew House was in the ground floor of an old house, only this one, a block off Rock Point's main drag, had been built as a guest house in the 1920s and had the wide, low porch and arts-and-crafts details to prove it. Wooden tables surrounded by mission-style oak chairs dotted the main room. The coffee bar dominated the back, where a teenaged girl was ringing up a to-go latte for a tourist.

Dave waved from a center table. With relief, I joined him. "Where's Avery?" I asked.

Dave nodded toward the kitchen, beyond the coffee bar,

and stroked his beard anxiously. Avery was toward the rear, talking with Sheriff Koppen. She was turned away from us, and the sheriff's face bore the implacable expression I'd seen that morning.

"You've heard, then?" I said.

"Yes." He pushed part of a sandwich around on his plate but didn't take a bite. "Koppen's been talking to her for at least half an hour. I don't know why he's so interested in her."

"Me, neither." After all, I was the one who'd found the body. The sheriff hadn't even come to take a statement yet. Besides, Avery and Miles had broken up ages ago. The back of Avery's head nodded yes. Then shook no. I couldn't tell what was going on in there, but Dave was clearly as concerned as I was. I decided to lighten the mood. "Hey, I finally made it down to Sullivan Kites this morning. Old man Sullivan, huh?"

It was good to see Dave laugh. "Jack's a good friend."

Which meant I'd likely be seeing more of him. And those amazing gray eyes. Not that he'd exactly seemed overwhelmed by me or by Strings Attached. And why should he be when he had Annabelle Black pursing her lips at him? I plucked at my woolly sweater. It was going straight to the back of the closet.

At last, Avery and Sheriff Koppen emerged from the kitchen. "Hi, Emmy," Avery said.

"I left you a phone message. You were asleep when I left the house, so I—"

The sheriff pulled me away. "Let's talk. Out on the porch."

I left Dave to console Avery and followed Koppen to the wide porch overlooking the beach. He led me to a corner and perched on the solid railing. Behind him, just down the hill, the beach was filling with people mounding sand into elaborate structures. A replica of Cinderella's castle, complete with central spire, had earned a small crowd of admirers. Just beyond it loomed a Gothic cathedral. Its creator was adding a flying buttress. Colorful kites bobbed through the sky, and I was pleased to recognize two as mine.

The sheriff slipped a notebook from his shirt pocket. "Tell me about last night."

"Last night? But it was this morning that I found the— Miles Logan."

"I'd like to hear about last night. Start with dinner."

I plunged my hands into my pockets. Even with the sun, the ocean breeze was cool. "Well, my parents came to visit yesterday, and my mother left us a casserole." Vegan, naturally. Heavy on the quinoa. "So Dave and Avery and I ate some of that. Dave—Dave Reed—was over, helping set up furniture."

"And?"

"I guess it was eight o'clock or so when we decided to build a bonfire down on the beach. It was just getting dark."

"Directly below the house?"

"More or less. In the big stone circle. It's been there for years—just to the right of where the trail lets out." It was habit in Avery's family to collect driftwood on beach walks, then leave it at the foot of the trail to dry for bonfires, and Avery had continued the tradition. A few big rocks, perfect as seats, surrounded the old fire pit.

"So you built a fire."

"Yes. Seemed like a good way to relax after a long day." Koppen nodded. "And Avery?"

Of course, this was where he was headed. "Avery had

a headache and went back up to the house. Dave and I sat by the fire."

"How long?"

"Oh, a couple of hours? I don't know. When I got back to the house, Avery was asleep."

"Did you see her?"

The sheriff's lack of emotion was starting to get to me. "What are you implying?" A fist clenched in my pocket.

"I asked you a question. Did you see her?"

"No." The word came out with more force than I'd intended. "But her bedroom door was shut. It's not like I was going to barge in and shake her to see if she was sleeping."

The sheriff simply stared at me.

I took a deep breath. "I'm sorry. It's just—"

"I know," he said, and let a moment pass. "You found a dead body this morning." He gave me another moment to compose myself. "When you were on the beach last night, would you have been able to tell if a car came or went from the house?"

My jaw dropped. He couldn't possibly think Avery had left the house.

"Could you?" he repeated.

"No. No, I suppose not." The ocean's continuous roar would have smothered any noise I might have heard. Of course, Bear would have noticed and barked. Or would he? But this was simply ridiculous. "Look. I see where you're going, and let me stop you right now. Avery had a headache. She went up to the house and drank some herbal tea that my mother made to help her relax. My mom's teas are pretty potent. Obviously, she conked out until morning."

"I see. You have proof that she drank the tea, correct?"

My stomach dropped. The tea cup. I'd washed it that morning and put it away. All he had was my word.

Koppen seemed to register my dismay and nodded slowly. "We'll talk more. In the meantime, take my advice and stay in Rock Point. We have a lot to sort through here, and I'm not sure where the investigation will lead."

Still in shock, I watched him descend the steps to the street. Beyond him, the beach had filled with a fantasy city of castles, skyscrapers, and Victorian mansions. All that work, all that detail. And in a few hours the tide would destroy them all.

chapter four

❧

I WAS WAITING FOR AVERY AT THE HOUSE WHEN SHE came home that evening. Opening day for Strings Attached had been a success as far as sales were concerned, but I'd found it hard to concentrate. Luckily, customers had seemed too interested in browsing the kites to notice how distracted I was. When the last customer had left, I'd flipped the sign to "Closed" and reached for my phone to try Avery again. And again she hadn't answered. I was dying to know what the sheriff had wanted from her.

At last, her mud-splashed Honda CR-V bumped up the driveway. Bear barked and danced in a circle. When I opened the front door, he bounded down the steps to the car.

"Whoa, buddy." Avery smiled at the dog, although her skin was drawn. "Hi, Emmy."

"Avery, you're home."

She tossed her purse on a side table and slumped into

an easy chair. "You mean, I'm here and not in jail? I guess I should be happy for that."

"No, that's not what I meant." I glanced around the room at the plump couch, perfect for naps; the cheerful vase of pussy willows; the family photos on the fireplace mantel, including one of me and Avery at four years old—I was the curly brunette still sporting baby fat, and Avery the fairylike blond. Just this morning this room had been so soothing, so like home. Now everything felt different. "It's just, well, with the sheriff and all, I wanted to see how you're doing." She didn't respond. "Would you like some dinner?"

"I don't know." Avery wouldn't look at me. She just kept staring to the side. I followed her gaze to the thermostat and realized she wasn't really looking at that. She wasn't really looking at anything.

I went to the kitchen, Bear at my heels, and opened the refrigerator. The bottle of champagne I'd intended to celebrate Strings Attached's first day lay on its side, its festive foil-wrapped neck butting against Mom's casserole dish.

"How about some quinoa?" I asked. "Or I could make you a grilled cheese sandwich." Once she was relaxed, she'd tell me about her conversation with the sheriff.

"You want to hear about today, don't you?"

I shut the refrigerator door and stood in the living room's entrance. "I don't want to stress you out. I mean, we don't have to talk about it. I'm fine just letting it be," I lied.

"Emmy, you left me five messages today."

She knew me too well. "All right. If you're sure you feel like talking about it."

She stood. "Grab a blanket, and let's sit on the porch. The sun is just starting to set."

She didn't have to ask twice. I lifted a thick wool blanket for each of us from the cedar chest. We sat side by side on the wicker sofa, just as we had for so many years. As kids, we'd fallen asleep on the sofa on summer nights while our parents murmured about mortgages and politics and other adult things we didn't understand. In middle school, we talked about our crushes and tried different hairstyles on each other. In college, work and school meant I hadn't visited Rock Point as often as I'd liked, but we were roommates in art school in Portland.

Then Avery's parents were killed in a car crash. Joy riders speeding up the coastal highway had taken a wide turn and swiped her parents' sedan off the rocky cliff, where it landed upside down, just above the shore. Afterward, Avery had insisted on staying at their family home, even alone. I'd visited weekends when I could. I hoped that she—an only child—thought me the sister I considered her to be.

"Comfortable?" I asked. The sky was just taking on the lavender cast it did before orange tinted the horizon.

"I'm fine," Avery said. "So strange."

For a moment, that was all she said. I knew it was just the start, the opening to more when she was ready. Bear hopped into the armchair next to me and sighed loudly as he curled into nap position.

At last Avery spoke. "I can't believe Miles is dead. We used to sit right here, you know. He'd have a beer and tell me about things at the restaurant. He loved the view. Even in the winter he'd insist on bundling up and sitting here."

I knew they'd only dated three or four months, which meant they'd been together last fall and winter. Chilly months to be outside, but somehow more wonderful, too, thanks to the protection of the porch's broad roof from winter rains, and the fireplace inside.

"I haven't had the chance to tell you this yet, Avery, but I'm so sorry about Miles. It has to be awful." She didn't respond. Whether it was because of a lump in her throat or simply having nothing to say, I didn't know. "How did you meet?"

"I'd noticed him around town, of course. Everyone did. You should have seen him when he was working. The Tidal Basin has an open kitchen. When he was behind the stove, he was completely focused. He moved so fast, so deliberately, plating food, shaking a pan on the stove, sprinkling parsley just so before a plate left the counter. I think most the women in town were in love with him."

"And all the female tourists," I added. "Or at least the restaurant critics."

"Yeah, he was a pretty decent chef, too."

"So, how did you introduce yourself? Did you dream up an excuse that had to do with the Brew House so you could talk to him?" I asked.

"No. Actually, he found me. I used to see his pickup sometimes coming up the road, but he'd take the cutoff at Perkins Road and go into the woods. Later he told me he went there to gather mushrooms. But one day he didn't turn off. He came straight to the house. He asked if he could go down to the beach to dig for clams." Her gaze lost focus again.

The horizon spilled rich tangerine. This was the moment that tourists tried in vain to capture on film. A thousand sunset shots like this had graced calendars through the decades. But a photograph could only hint at the real thing's breath-snatching beauty.

"Did he ask you out then?" I said.

"He did. Just about right away. He said, 'I'd love to have coffee with you or a drink sometime.' Just like that."

"Seems kind of forward if you hadn't talked much before."

"It was. But you know what the really strange thing was?"

"What?"

"It wasn't clam season."

I smiled. Clearly Avery had no idea of her attractiveness to guys, and that was part of what made her such a catch. "Well, he'd clearly noticed you and wanted to get to know you better."

"It seemed that way at first, I admit. He came on pretty heavy, although his schedule at the Tidal Basin put a damper on that. I was flattered. I mean, a local-celeb chef interested in me—who wouldn't be a little light-headed about it?"

"No kidding. I bet Annabelle Black wasn't thrilled, though." Or Dave, I thought.

Avery nearly smiled. "You heard about her and Miles?"

"Met her this morning at Sullivan's Kites."

"She was truly put out. You know the expression about 'looking daggers' at someone?"

"That was her, I bet."

"Miles told me they dated in high school, then again a year or so ago, but he said he had an extreme allergy to chintz and left it at that."

Bear lifted his head, then jumped between us, where it was warmer. Night was beginning to fall, and already a few stars glittered overhead. I always forgot how vivid the stars shined on the coast, with no city lights over the ocean to compete with them.

"Sounds like he had a thing for you. What happened?" I asked.

A long time passed before she answered. "I guess it wasn't meant to be."

What a frustrating answer. A nonanswer, really. She wasn't telling me everything. "But he kept coming by."

"Oh, sure. He had all sorts of plans for me. Thought I should sell the house and buy the Brew House's building. Move upstairs. I told him no way."

Of course not. This was her home. "That must have been heartbreaking. You cared about him, and he kind of cooled off."

Again, Avery didn't speak. This wasn't like her. I'd never known her not to be eager to get to the bottom of an emotional situation with me. She ran the edges of the wool blanket against her fingers.

"So maybe you didn't get along?" I said, hoping for more.

"I wouldn't say that. He was a sweet guy." She hugged her knees and pulled up her blanket. "I can't believe I'm saying 'was' a sweet guy." Exhaustion etched lines near her eyes. "Eventually, we stopped seeing each other. We never had any big talk or formal breakup—our relationship just petered out. But I was always happy to wave at him in town or when he drove by. No hard feelings." She stroked Bear's head. "I wish you could have met Miles."

So did I. Waves crashed below, now likely enveloping the cluster of rocks where I'd found him. I couldn't help but remember Sheriff Koppen turning his body over and the red gash against the chef's sea-bleached skin.

"Does the sheriff really think you had some fit of rage and stabbed him and tossed him in the ocean? I mean, you guys broke up six months ago. I know that dating is cutthroat—" I couldn't finish my sentence.

Even in the bare light the moon gave, I saw Avery's tightened expression.

"Sheriff Koppen says so. Says he has proof." She flopped her head against the back of the sofa. "Says Miles and I had an appointment to meet last night."

What? My hand hit the sofa's arm with a clunk. "But he can't have proof," I said. "You were here with us. It was my first day in the house."

"Let's go in," Avery said. She tossed the blanket on the sofa and went in the living room, Bear close behind. Proof? I stood on the porch in disbelief. And why wasn't Avery coming clean with me about Miles? A lamp clicked on inside, casting its yellow glow to the porch.

I picked up the blankets and followed her. "Did he tell you what this proof was?"

"Miles's calendar. He'd penciled in a meeting with me at the dock."

Avery's family shared a dock with a few other families. Her dad used to love to fish, but Avery didn't use the boat much. I was surprised she hadn't sold it, frankly, but she said Dave liked to take it out from time to time.

"So they must have found his phone," I said, assuming that's where Miles kept his calendar.

"Oh no," Avery said. "He had a paper calendar, a little spiral-bound one, at his cabin. The sheriff must have found it."

"You . . ." I hesitated. "You didn't have a meeting with him, did you? Maybe something you forgot?"

Her whole body sagged with exhaustion. "No. I didn't see him."

"Then you were set up." I'd spoken a little louder than I'd intended, and Bear raised his head. "Sorry. It just makes me mad."

"I can't think about it anymore. I'm so tired. All I want to do is go to bed and hope it all goes away."

"But you're being framed. You can't give up," I said.

"Can you prove I didn't go anywhere last night? You and Dave were down on the beach. The surf pounds down there. You couldn't have heard me if I drove away."

"But you didn't. You had a headache, drank some of Mom's tea, and fell asleep." When she remained silent, I added, "There's some kind of misunderstanding."

"Maybe."

I'd never seen Avery so defeated, so devoid of hope, except after her parents' accident. I wondered if her grief had lingered. "Is there something you're not telling me?"

Avery didn't reply. She laid her head on the arm of the couch and closed her eyes.

"Oh, Avery. Someone must have pretended to be you and set up the date at the dock. Either that, or the sheriff is leading you on to try to get you to admit to something you didn't do. Can't you see? We have to figure out who's behind this."

"I don't know. I hadn't seen Miles one-on-one for weeks." She rubbed her eyes. "I can't think anymore. Will you make me some of that relaxing tea?"

"No. No more of Mom's tea." I winced at the memory of cleaning out Avery's cup that morning. I could have shown the sheriff. My cell phone trilled to Abba's "Mamma Mia." Yes, somehow I'd conjured my mother just by mentioning her name. "I'd better get this."

Avery didn't move.

"How was your first day, honey?" Mom asked. "Did people like your kites? I wish we could have stayed longer."

I looked at Avery slumped on the couch and thought through the day, from finding Miles's body to the sheriff's evidence against her. "Everything's fine, Mom," I said. "Just fine."

chapter five

WITH THE CONSTANT JINGLING OF THE BELL AT THE shop's front door, helping customers, and the repair of a lovely sunrise-pink kite that had taken a nearly fatal dive into a sand dune, I was busy all day. You'd think I'd be thrilled, but I was still antsy about Avery. She'd asked me to let the matter rest, but I couldn't help wondering if I should at least recommend she get an attorney.

Thanks to poetry night at the Brew House, she wouldn't be home until late. I decided to burn off some of my anxiety with a walk on the beach. Yesterday's sunny weather hadn't lasted, and now the breeze held misty rain. My thoughts kept returning to Avery. She wasn't telling me everything about her and Miles. I was sure of it.

A familiar figure, shoulders draped in a cerise shawl, came toward me from down the beach. Stella. She looked distracted and didn't see me, and I didn't want to disturb her while she was so absorbed. We passed so close, though, that it wasn't civil not to greet her.

"Hi, Stella. Nice evening for a walk, huh?"

"Oh. Emmy." Stella was somewhere else completely, and wherever it was, it wasn't a happy place.

"Is everything all right?"

She stopped and turned toward the ocean. With each wave, the sea drifted lazily toward our feet. But the meandering water was deceptive. The ocean's real force showed in the waves that shattered over the rocky outcroppings just offshore.

"I didn't know it was Miles you'd found."

"That's right. You knew him from the Tidal Basin. I'm sorry." No wonder Stella was so despondent. There was no leaning in for gossip or urging me for gruesome details, either. No, this was pure grief. Stella and Miles must have been close.

"Why don't we walk together? I wouldn't mind the company," she said. I turned back to town with her. She linked her arm in mine. "I was getting a little melancholy on my own."

"If you're sure."

"Absolutely. Usually the ocean helps me sort out my thoughts, but sometimes it simply makes me maudlin. Besides, I had an idea for a kite that I wanted to talk to you about."

"Really?"

"Inspired by a fishing net. In fact"—she stopped and turned to me—"why don't you come up to my place and I'll show you? Or maybe you have plans."

The breeze blew a few strands of white gray hair across her mouth, and she pulled them away. I had the feeling

Stella was honest. Straightforward. What you saw was
what you got, and I saw a refined, openhearted woman.
After the last couple of days, I'd welcome her company.

"I don't have plans, and Avery's out for the evening. I'll
need to check on my dog, but I could meet you in, say, an
hour?"

Stella jotted down her address, and we parted ways by
the docks.

After an hour nearly to the minute, I arrived at Stella's.
She lived in a 1950s ranch-style house high enough on the
bluff above Rock Point to have a sweeping view of the
ocean and far enough that I couldn't hear the surf—only
the occasional shrieks of seagulls. I climbed the steps up
to the front door and didn't even have to ring the bell. Stella
was already at the open door, smiling widely, but still with
a hint of the sadness I'd seen earlier. She held a paintbrush
and wore paint-smeared overalls.

"I saw you coming up the street. Come in," she said.
"Would you like some tea, or maybe a glass of pinot gris?
I was just opening a bottle."

"Wine would be nice." Stella's front room was flooded
with light. In front of the stone fireplace, instead of the
traditional couch and matching side chairs was a circle of
armchairs from different eras, surrounding a low, round
coffee table stacked with books and framed photographs.
A white cat with one blue and one amber eye lounged in
a Swedish-style teak-framed chair. Nothing matched, but
all the same the room's feeling was harmonious.

Stella noticed me surveying her decor. She picked up a
silver-framed photo and handed it to me. "My husband."

The photo showed a tall man with kind features and

thick white hair leaning against a brick wall. I replaced the photo on the table. "Do you miss him?"

"Every day."

"I'm sorry." After a moment, I turned to the seating area. "I love the mix of chairs."

"I thought a couch would be too stuffy. I so much prefer everyone to have their own armchair. More convivial, don't you think? Have a seat. I put my kite sketch there, next to the candle. And that's Madame Lucy." She nodded toward the cat.

"Bonjour, Madame," I said. The cat stood and stretched, then circled in the chair to settle with her back facing me. Well. She knew a dog person when she saw one, I guessed. I chose the rocking chair and gratefully took the glass of wine Stella offered. It was crisp and floral, like spring. "This is nice."

Stella lowered herself into a leather deco club chair with a mohair throw tossed across its back. "Willamette Valley vintner. I traded him a painting for an annual case of his pinot gris."

Stella handed me a sketch pad. She'd drawn a stunt kite—the kind that you handle with two lines, but which can dip and swoop—with net joining the kite's wings in a long, braidlike tail. She'd wisely left off trying to sketch in the kite's mechanics.

"This is good," I said. "The trick would be to make sure the nylon doesn't weigh it down. I could even weave the net from different colors." My fingers itched for a pencil to jot down a few details. "Do you—"

"Right here." Stella pulled a pencil from the front pocket of her overalls.

I sketched in the placement of the bridle to counterbal-
ance the net tail. Nice. "If you'd like, we could work on
this together in my workshop."

Stella's face softened. "I'd love it."

"Where's your studio?" The scent of turpentine and oil
paint that I remembered so well from art school lingered
in the air, but I didn't see an easel.

"Downstairs. Since the house is built on a hill, I have
a nice bank of windows down there and a few big walls
for my larger pieces. Would you like to see it?"

"I would."

She led me past the kitchen and down a staircase on the
hall's right. The house's ground floor, open in the front,
glowed with the west sun. The trappings of a painting
studio—utility sink, jars of paintbrushes, primed canvases—
were there, sure, but what caught my attention were the land-
scapes in various stages of completion lining the walls. The
paintings were vivid and wild, churning with emotion.

Stella set her wineglass on the paint-stained table holding her palette. "What do you think?"

"I love it." The paintings were so rich that they almost
seemed to move on their own.

"The light's from the west. It's not ideal, but when the
Realtor brought me down here, I knew this was the house
for me."

"I don't mean the studio, although it's great. I mean
your paintings. They're wonderful."

"Thank you."

I took in the sweeping view of Rock Point, down the sloped
streets of the northern edge of town to the ocean. The sunsets
here must be almost as gripping as those from Avery's porch.
That, at least, hadn't changed since yesterday morning.

"I hate to bring it up," Stella said, "but how are you doing? I mean, with everything. As you might imagine, people are talking about Miles—and your friend."

"Honestly?"

Stella nodded. "I worked at the Tidal Basin last night, and the staff was feeling down. Chef Miles." The light in her face vanished.

"It's awful. Poor Avery. The sheriff seems to have made her his number-one suspect, and she's not even fighting it. She's walking through it all like a zombie. Just kind of stunned."

"Did you—could you—?"

I remembered her tact the morning before, when she didn't press me on finding the body. Of course she'd want to know more now. "I was taking the dog for a walk on the beach, and I found him washed up on a cluster of rocks just below the house." It sounded so simple, almost clinical. "He was facedown. When the sheriff came, he rolled him over, and, well—" My voice dropped off.

"It was clear he was murdered. No doubt," she said.

"Yes."

Stella seemed to withdraw. Her expression closed down, and she gazed out the studio's windows toward the ocean. "Avery lost her parents not long ago, am I right?"

"A little more than two years ago." I understood where Stella was headed and nodded. "Miles's death on the heels of that—well, it's a lot to take."

"She clearly didn't do it, though."

"Of course she didn't." I paused. "I know that, but not everyone else is convinced."

"Well, why should she have killed him?" The violence in Stella's response startled me. Until now, she'd seemed despondent. Anger clearly burned under her grief.

Madame Lucy emerged from the stairwell and hopped onto a chair.

"No reason. No reason at all." Motive. That was the one thing the sheriff seemed determined to ignore. Avery had no motive to kill Miles. "But, then, who would want to kill Miles?"

Stella rested a hand on Madame Lucy's back. "I've been thinking about that. Miles and Annabelle dated way back in high school, and Annabelle's had her eye on him ever since. They even started seeing each other again before he started dating Avery, but I think Miles called it off for good. At least, that's the word on the street."

"Word does hit the street pretty quickly around here."

"It's a small town. Lenny, down at the filling station, listens to the police radio and keeps his eyes on people's comings and goings. Jeanette at the post office generally stops by the filling station on her way to work for a coffee and gets the lowdown. Then she's the info relay during the day. Everyone who checks their mail or buys stamps either gives or gets the latest gossip."

"She doesn't go to the Brew House for coffee?" Around these parts, most residents were pretty choosy about their morning java.

"Oh yes, but that's during her afternoon break. That way she's plugged into all the major news outlets."

So Avery couldn't so much as buy a can of tuna in Rock Point without everyone knowing her business. "Is there any talk about Annabelle? Or anyone else for that matter?"

"Of course there is. Everyone's speculating, and I've seen enough of humankind in my time as a teacher to know Annabelle's type. She's proud, and she bears a grudge. Unfortunately, the money seems to be on Avery right now."

Stella shifted on her feet. "I think the sheriff would be wise to pay a little more attention to the Tidal Basin, though."

Madame Lucy had removed herself to the floor and was vigorously grooming her hindquarters.

"Why's that?" I asked.

"Well, Miles didn't seem fully committed to the job. Every once in a while he'd simply not show up for work, and the restaurant's owner, Sam, wasn't keen on it."

"You're kidding." The Tidal Basin had garnered national reviews. Any foodie passing within a hundred-mile radius made dinner reservations. The chef simply not showing up for work—well, that was serious. "Did he have health problems or something?"

"No. Every few months he'd go hiking and lose track of time. Or he'd be scouring antiques malls in Lincoln City for old cookbooks. He didn't share Sam's urgency."

"But someone had to lead the kitchen, right?"

"The sous chef is decent, and Miles usually had the upcoming week's dishes planned out, so the restaurant could limp through on those days."

Interesting. "Avery said Miles could be kind of dreamy, sort of do his own thing."

"That's a fact," Stella said. "It's one of the things I appreciated most about him, actually. We were simpatico that way." She wandered to the window and took in the view before facing me again. "There's more. Last week, some strangers showed up at the kitchen door, and there was a kerfuffle. The dishwasher—he's a beefy guy—had to throw them out."

"Could you tell what it was about?"

"I'm at the front of the house and can't hear everything,

but one of the line cooks said they threatened Miles, said he'd 'pay for' what he'd done."

"The sheriff should be all over this."

Stella nodded. "I agree."

"I'm glad you're looking beyond Avery. I hate to think of the sheriff going any further down a dead-end trail. It wasn't her."

"I have my own reasons for wanting to know who killed Miles." I waited, but Stella didn't elaborate. Then, in an apparent change of subject, she said, "I'm thinking it's time I give up my job at the restaurant." Her voice sounded far away.

"I thought you liked the distraction from painting."

"I'll find something else." She seemed to snap to and now faced me.

An idea came to me. Right now my plan was to close the shop on Mondays and Tuesdays to take a break, but if Stella were willing to fill in, I could keep Strings Attached open all week. It would be great as tourist season picked up. Stella's kindness and schoolteacher's savvy would be a plus for the shop.

"Well, if you'd ever consider a few hours in a kite shop from time to time, I'd love to have you. It wouldn't be more than two days a week, but it would be less strenuous than hostessing."

An eyebrow lifted a notch. "That's not a bad idea. They're such lovely kites. I'd see more children, too."

I pushed my luck a little further. "It sounds like we share an interest, as well, in finding out who killed Miles."

She examined me a moment. "Perhaps, but what are you getting at?"

"I don't mean we should go all Nancy Drew, but maybe

if we had a few ideas to feed the sheriff, it could help point him in the right direction. Avery is not the right direction, and I hate to have people around town talking about her."

"The sheriff is good at his job. Fair. We can count on him."

"Sure, but how many murders does he investigate?" I waited for Stella's response, and getting none, I continued. I was starting to get excited about the idea now. Stella knew the residents of Rock Point better than I did, plus she had an in at the Tidal Basin. "If we happened to stumble over something that could help him find Miles's real murderer, we could let him know."

"You own a kite shop, and I used to teach middle schoolers. We're not FBI material."

"True." Madame Lucy nudged her head at my ankles. I knelt and scratched her white ears. "But we live right among Rock Point's residents. We see things that a sheriff wouldn't. I'm worried about Avery. And what about Miles?"

"Miles," Stella nearly whispered. She picked up her wineglass. She seemed to be turning something over in her mind. "Tell you what. Why don't you come have dinner at the Tidal Basin tonight, and we'll talk about it more?"

chapter six

❦

I RETURNED HOME ONCE AGAIN AND QUICKLY CHANGED into something more presentable than the jeans and blouse printed with tiny kites I'd worn during the day. Despite the low-key title of "gastropub," the Tidal Basin's prices were steep and its clientele tony. They might not be dripping diamonds, but their "casual" blue jeans probably cost more than my entire wardrobe.

As I drove my Prius toward town, I reflected that it wouldn't earn pride of place in the restaurant's parking lot, either. It was a first-generation model, in dirt-collecting white, that my dad drove for a few years before deciding he couldn't give up the VW bus. As a result, my bumper exhorted drivers to "Save Tibet" and "Kill Your Television." One bumper sticker curiously read "Bowl Naked," even though neither of my parents were bowlers.

The Tidal Basin commanded part of a new building on

the fancier side of the docks, the side the town called the "marina," where the small yachts and tourist fishing outfits were tied up, rather than the plain old "docks," where generations of fishermen anchored their crafts and where Avery's family's boat was. I opened the restaurant's front door to the sound of jazz and the murmur of conversation, punctuated by bursts of laughter here and there.

Stella had told me I could sit at the bar and pick on a salad for a few hours without breaking the bank. Plus, she'd said that from the bar I'd be able to get more of a feel for what was going on, anyway. I didn't know what I was looking for, exactly, but the artistic process was like this, too. Sometimes you had to pick up a pencil and trust that the concept would come. Maybe if I sat at the Tidal Basin and observed, I'd have some kind of hint to throw Sheriff Koppen's way. Stella said that during her break we could talk about setting her up with a few shifts at Strings Attached.

"Emmy." Stella stood at the podium just inside the door. She'd changed into a soft wrap dress and boots, and with her hair pulled into a loose chignon and a touch of rose lipstick, she could have walked from the set of a French movie. "I saved you a seat. Follow me."

Stella led me through the dining room to the bar toward the rear and pulled out a chair facing the open kitchen. This wasn't a bar as in "cocktail lounge," but rather a strip of seating facing one of the kitchen's stoves and a counter where kitchen staff quickly stacked fish and vegetables into mini-tableaux. Stella plucked a tiny "Reserved" sign from my seat and handed me a menu.

"The cioppino is really good today. Enjoy. I'll check in later," she said before returning to the front of the restaurant.

I ordered as Stella recommended, then looked around

the room. Most of my meals out in Rock Point had been in brewpubs or coffeehouses like the Brew House, and Mom's casseroles hadn't exactly prepared me for haute cuisine, so when the seafood stew I'd ordered was set in front of me, its aroma was exotic with herbs I didn't recognize. I could see getting used to this.

To my right, a door led presumably into the less diner-friendly areas of the kitchen, where onions were chopped and dishes scrubbed. Directly to my left at the bar was a middle-aged couple deep in conversation.

"It's just surfing, honey. It's no more dangerous than scuba diving," the man said.

"Maybe if you're twenty. I just don't see what you have to prove." The woman dabbed her mouth with her napkin.

In the kitchen, in the place Miles presumably held, a harried-looking man with curly hair and a bulldog posture checked a computer screen mounted above the table where plates sat, getting final swirls of sauce and pinches of chopped green herbs. He moved quickly and efficiently, clearly in charge. Would he have wanted this job enough to kill Miles for it?

Stella's voice broke into my thoughts. Standing next to her was a paunchy man with thinning red hair. "Emmy, I'd like you to meet Sam Anderson, the Tidal Basin's owner. Sam, this is Emmy Adler. She has the new kite shop in town, Strings Attached. I thought you should meet since you both own businesses in town."

"A pleasure," Sam said, but his glance skittered to the kitchen, then the dining room before returning to her. "Enjoying your evening?"

"I am. This cioppino is amazing."

At last his gaze settled on me. He smiled. "Thank you. It's one of Miles's recipes. It calls for grilling some of the seafood first on fir boughs. Oregon touch, you know?"

I remembered Stella's hint that Sam had been angry at Miles's flakiness. Not that he'd reveal it to me, a stranger. "I'm sorry about the chef. Losing him must be awful for you, personally and professionally."

"Well—" He looked away.

"And so suddenly," I prompted.

"I hated the guy," Sam said decisively.

My spoon hit the bowl with a clatter. "I'm sorry, I "

"Sure, I could tell you what a tragedy it is—not to say that it isn't—but he'd gotten on my last nerve."

"You hated him?" I still couldn't get past that.

Sam pulled up the stool next to me. "I shouldn't have said that. It's not true." He ran his fingers through the few strands of reddish hair stretched over his skull. "It's been a lot to take with everything else."

"I imagine," I said, having no idea what he was talking about.

"Miles was a brilliant chef, but I'm a businessman. You know, running a business yourself."

I nodded.

"I couldn't depend on him. I asked him time and again to run the menus by me, give me an idea of what food bills might be, but half the time he'd just show up with something he'd bought off some fisherman on the dock, and it would cost a fortune."

"I'm sure that could be frustrating for someone like you."

"I shouldn't have said 'hate,'" Sam repeated. "That's

the East Coaster in me talking. I just meant that he could drive me to distraction. I came out to Oregon to mellow out, not sweat bullets every night hoping that my chef would turn up."

How much would he tell me? "And then having to deal with the sheriff." I held my breath.

"Oh, sure. Sure. They wanted to see everything, talk to everyone. Looking for the murder weapon."

Miles had been stabbed, and the gash was wide. I shuddered. It could have been a kitchen knife. The Tidal Basin, "The Pride of Rock Point," according to the chamber of commerce, might be a lot deadlier than its upscale, easygoing decor indicated. "How did you know?"

"They asked a lot of questions. When I told them a knife was missing, they flipped out." Sam rose, and I swiveled in my seat to follow him.

"You mean the murder weapon came from here?" The couple next to us raised their heads. I mustered a smile and lowered my voice. "From your kitchen?"

"I doubt it. Stuff goes missing here all the time. Gets thrown out with the garbage, grows legs, you know. No biggie."

Sam Anderson was a talker. I bit my lip and plowed ahead. "I heard there was quite a scene here the other night."

He raised his eyebrows. "Where'd you hear about the mushroom hunters?"

Mushroom hunters? Bizarre. "Stella mentioned it."

He nodded. "Yeah? Well, there you have it." He glanced at the curly-headed chef, who'd taken a deep swig from a water bottle before reaching for another plate. Sam wasn't going to tell me more, whether it was because of the couple next to me clearly straining to hear more or because of the busy scene in the kitchen that drew his attention again and again. "Anyway, nice to have met you. Glad you enjoyed the cioppino."

A quick handshake, and he slipped back through the kitchen.

The woman next to me leaned over. "Was that the owner?"

"Uh-huh." He'd told me, a stranger, quite a lot. I hoped he was equally honest with the sheriff.

"I heard that the chef was murdered. Someone found his body yesterday." Surfing forgotten, the man was all ears.

"That's what I heard, too," I said.

"Grisly."

Miles's death had thrown ripples throughout Rock Point. It still remained to see what they would uncover.

BY THE TIME I LEFT THE TIDAL BASIN, THE CROWD WAS thinning. My landlord, Frank, occupied a table at the edge of the bar, where he could keep an eye on the basketball game. He waved a hand and smiled. Stella brought me my coat.

"Does Frank come here often?" I asked.

"He loves it here. He was one of the restaurant's first investors. Did you get anywhere with him—Sam, that is?" Stella said. "I was hoping that with a fresh audience he might tell you more than he'd tell me."

"He said it was mushroom hunters who threatened Miles the other night. Isn't that strange?"

"Mushroom hunters, huh? Not as strange as it sounds.

Mushroom hunting draws a queer crowd, and they get testy about their territory. I've heard stories . . ." She shook her head.

"Sam was frustrated with Miles, too, although he wouldn't get into details."

"That's not news. He's talking to you, though. That's good."

"One last thing. The sheriff wanted to know if any of the kitchen's knives were missing."

"So Koppen is looking into this angle. We can take comfort there."

I still bubbled with adrenaline from questioning Sam, but I hadn't uncovered anything new, except possibly the mushroom-hunting detail. That was a drag. "Nothing new to tell the sheriff."

We were running through the details of having Stella work at Strings Attached, when a fleece-bedecked couple hesitantly pushed open the front door. "Are you still open?"

"For another half hour," Stella said. "I'd be happy to seat you." Then, to me, "I'll let you know if anything else comes up. Drive safely."

On the street, a wind had kicked up from the ocean. It could mean a change in the weather—not a surprise in spring in coastal Oregon. I thought about Sam's changing moods and the mysterious mushroom hunters. Each had shown strong feelings about Miles—stronger than Avery's, or at least stronger than she'd admit to. But it was Avery's name Miles had written in his calendar. Besides the surf's constant grumble, the night was quiet. Probably much like two nights ago, the night Miles had come down to the docks.

I looked toward the darkened pier. If the sheriff was right, and Miles thought he was meeting Avery here, he would have walked from the parking lot, past the vacant office at the dock's mouth, and toward Avery's boat. Did he have a flashlight? A flickering mercury lamp over the office was the dock's only illumination. It would have been easy for the murderer to hide in the shadows, to loop an arm around the chef's neck . . .

"Emmy." A man's voice shattered the silence. Heart in my throat, I slammed against the Prius. "I'm sorry, did I startle you?" The man stepped into the streetlight. It was Jack Sullivan.

"No, I—" It took me a minute to regain my breath. "I just didn't expect to see anyone, that's all."

He stood a moment, hands in pockets. We looked at each other. The gray in his eyes had turned almost steely in the dark. "Well," he said finally. "Take care."

He turned to enter the Tidal Basin.

chapter seven

~◆~

THE NEXT DAY WAS MONDAY, MY DAY OFF, AND I WAS AT loose ends. I'd already taken Bear on his morning walk, studiously avoiding the spot Miles's body had washed up, and returned to the house for breakfast. I kept thinking there was something I should be doing, but I simply paced the living room, hearing the old planks creak beneath my feet. I couldn't shake my cloak of anxiety.

Worse, Avery wasn't out of bed. Usually she was an early riser, and it was the scent of her coffee brewing that woke me. At last, I knocked on her bedroom door. At her faint "Yes?" I barged in.

"Avery, I'm worried about you. Aren't you going to get up and go to work?"

The curtains were drawn, but I made out her figure twisting in the sheets as she rolled to face me. "They're covering for me today. I just don't feel like going in."

Bear jumped on the bed, and Avery reached a hand toward him. Good old Bear. I drew back the curtains. "What's your story, morning glory? Rise and shine, turpentine." It was a saying we'd started when we were in art school. It had seemed funny at one point, and now it was habit.

Avery merely groaned in reply.

"Maybe you'd feel better if you went on a walk. It's raining, but not hard. There's coffee downstairs. I could make you some eggs."

"No, I just want to rest."

I moved closer. "Miles's death is hitting you hard. I get that. But there's no reason you should sink into a black hole." I didn't want to say it, but I wondered if I should call her doctor. "I mean, you're not sick, right?"

"They think I killed him. Everyone does. You should see them looking at me at the Brew House."

"They're just curious. You didn't kill Miles. You know that. Sheriff Koppen will figure it out, too." God willing.

"You should have seen them at poetry night. Mrs. Mendez recited a poem that had a line about 'murdered dreams,' and everyone swiveled to look at me. One of the customers even had the gall to ask what the body looked like. As if I knew." She pulled the sheet over her head. "I can't go back. Not right now."

"They'll be sorry once the truth comes out. If you stay away, it'll only make them think you're guilty," I said. Avery didn't respond. "You can't stay in bed all day, you know."

She pulled up the sheet and ignored me.

"Avery," I said.

"There's one thing you could do for me."

"Sure," I answered eagerly.

"Could you make me some of your mom's tea—that one that puts you to sleep?"

I sighed in exasperation. "I'll bring you a cup of coffee. Black." I sat on the edge of the bed. "I know this is bringing up a lot of grief for you, so take it easy. But don't let it defeat you, either."

"Thanks."

I couldn't tell if she really heard me or not. "When I come back this afternoon, I expect to find you up and showered." Maybe I'd been a little harsh. I softened my voice. "Listen. I'm sorry. I can't possibly know how you feel. But there's no reason you should bear all this pain. They'll find the murderer. They will."

She said something unintelligible, then rolled to face the wall and pulled Bear closer. I gave up.

I rode my bicycle to Strings Attached, hiding the rest of the Lassitude Tea in the shop's kitchen so Avery wouldn't be tempted by it. Then I went to the Brew House for a booster cup of joe and ran into Dave, whose store was also closed on Mondays this early in the season.

He leapt to his feet when he saw me. "Avery isn't working today."

"She's still in bed."

"Still?" The circles under his eyes showed that Dave hadn't slept all that well himself. It wasn't Miles's death that had kept him up, though. It was Avery. I knew that. Dave was fair, and I'm sure he was always friendly when Miles came to rent a kayak or saw him at the Tidal Basin—heck, he'd even referred to Miles as a "friend"—but he couldn't have been happy thinking of Avery and Miles together. At least I could cross Dave off the suspect list since he was with me when Miles was murdered.

"She's taking . . . all this . . . hard."

He rubbed his fingers over his close-cut beard. "I wish there was something I could do."

A few locals had looked up from their coffee and were unnaturally quiet. Undoubtedly, they hoped to catch some scoop on the murder. I didn't want to stick around.

"Is that coffee to go?" With meaning, I looked at the people at the next table, then back to Dave. "Why don't we take a walk to the old part of town?"

Understanding passed over his face, and he slipped on his jacket. "Good idea."

Above Main Street, where the streets sloped up to the bluff, was Old Town. It was really just four or five blocks of Victorian homes. A few of the homes had remained in their families over the years, but many had been converted to guesthouses or offices. The street's trees were bright green with new growth, and daffodils splashed gold in many front gardens. The salty tang of the breeze reminded me that the ocean was only a short walk away.

"I'd been hoping to see Avery this morning," Dave said.

"Like I said, she's in bed. Doesn't want to get up. She says everyone is looking at her like she's guilty." I tossed my paper cup in a street garbage can and buried my hands in my pockets. "Dave?"

"Yes?"

He was so deliberate, a clear thinker. "Do you have any ideas of who might have killed Miles?"

We walked a few more steps before he replied. "I've thought about it, even wondered if it might have been a random killing. I can't think of anyone in Rock Point who would have done it."

"I don't see a random killer taking his body out on a

boat and dumping it in the ocean, then planting an obviously fake meeting with Avery."

"No. Someone planned it." His shoulders tightened, probably at the mention of Avery.

"I'm worried the sheriff won't look any further than her," I said.

"That bothers me, too. He's a good sheriff, though."

Good sheriff, fair sheriff. That's all anyone said about Koppen. All I knew was that he suspected Avery, and he was wrong. "I think he's way off base. I wonder—have you ever thought of looking around for a little information that could set him back on track?"

Dave shot me a sideways glance. "What do you mean?"

He knew what I meant. I simply returned his look.

He shook his head. "No way. We could make a lot more trouble for Avery that way."

"What do you mean?"

He stopped on the sidewalk and turned to me. "Say we found some terrific piece of evidence—a letter, or a conversation with someone—that nailed the murderer. Well, both of us obviously want to protect Avery."

"Sure." I wasn't sure where he was going.

"The prosecutor could say we tampered with the evidence or influenced a witness. We'd mess up the case."

Damn it. He was so logical. "We can't just sit around, though. What if we look for hints, then feed them to the sheriff? That's all."

"Not a good idea. The best thing we can do is stay clear of the investigation."

To Dave, it was open and shut. Wait and expect that justice would prevail. Well, life wasn't a Frank Capra movie. Happy endings were not guaranteed. "Fine." At least Stella saw things my way.

Dave's thoughts had moved on, and we continued our walk up the hill. "Poor Avery. I wish there was something I could do."

I bit my tongue. He'd nixed my suggestion, but that didn't mean he couldn't do something. "She needs to get out of the house. At work, she'll just run into nosy people who'll ask upsetting questions."

Dave's pace slowed. "What she needs is to get outside. She loves the outdoors."

"Yes. That's a great idea."

His pace picked up. "I'll take her kayaking. There's a spot up the river where the cormorants are nesting now. She'd love that."

"That's perfect. Exactly what she needs. Take some sandwiches with you—it's getting close to lunchtime."

Now Dave was antsy and started down the hill. He'd only gone a few steps before he stopped. "You coming with me?"

I'd noticed the sign on the especially gaudy Victorian mansion behind me. "Morning Glory Inn & Teahouse," it read. Annabelle Black's place.

"No," I replied. "I'll stay up here."

ANNABELLE AND I HADN'T EXACTLY HIT IT OFF DURING our first, brief meeting, and now seemed as good a time as any to mend fences. Rock Point was a small town, and the smallest grudge could escalate into years of tension if it wasn't nipped in the bud. Besides, the Morning Glory

Inn attracted out-of-towners, some of whom surely would enjoy flying kites. It was lunchtime. Why not stop in?

My enchantment with the Victorian house's gingerbread facade and old-fashioned screen door came to a screeching halt once I'd passed into the main hall. The place was festooned with doilies. Seriously. It would take a dozen tatting clubs a decade to churn out the number of doilies Annabelle had strewn on chairs, slung over end tables, and even framed on the walls.

"May I help you?" came a voice from the adjoining room. Annabelle appeared from a broad-arched doorway that must have once led to the living room and now housed a lounge. She wore a flowered apron over a prairie-style dress with an obscenely low neckline—like what a burlesque performer might have worn in a covered-wagon routine.

"Emmy Adler," I said and extended a hand. "We met at Sullivan's Kites over the weekend. What a beautiful inn you have."

"Oh yes." Annabelle's unchanged expression told me that she'd recognized me right away. "Thank you. You're not looking for a place to stay, are you?"

"No, no," I said. "I thought I might get a bite to eat. Your inn has such a great reputation, I've been looking forward to stopping by." I might have been laying it on thick, but I wasn't sure what else to say. A natural rapport wasn't exactly cropping up. I decided to try honesty. "Plus, well, I feel like we didn't get off on the right foot, and I wanted to get to know you a bit better."

"Come in." She hadn't acknowledged my extended olive branch. She stepped into the lounge and gestured toward a floral upholstered Queen Anne chair with a doily over its back. "I'll get you a menu."

I was getting hungry for lunch. A fat sandwich would be good. Annabelle handed me a pink menu with flowery script. "I'll bring you some tea," she said, and without waiting for my reply trotted through the dining room into what must be the kitchen.

Well, all right, it looked like I'd be having a pot of tea. Once I saw the menu, I understood why. It was all tea cakes, petit fours, and scones. I turned the menu over, hoping soup and sandwiches might be listed on the back. Nope. When Annabelle returned with a pansy-sprigged teapot, I asked if she served sandwiches.

"You want sandwiches? No problem." She again returned to the kitchen.

Her attitude might have been curt, and the floral patterns and powder tones in the lounge might have made me a little itchy, but at least I had a nice view down the tree-lined street to Rock Point's main street, and just beyond that a slice of the ocean muffled with clouds. I wasn't giving up yet on my efforts to at least restore civility with Annabelle.

An elderly couple lounged at one of the other five tables. They rose, pushing away their scone-crumbed plates.

"Thank you, Mr. and Mrs. Orr," Annabelle said. "Enjoy your day in Rock Point."

"We will, honey. Maybe we'll drive up to the cheese factory," the wife said, brandishing a brochure.

"Don't forget the cranberry bogs. I really think you'd enjoy them."

"See you this evening," the husband said. The front door shut a moment later.

Annabelle set a plate on my table. Yes, she'd given me sandwiches, but they were all finger-sized on white bread with the crusts cut off.

"Smoked salmon and cream cheese." She pointed at two of the sandwiches. "And cucumber. Enjoy."

Definitely not one to be overly friendly, I thought. As she cleared the elderly couple's plates, I tried again. "Such lovely moldings in this room." The cream-painted ceiling moldings depicted fish jumping and swimming, and in one case, appearing to do the limbo. "And amazing lacework."

For the first time, I got a smile. "This house was built by Rock Point's founder. I was lucky to buy it. He came over on the Oregon Trail, like my family did."

"It's a grand house. He must have done well for himself."

She nodded, wiping the table the couple had left. Despite the delicacy of her face, her hands were strong and reddened. Working hands. "Made his money in fish fertilizer. Sold it across the country." She set down her sponge and lowered herself into one of the chairs. "One of his grandsons owned the house when I bought it. He was going a little batty and moved to New York into some high-rise. Said he couldn't stand all this 'frippery.'" She laughed. "Imagine that. His loss, my gain, I guess."

"And the Oregon Trail. You must be pioneer stock." At last, the *Little House on the Prairie* look made sense. It was branding. Annabelle actually dressed to match her business.

"Oh yes. It's the Black way. We go after what we want, and nothing stands in our way. Of course, honor and community service are key."

"Wow." I wasn't sure what else to say.

"I've done the whole family tree."

"It must be nice to know a lot about your family—you know, family stories and legend." Because I knew how lame that sounded, I glanced around the lounge. "And share that in how you've created the inn."

"My ancestors inspire me. The Morning Glory has been a lot of work, and I haven't seen a profit yet, but I think about my ancestors who never gave up, and it keeps me going. If they could make it across the whole nation in a rickety wagon, I can get a bed-and-breakfast up and running."

At least she was beginning to relax now. If I could keep the questions flowing, we might part ways a lot friendlier. "You've really built something here."

"Rock Point is growing, and I wanted to establish myself before it turns resort," she said.

I kind of liked the fishing village charm, myself. "What do you mean about 'turning resort'?"

"It's inevitable. The town has to grow, and it will be tourist trade. It won't be long before we'll need more lodging and restaurants."

"I like Rock Point, too, but there are plenty of towns along the coast."

"Plenty that are not Rock Point," she said. "Look." As if explaining to a kindergartner, she held up a hand and began ticking off reasons on her fingers. "One, Rock Point is close to Portland. That means weekend traffic from the city. Two, Rock Point is unspoiled. We don't have that seedy taffy-and-bikinis feel some towns have."

"If we grow, there's no avoiding fudge shops," I said.

"Growth can be controlled, and we can maintain a first-class atmosphere. I've talked about this at length with Frank."

Frank Hopkins, my landlord. "We already have the Tidal Basin. I guess that's a step in the right direction." I just wanted to sell kites, not take over the pages of *Travel and Leisure*, but I was glad to know someone was on the job.

"And the Morning Glory. I feel like I'm helping to set a direction for Rock Point." She lovingly stroked the edge of a velvet cushion. "It's taken the better part of two years, but it's worth it."

"You must have worked like crazy to get the house ready for guests."

"Oh yes. While contractors were working, I was at auctions and estate sales everywhere."

"The teapots alone—"

"Exactly. It's not easy to manufacture this kind of charm, but I was determined. My mother always said that when I want something, I get it, and she was right." She scanned the room, then, apparently satisfied with what she saw, returned her gaze to me.

"The Black family way," I said.

"Exactly."

My sandwiches were nearly half-gone already and hadn't even started to satisfy my appetite. I slowed myself down by pouring another cup of tea. At least Annabelle was starting to open up. "Have you known Jack Sullivan long?" I asked, mostly to continue the conversation.

Her manner iced over. "Of course."

Whoops. Wrong turn. "Naturally you would, with both of you living here and all."

"Why do you want to know, anyway?"

Wow. "No reason. Just talking." I picked up my remaining finger sandwich. I'd have to stop by the Brew House for a real lunch later.

She slipped into the chair at my table. "How's Avery?

I couldn't help but hear she's a suspect. It can't be easy for her."

I tread cautiously. "She's upset, of course. Dave's taking her kayaking this afternoon to cheer her up."

"You're not going with them? Dave's not a bad-looking guy."

She apparently hadn't got the message about Dave and Avery. "No, I have an idea for a new kite, and I thought I'd work on it at the shop." Everything seemed to be about men with her. I leaned forward. "Listen, Annabelle, I'm sorry we had to meet under such"—I searched for the words—"upsetting circumstances."

For a moment she looked blank; then her eyes narrowed. "We were meant to be together. I still can't believe he's—he's gone."

"I'm so sorry," I said, confused. I'd expected Annabelle to break into tears, but she almost seemed angry. I thought of Avery's grief and how different—and profound—it seemed.

Annabelle seemed to realize her at-odds attitude, too. She dropped her head and heaved a sigh. "It's so hard. You can't understand. I feel so helpless."

I felt helpless, too, but for different reasons. "I'm sorry," I repeated.

"I guess I could offer to host the reception after the funeral." Her gaze darted through the room, as if already laying out the buffet in her mind.

"It's true. I can't understand how Miles's death hurts you." I hoped my voice didn't sound as curt as I suspected it did. "But I've seen how it's affected Avery—"

Annabelle leaned forward, and I prepared for a self-pitying remark. Instead, her words, delivered low and calm, chilled me. "If she killed Miles, she can spend her years in prison making lattes for convicts for all I care."

"What?" Where did this come from? I pushed to my feet. "She's my friend. Watch it. No one's been charged with anything yet."

Surprised, she stopped and examined me. Maybe she wasn't sure where to go next with this conversation. All I knew was that if she made one more comment about Avery, I'd stuff her craw with doilies.

"Maybe Avery is your friend, but Miles was my friend," she said. "More than that."

I was leaving, but I wouldn't give her the satisfaction of seeing how much she'd infuriated me. To ramp down, I mentally counted to three. "Thank you for the tea. I guess I'd better pay my check now," I managed to spit out.

"No problem. Stop by again soon."

"Real soon."

chapter eight

~~~

FUMING, I LEFT THE MORNING GLORY INN. HOW DARE
she? I'd visited to try to make nice, and Annabelle had to
go and insult Avery. For all I knew, she'd been jealous that
Miles wasn't falling at her feet and had killed him herself.
And I was sure she wasn't the only possibility. Sam Anderson down at the Tidal Basin, for instance. And the
mushroom hunters. Where was the sheriff in all this?

I remembered seeing his local office—the main office
was at the county seat in Astoria—in a small storefront
down on Main Street next to Martino's Pizza. He and I
had some talking to do.

I stomped to the sheriff's office and only paused a
second at the door before pushing it open.

"Can I help you?" a woman at the front desk asked. She
must have been about forty or so and was dressed in practical short hair and a khaki uniform.

"I'm here to see Sheriff Koppen." The aroma of garlic and yeast floated in from Martino's. My stomach rumbled after Annabelle's Barbie-sized sandwiches. Avery had told me that a local named Marty owned the place, and he'd Italianed up his name for show.

"I'm Deputy Goff. What's the problem?"

"Emmy Adler," I said. "I need to know where he is with Miles Logan's death."

The deputy looked me over and didn't appear to like what she saw. "You're the one who found the body, right? Avery Cook's roommate?"

"That's another thing. What's all this suspicion with Avery? I don't care what Miles's calendar said. She was home, in bed, when he was killed."

Sheriff Koppen emerged from a back room. "What's going on out here?"

"I came to find out what you're doing about Miles's murder."

The deputy looked at Koppen and shrugged. "She came in here demanding to see you."

"I want you to leave Avery alone and find the real murderer."

"I told her she could tell me, but—" the deputy started.

"It's all right, Denise. I'll take care of this."

"She shouldn't be bothering you."

"I've got it," the sheriff said. The deputy reluctantly turned away, but not without giving me the stink eye first.

Koppen raised a brow. "Follow me."

The sheriff had a small, windowless office at the back of the storefront. The vines from a philodendron plant on top of a filing cabinet wound around the room at least twice, held in place by pushpins and string. Koppen lifted his jacket from a chair and motioned for me to sit. The aroma from Martino's was even more potent here.

"You have some reason to doubt my ability to solve this murder?" Sheriff Koppen leaned back, his face inscrutable as always. On his desk was a framed photo showing a dark-haired woman and two boys in what looked like tribal costumes. Strange to think of him with a family, laughing and loving. All I'd seen was his brick wall of an expression.

"If you suspect Avery, I do. She's not a killer. Besides, all you've got against her is that Miles mistakenly thought he was meeting her, and she used to date him. But that was a long time ago."

He didn't speak. His face was stone solid.

I continued. "Think about it. Why would she kill him? Why now? If people just knocked off their exes, undertakers wouldn't have time to sleep." Now I was really picking up steam. The pungent scent of sausage gnawed at my stomach and fueled my anger. "Besides, what about Annabelle Black? I just saw her, and she's a nutcase. Dresses like an extra from *Gunsmoke*. She dated Miles, too, you know. You don't seem to care about her." We stared at each other. Koppen's expression was still infuriatingly unmoved. "Well?" I said.

"Are you finished?"

I nodded and looked away to keep from getting even more upset.

"You're right," the sheriff said.

My gaze snapped to him. He agreed with me?

"The evidence against Avery is weak. That's why we haven't taken her in. But we do have to investigate it. You know that, don't you?"

"But you're following up other leads, right? I mean, you don't even have a murder weapon."

"Emmy, this is my job. Admittedly, murders don't turn up every day in Rock Point. But we have a protocol, and we're meticulous about it."

"Like what? Who are you talking to?" I moved to the edge of my seat.

"Right now, a crime-scene team is examining the Cook family's boat, for instance."

I sat up straighter. "Avery's boat? What's that got to do with anything?" Damn. Of course they'd examine the boat.

"Miles had an appointment to meet Avery there. Besides, his body had to have been disposed of at sea. That's why it washed up where you found it."

"Well, you won't find anything." That, at least, was a comfort. "But who are you talking to besides Avery? I can think of three suspects with better motives than hers."

"At the risk of sounding rude, that's our business and not yours."

"But how do I know that you're—"

"Listen. The best thing you can do is butt out and let us do our job. We're talking to everyone and anyone in Miles's life. Upholding the peace is my job. Not yours."

"But people are talking. Avery doesn't even want to go into work, because everyone stares at her."

"Sounds like the Brew House might pick up some new business."

"That's not the point." I was aware I might be coming off like a three-year-old who'd lost her blankie. I thought about Stella and our promise. "Would it help you if I passed along things I'd heard that might help your investigation?"

"If you have something to tell me about Avery, I'm listening. You do live with her."

"Not Avery." Lord, he was dense. "I mean, maybe I'll hear things, like about Sam Anderson, Miles's boss."

"We've questioned Sam."

"Did you know that he was upset with Miles for not showing up to work?"

"Not only do I know it; I have his work schedule, with his absences noted, for the past six months."

"I just thought that . . ." My voice petered out. "Well, what about the mushroom hunters? The ones who threatened him?"

He leaned back in his chair. "Look. Sure, if you stumble upon something that has to do with the investigation, let us know. But don't go making trouble by getting involved. That's not your job." His gaze drilled into me. "Maybe your job is taking care of your friend. Seems like the past few days have been pretty rough on her. You could do more good at home with her than blowing off steam at me."

My face burned. He was right, of course. Avery might be home now. I'd take her a pizza from Martino's.

BEAR GREETED ME WITH A FEW JOYOUS BARKS AND A clattering of nails as he ran to the door.

Avery looked much happier than when I'd left her in the morning. She stood straighter, and her eyes were brighter. I pushed my sketch pad away and rose to hug her.

"How was the kayaking?"

"Great. Dave took me up the river. I'd forgotten how much I love spring. There's a storm coming in, though.

Good thing we got home when we did." She kicked off her shoes and plopped onto the sofa. "Have you eaten yet?"

Food. She wanted food. This was a good sign. "I brought us a pizza. I'll go heat up the oven."

"Somehow seeing those baby cormorants brought it all home for me. Life goes on, you know what I mean?"

"Yes." I smiled but kept most of my jubilation—and relief—inside. I didn't want Avery to feel self-conscious. "We'll get past this. The sheriff is doing everything he can."

Avery's smile melted. "You talked to the sheriff?"

"He didn't come to find me," I hurried to say. "I just happened to be near his office and thought I'd drop in, you know, to see if anything new came up."

"Right." Clearly Avery knew me too well.

"I couldn't help it. He's wrong about suspecting you."

"But, Miles's calendar—"

"It was some kind of mistake." Why wasn't Avery defending herself? "He accidentally jotted down a date on the wrong month. Or someone planted it. We don't know."

I couldn't tell if Avery was listening. She absently stroked Bear between his ears.

"Avery?"

"You're right." She smiled again, and my shoulders relaxed. "New evidence will come up. It'll work itself out."

A much better attitude. Why she refused to stand up for herself, I had no idea, but at least she was sounding optimistic.

"Very true." I rose to slide the pizza into the oven. "After all, they don't even have the knife that killed him. It's probably loaded with fingerprints." I returned and plunked on the couch next to her.

"Maybe it is. Or something else will appear." At last she seemed to be getting back to normal. "But Emmy, when we were talking about Miles the other night, I didn't tell you everything."

She hadn't. I knew she hadn't. At last she'd finish her story about Miles. "I'm listening."

The old fir trees behind the house swished in the wind, and the house groaned in response. Bear was starting to get used to the house's grumblings and didn't even raise his head this time. I settled back. As with a kite that barely began to catch the wind, I had to let Avery find her own pace.

"It's hard to talk about it. I think—I think with everything else, it was simply easier to bury the whole thing. But I want to tell you." Her tone was low and serious.

"I get it," I said. The rain, which had been soft during the day, now blew hard and sharp against the windows.

Avery looked me in the eyes. I almost held my breath. "You know how I was telling you that Miles and I—we—"

I nodded, and she looked away. "Well . . . ," she started. "Just a minute. It's getting cool. Let me get my slippers." She rose from the couch and headed toward the hall. I crossed my fingers that she hadn't lost her courage and would tell me the whole story. "Have you seen them? The ones with the sheepskin lining?" Her voice was muffled. She must have moved into the bedroom.

Bear had a reputation for hoarding shoes. "Did you check Bear's bed?" Avery didn't reply. "You've got to watch him with socks, too." Still nothing. Tension gripped my stomach. "Avery?" Silence.

I leapt from the couch and went to find Avery. Dread crept over me as I rounded the corner to her bedroom.

"Avery?" I repeated.

I found her kneeling by her bed. She looked up, her features frozen in fear. She lifted a hand. In it was a knife.

chapter nine

AVERY STOOD IN THE DOORWAY OF HER BEDROOM, dangling the knife between her thumb and forefinger as if it were a dead animal.

"Where'd you find it?" My lungs had tightened, and my voice was barely a squeak.

"Under my bed. I was looking for my slippers, and—"

We stared at the knife. I know we both thought the same thing. This was the knife that killed Miles. It had an industrial plastic handle battered by use. Rust-colored stains I prayed were only rust marred its long, narrow blade. The pounding wind and rain echoed my state of mind.

"You don't happen to have—"

"No," Avery said, anticipating the rest of my sentence. She didn't have a knife like that.

"Or do you think it—"

"Don't know." Avery let out a long breath. Her hand

dropped to her side, still holding the knife. "What should we do?"

I met Avery's gaze. We both knew what we had to do. For a split second I considered urging her to throw the knife into the ocean. But we couldn't. There was only one real option. I ached right through.

"I'll call the sheriff," I said.

SHERIFF KOPPEN AND DEPUTY GOFF WERE AT THE DOOR within minutes. I'd barely answered his knock, and they'd wiped their feet on the mat, then pushed past me, shaking the rain from their coats. Avery sat, stunned, on the couch, Bear beside her.

"Where is it?" the sheriff asked.

Avery lifted a hand to the coffee table, where the knife lay.

The sheriff pulled on a pair of latex gloves and held the knife gingerly from its top, probably to avoid where fingerprints might still be had—if any fingerprints remained except Avery's.

"Denise, hand me the evidence bag," he said to the deputy before turning back to us. "A filet knife. Restaurant grade. Listen"—he looked at each of us in turn—"I'm asking you to keep to yourselves what type of knife this is. It's important to the investigation that the public not know every detail." We both nodded. "I can trust you, right?" He seemed to direct that last portion to me. "It's critical."

"Definitely," I said.

Deputy Goff took in the room, and her gaze rested on me. She might have curled her lip just a bit. Even Bear, who usually made the rounds with a wagging tail, kept his distance.

"Now, tell me where you found the knife," Sheriff Koppen said.

"It was under her bed," I started, but the sheriff cut me off.

"You found the knife?" he asked me.

"Well, no, but—"

"Then let Ms. Cook answer." He handed the knife to Goff, who slipped it into a clear plastic bag. She jotted something on a small piece of paper, almost like a label.

"I was looking under my bed for my slippers, and there it was," Avery said.

"Start at the beginning," the sheriff said. "When you got home. When was that?"

"I went kayaking with Dave Reed and got back midafternoon—about three."

"Was Emmy home?"

"No," I said.

"Didn't you hear him? He's asking Avery," the deputy chided. "When he wants you to tell him something, he'll let you know."

The sheriff cast her a curious glance, then returned to Avery. "Was Emmy home?"

"No. She didn't get home until six or so."

"What did you do this afternoon at home?"

"Nothing interesting, I guess. Laundry. Dishes. I took Bear for a walk."

Despite the dire situation, I felt some satisfaction. She'd been feeling good enough to work around the house. Good enough until now, that is. I took comfort, though, in knowing the sheriff was trying to figure out if there was a time someone could have planted the knife.

Deputy Goff lifted her head from taking notes long

enough to give me a dirty look. Why she disliked me so much, I didn't have a clue.

"So the only time you were out of the house was while you were kayaking and when you took out the dog," the sheriff said.

"Yes. Bear and I were only gone for about half an hour."

"Bear could easily run—" I began.

The sheriff shot me a warning glance. I clamped my mouth shut.

"Then Emmy came home, and you were looking for your slippers," he said.

"Yes."

"You don't know where your slippers are?" the sheriff asked.

"Normally I do. Normally they're by the side of my bed. But they weren't there."

"Bear likes shoes," I said. "Sometimes he stockpiles them somewhere."

The deputy tapped her pen on the side table. "If you won't be quiet, you'll have to leave. Nick, should I take her to the patrol car?"

Again, an eyebrow raised a touch, he looked at Goff. "No, that won't be necessary."

"I'll be quiet." I took an armchair across from Avery and clutched a throw pillow to my lap.

"I couldn't find my slippers, so I looked under the bed. I saw the knife's handle," Avery said. "I pulled it out."

"Have you seen the knife before?" the sheriff asked.

"No." Avery shook her head to emphasize it. "Never."

"Now let's go back to when you left this morning. What time did you leave?"

"It was about one in the afternoon," Avery said. "Dave

drove here with the kayaks already loaded up. I didn't think I wanted to leave the house, but he convinced me. Told me cormorants were hatching upriver. He'd even brought sandwiches."

Dave was a good man. I knew he would have had his reward when he'd seen Avery perk up.

Goff flipped the page of her notebook. "Tell me again when you returned?"

The sheriff had already asked this question. Was it a trick? I opened my mouth to say when Avery had returned home, but at a look from Goff, I shut it.

"Like I said, around three, I guess."

Koppen was hard to read. His jaw was set tight, but it could have been from anything from worry to anger. I couldn't tell.

"And you," he said to me. "Were you home when Ms. Cook arrived?"

"No." I leapt at the chance to speak. "I came home after I talked to you. Less than an hour ago." Goff made notes, but neither the sheriff nor deputy responded. "Don't you see?" I said. "Someone saw the house was empty and planted evidence against Avery. It's a setup."

Goff swung her gaze toward me. "You're doing our job?"

"If it was Avery, why would she call about the knife? I mean, that would be stupid, right?"

The sheriff looked at me, those clear black eyes boring into me. "Or clever," he replied. "The judge signed a warrant this afternoon. We would have searched the house first thing in the morning. And found the knife."

"But why would we have kept it? Why not just get rid of it?"

"We?" Koppen asked. "What do you have to do with it?"

My insides sizzled with frustration. "I mean Avery. She's not stupid. If she killed Miles, I'm sure she would have thrown the knife away, not suddenly pretended to find it tonight."

"Stop it!" Avery said. Somehow I'd forgotten about her sitting on the couch. "Stop arguing. The sheriff is asking legitimate questions. Leave him alone. This is between him and me."

My jaw dropped. Avery was asking me to back off. Bear seemed to sense the tension. He slunk off the couch and trotted toward his bed.

"I'm afraid we're going to have to take you in," the sheriff said.

Take her in? To jail? "You can't be serious," I said.

As if in response, against the steady whistling of the eaves from the wind, something hit the back of the house. Probably a blown-down branch.

"We have too much evidence against her at this point to let her remain out of custody. Maybe the knife will reveal other fingerprints, but until then, you'll need to come with us."

"But all you have is this knife—which we reported— and some mistaken calendar entry." My voice had leapt a few notes. I tried to rein it in, appear calm. "How can you arrest someone on that?"

Avery was silent. Not a peep out of her. Not a single word of defense.

Koppen rose. "There are bloodstains on the deck of the Cooks' boat. We haven't tested them yet, but forensics says they're new. And a witness saw Avery at the dock."

A witness? It had to be a mistake. "I'll get you a lawyer,"

I told her. "This is ridiculous. You'll be out of jail in no time, and he—" I narrowed my eyes. "He'll be sorry."

Koppen rose and so did Avery.

"You'll be sorry if you don't check the oven. Something is burning," Deputy Goff said with evident satisfaction.

The pizza. "Don't go!" I yelled, and dashed to the kitchen to yank open the oven door. Acrid smoke billowed out. Despite the driving rain, I pulled up the kitchen window and waved my way through the smoke to the living room, where Avery was shrugging on her purse. At least she wasn't in handcuffs.

The sheriff faced Avery. "Ms. Cook, you have the right to remain silent—"

"I'll find you a lawyer!" I shouted.

Flanked by the sheriff and deputy, Avery didn't reply, didn't even turn back as sheets of rain blew past.

I stood at the door, the smell of charred pizza streaming around me, as Koppen's taillights faded into the distance.

chapter ten

THE NEXT MORNING I ROSE EARLY. I HAD WORK TO DO.
It seemed like the wind itself had felt Avery's absence, and
the house creaked and moaned like a pirate's galleon all
night. But the storm had blown over, and the morning was
still.

Dodging fallen branches, I loaded Bear into the car and
drove into town, parking near the Brew House and leaving
Bear in the back with the window rolled partway down. I'd
only be a minute. The café was just opening. Trudy, the manager, was wiping down tables and listening to Neil Young.

"Hey," Trudy said. "I thought you were Avery."

"She's not coming in today," I said.

Something about my expression must have alarmed her,
because she straightened and tossed her bleach-water rag
onto the counter. "Is everything all right?"

"Everything's fine. It's just that—well—something

unexpected has come up, and she'll be out for a few days. Can you hold down the fort without her?" I felt bad lying to Trudy. She'd been with the Brew House since it had opened, and I knew Avery trusted her completely. But I hoped that Avery would be home soon. Why complicate things by telling her that her boss was in jail?

"Sure. No problem at all. Tell her I said hi, and that Matt changed the rings on the espresso machine last night."

"No storm damage?"

"No. The old building held up pretty well. I don't think we lost a single roof shingle."

That was something, at least. "Thanks, Trudy. Could you spare a large Americano for me? Leave room for milk, please."

The espresso machine hissed as it delivered its shot. Trudy steamed water for it and slid the cup across the counter. "Is that Bear out there?" I nodded. "Take him this." She reached into a jar Avery kept under the counter and placed a dog biscuit next to my coffee.

"He'll love it."

Task number one completed. Task number two had to wait until I was back at Strings Attached with Bear curled up on his cushion in the kitchen, crunching on his Milk-Bone. Half an hour later, I was in the shop, punching the jail's number on my phone. I got a recording listing visiting hours and made a note of the evening slot. I had to see Avery and find out what was going on.

The last task was the trickiest. "Mom?" I knew she'd be up meditating, despite the early hour.

"Honey? Is anything wrong?"

I gulped some of the Americano. "No. Not wrong. It's just that I—I have a friend who needs some legal help."

"Are you in trouble with the law?" My mother's voice leapt.

"No, Mom. Not me. I told you, a friend." My father was a retired attorney. True, he'd mostly prosecuted environmental cases, but he surely knew the local talent. "I have a friend who might need a criminal-defense attorney. Can you ask Dad who's good?"

"What did your friend do?"

"That's personal."

"You weren't involved, were you?"

"No. Not at all." I crossed my fingers as we spoke. "I just need a referral, that's all."

A moment passed. "Well, I'm glad to know it isn't you, Em. You might be bullheaded at times, but you're no felon."

"Thanks, Ma."

"He's still in bed, but I'll give him the message. He's worn out. Did you know there are thirty-seven hundred hours of Nixon tapes? I'm making your father a tincture for his throat. Poor man."

THE EERIE, DIPPING SONG OF A ROBIN PIERCED THE morning's quiet. Later, Stella would be coming by to get the lowdown on how to run Strings Attached, but that wouldn't be for a few hours yet, when the shop opened. To pass the time and distract me from this nightmare with Avery, I turned to the one thing I knew would absorb me: kite making.

I finally had a design for a promising kite shaped like a comet. The next step was to make a pattern so I could sew a prototype. Since I was simply testing the design, I'd draw it freehand on the stiff paper I used for cutting patterns. After that, I'd weight the pattern down on ripstop nylon and cut its pieces. Then I'd sew the kite, thread the spars that gave it shape, and attach a bridle.

The catch with the comet kite was that it was asymmetrical. I hoped the kite wouldn't pull to one side or, worse, refuse to rise at all. The trick was to create enough surface to lift the kite, but also balance so that it wouldn't veer and crash.

My sewing machine hummed as light washed through the windows. Now I just needed to position the bridle, and it would be ready to test. The bridle's placement was critical to its flightworthiness. Some kite makers say you can fly anything if you bridle it right. My slapdash prototype would test that theory. The store wasn't opening for another half hour. I still had time to take the kite to the beach and give it a whirl.

"Come on, Bear," I said.

He leapt to his feet and trotted after me down to the still-quiet beach.

A stiff breeze blew in from the ocean. Here on the sand was little evidence of last night's storm. I wondered how Avery had slept. Sheriff Koppen wasn't a monster. He would have made sure she was comfortable. But how comfortable could she be, locked up for a crime she didn't commit? Koppen had been so confident as he rattled off the evidence against her: calendar, boat, knife. Avery had been about to tell her something last night, too, before she found the knife.

And how many locals already knew she'd been taken in? I suspected the Brew House would be busy this morning.

"That kite will never fly," came a voice from behind me.

I spun around. Jack Sullivan. A lock of dark hair blew over his eyes. He pushed it back.

"How do you know? Have you ever flown a kite like this?" I said, indignant. He'd chosen the wrong morning to pick a fight.

"No, and I doubt anyone else has, either. That shape—"

"Comet," I said. "It's a comet."

"Yeah, well it doesn't have the surface area to catch the wind. Your updraft won't be strong enough to hoist the whole kite. I get where you're going with it, but maybe you should try a different shape. Something three dimensional. Maybe a sock."

"You don't know it won't fly," I said. I didn't want to admit that I'd had the same concern. I had to try, anyway.

"Then give it a go."

Smart aleck. I made a production of turning away from him and lifted the kite in both arms. Walking briskly backward, I let the kite go, silently begging it to lift. It held on a few feet off the ground, but I knew that was only because I was walking so fast. The kite clumped to the sand.

I looked at Jack with a stern expression. If he said "I told you so," I'd send Bear to his house to hide all his shoes and chew up the best ones.

Instead, he said something worse. "So I hear Avery is down at the jail."

"Where did you hear that?" I practically shouted.

"I guess someone saw her and the sheriff headed north to Astoria, and Lenny listens to the police band twenty-four seven."

"She won't be there long. Sheriff Koppen will figure it out."

"It's his job to find who murdered Miles," he said.

I stared at him. "That's right. It is."

"And he thinks it's Avery. Word is that someone saw Avery down at the dock the night Miles died."

"Did you see her?"

"No, but—"

"Then you should be quiet." I cast him a look that might crack stone. "I happen to know exactly where she was. At home, in bed." Young man Sullivan was ten times worse than old man Sullivan.

"Is that so?" he said. "People don't get charged with murder for no reason. Dave told me that the two of you were down at the bonfire most of the evening."

"And Avery was in bed. She had a headache. I'm sure he told you that, too." God, he was irritating. How could I have ever found him attractive? "Back off. Go back to wherever you came from, and leave me alone." Bear had wandered down the beach to play with a golden retriever. "Bear!" I yelled. I was getting out of there.

"Look," Jack said. "I'm sorry. Don't go. I'm being a jerk."

I paused and examined his face. He bit his lip. Maybe he did have a conscience after all. "Why, then? Why be a jerk?" I asked.

He looked toward the ocean, squinting into the wind. "I just want Miles's killer caught, that's all."

"And I don't?" I was so mad I was on the verge of tears, but I'd be damned if he'd see it.

"He was my friend. I can't stand it that someone did this to him and is going free."

All at once, I saw the strain around his eyes. He was hurting, too. I still didn't trust myself to speak. Bear ran up and nuzzled my palm with his wet nose.

"Miles and I had been friends since grade school. When he died, and they said he was murdered—" He thrust his hands deeper into his pocket. "I just want whoever did it put away for good. That's all."

"You know Avery didn't kill him."

He caught my gaze and held it a moment. A muscle twitched in his jaw. "I believe that the truth will come out." His voice had softened.

It was an imperfect truce, but one I could accept. "Yes. It will."

He zipped his jacket up a few more inches and turned to climb the bluff toward town. The gray morning blew around me, and the surf crashed deep, then gentled as it unrolled over the sand.

I would find the person who killed Miles. I would. By God, I would.

Bear lifted a leg and peed on the comet kite.

STELLA WAS AT STRINGS ATTACHED AT NINE O'CLOCK, just as she'd promised.

"Come in." I held the door open. "Would you like some tea? I put water on."

"Don't mind if I do," Stella said. Today she wore a modern dress cut as simply as a T-shirt. It swished around her calves. A chunky knit shrug kept her shoulders warm.

I led her into the kitchen-slash-workshop and took two mugs from the cupboard.

"I know you've seen the store before—" I began.

"But not as if I were responsible for it," Stella finished. "Is this the tea?" She reached for the Lapsang souchong tin where I'd stashed Mom's Lassitude Tea.

"Not that one," I warned. "That stuff will knock you out. It's one of my mother's herbal remedies." I moved the tin to the back. "The others are labeled correctly, though. How about Darjeeling?"

"Sounds lovely."

"While it steeps, let's go back into the shop, and I'll show you around." I pointed to a wall of simple kites packaged in long bundles. "Those are the diamond kites. They're the easiest to fly and the least likely to get out of hand in the wind. Best for children and for people who haven't flown a kite since they were kids."

"Probably a lot of your customers."

"Right. I order those kites. But here"—with a flush of pride, I pointed to the ceiling, where I'd suspended the kites I'd designed—"are the custom kites. I make each one by hand. They're quite a bit more expensive than the pre-packaged kites, and not everyone will understand why, but real kite fanatics will get it."

"I certainly get it."

"Kite lovers seem to fall into two camps: people who want to maneuver their kites, do tricks; and people who love flying a beautiful kite." Jack didn't understand her need to fly the comet kite just to watch it sail through the sky, its tail stretched behind it. He probably liked kite fighting, where people tried to slice the line of their opponents' kites. To me, that was not what kites were about.

"And we have the beautiful kites," Stella said. I loved her use of "we."

"You can send people really into sport kites to Sullivan's." Maybe Jack was more about kite engineering than art, but his attachment to Miles Logan was real. My attention slipped to Avery. "Over here . . ." Avery, alone in jail.

Stella looked toward where my hand pointed and waited. "Over here what?"

"Sorry. That's where the stakes are for anchoring kites in the sand."

"Emmy, what's wrong?" Stella asked. God bless her no-nonsense approach.

"It's Avery," I said. "The sheriff took her in."

"Oh, darling," Stella said, and touched a hand to my arm. "I'm so sorry."

I stood for a moment, unable to respond. "Let's get our tea," I said finally. I pushed open the door to the kitchen and filled our mugs. "Avery found a fil—" I stopped myself before I gave it away. "A knife under her bed, and Sheriff Koppen thinks it was used to kill Miles. He's so wrong. I have no idea where the knife came from."

"Avery didn't have a knife like that?"

"No. Besides, even if she did, why would she hide it under her bed?"

"Good point. If I killed someone, the first thing I'd do is get rid of the murder weapon."

I fell into a chair. "If I could understand Miles better, maybe I could get an idea of who else might have wanted to kill him. Get Koppen on another trail."

"I didn't really know Miles well. I worked at the front of the house, and he was in the kitchen." She kept her gaze on her mug.

"But what about his personality? Was he quick to anger, or could he have made someone else mad?"

"I didn't find him any angrier than anyone else. He was an odd man, though. In the best way. Followed his own star." She smiled. "I admired that. I saw him as a fellow artist. He even lived like an artist, in a cabin apart from other houses."

I set down my mug. "Apart? What do you mean?"

"He had a place in the woods south of town. Off Myers Road. I think he liked the peace and quiet."

"I see," I said. His cabin probably told a lot about how he lived his life, what was important to him. Maybe it even held clues as to why he died. I lifted my eyes to Stella's.

She raised an eyebrow. "You're not thinking of going out there, are you?"

"Why would I do that?" Neither a yes nor a no.

"Because you want to find something to get Avery off the hook."

"That sounds foolish. I'm sure the sheriff has been out there, and he'd have my hide if he knew I was planning something like that."

"And don't forget it, either," Stella said. She brushed a foot over the kitchen's old linoleum floor. "Of course, if you were thinking of going down there . . ."

"What?" I held my breath. I planned on visiting Avery that night but had a few empty hours between when the shop closed and my slot for visiting her opened.

"Maybe we could go together."

chapter eleven

AFTER THE SHOP CLOSED, I DROPPED BEAR AT HOME AND drove up the hill to Stella's house. Madame Lucy's white face peered from the living room window above, but Stella was waiting for me by the garage door.

"You're sure you don't mind driving?" I asked.

"It'll save us time to take my car." She pointed the opener at the garage door, and the door lifted, revealing a James Bond–worthy sports car. Its sleek lines looked like they'd be right at home hugging the curves of a road twisting through the Tuscan hills. Or maybe dashing after a jewel thief who'd just carried off a heist in the Riviera. Better yet, driven by the jewel thief.

"Wow." I hoped I didn't sound too shocked, but this car was not what I'd expected.

"Corvette," she said. "Nineteen sixty-seven. I was glad

to find one in black. Red is so clichéd, don't you agree?
Get in."

I slid into the leather seat, and Stella expertly backed
out, her fingers light on the gearshift. In minutes we were
on the highway headed south of town. I ran my fingers
over the Corvette's dashboard.

"How fast can this car go?"

A smile spread over Stella's face. "You want to find
out?"

"No, I was just—"

She nudged the gearshift, and the car's engine tightened.
We thrust ahead, fast and low to the ground, while the
speedometer climbed to seventy, then ninety miles an hour.
Centrifugal force pressed me against the seat, and my smile
turned into a full-on laugh.

And then we heard the siren.

"Damn." Stella shifted down and pulled the Corvette
to the shoulder. A policeman parked behind us, his lights
still pulsing. Stella tapped my knee. "Don't worry. It won't
be my first speeding ticket." She rolled down the
window.

"License and registration," the officer said. If he was
surprised to see a gray-haired woman behind the wheel,
he didn't show it. Reading the license, he rose to return to
his car, then stopped. He came back to the window. "Mrs.
Hart?"

"Yes," Stella said in a ladylike voice.

"Did you teach at Carsonville Middle School?"

"Yes. Yes, I did." Recognition came over her face.
"You're one of the Dolby twins, aren't you?"

Officer Larry Dolby, his name tag read. I was waiting

for him to break into a smile, maybe reminisce over some eighth-grade antic, and let us go. Instead, he pulled a pad and pen from his breast pocket.

"You flunked me in history," he said.

Uh-oh.

"Oh dear," Stella said.

Not that my Prius was in danger of breaking any land-speed records, but I knew speeding tickets were serious business on the coast. The stretch we were on was straight and fairly safe, but each year speeding along the coastal highway totaled several cars and cost a few lives. I shouldn't have asked Stella about the Corvette's speed. And if she had prior speeding tickets, there was no telling how steep this one would be.

Officer Dolby glanced at Stella's license again and scratched something else on the pad. He ripped the top sheet off and handed it through the window. "Best thing that ever happened to me, flunking history," he said. "I met my future wife the next year when I took it again." He winked and touched the brim of his hat. "That's a warning, not a citation. Keep an eye on the speedometer, Mrs. Hart."

"Yes, Officer Dolby. I will."

Once the policeman pulled away, Stella shoved the warning into the glovebox. "I always did like that boy. Didn't know William the Conqueror from William McKinley, but he was a good kid." She turned the key in the ignition and shrugged. We were a few miles down the road before we stopped laughing.

THE HIGHWAY DIPPED INTO THE FOREST, LEAVING THE ocean view behind. Stella slowed and pulled into an unmarked road. Good thing she was driving. I would have missed it.

"Myers Road," she said.

"I barely noticed the turnoff. You must have been here before."

"What? Oh no." She didn't look at me. "It's an old logging road. Leads up to Myers Lake. They say there's good fishing up there."

She'd slowed the Corvette to a crawl, circumventing a few potholes that might have earned "lake" designation on their own. Nearly half a mile in, we approached a mailbox by the side of the road. "Logan," it read in painted-on block letters.

"Here," Stella said, and took the rutted driveway next to it.

Miles's cabin—it had to be his; a stretch of yellow police tape cordoned off its front entrance—was dark. And small. Standing outside the car, I realized how isolated it was, too. The ocean was too far away to hear, as was the highway to the west. The air was piney instead of tinged with salt.

But something was strange about the cabin. Instead of being a simple shoebox, a bulbous metal shape protruded from the side. I stepped around the cabin's side and nearly laughed out loud. Miles had built his cabin around an old Airstream trailer. He must have intended to live in the Airstream, then decided to build it a canopy to keep out the damp, then eventually enclosed the canopy. And added at least one more small room. The trailer's end poked from the cabin's side as if it had been driven, nose-in, to a building.

"What do we do now?" Stella asked.

I wasn't sure I had an answer to Stella's question. It had simply seemed like a good idea to see Miles's place for real. "Let's try the door."

I pulled my sleeve over my hand to protect it from fingerprints, and I rattled the doorknob. Locked. Naturally. We couldn't go inside—not with the police tape. The tape had sagged on one side. And yet, surely Sheriff Koppen was finished with the cabin by now. He and his team had searched it and were done. What could it hurt if we looked around a bit, too?

"We could break in," Stella said. She was full of surprises tonight. I wondered if the school board had any hint of what they had been getting when they'd hired her.

"I didn't know Miles, but from what I've heard, he didn't seem the type to have Fort Knox–level security measures in place," I said. "Maybe we won't have to break anything." And maybe we wouldn't have to cement our spots on the sheriff's blacklist.

"I'll try the windows," Stella said.

"Good idea. I'll see if he hid a spare key anywhere."

I scanned the clearing around the cabin. If Miles were to hide a key, where would it be? To the left was an oak tree with a clearing under it, probably for sitting in summer with a beer and a friend. Nothing was there now except a large can—looked like it had once held pickles—with a few cigarette butts in it. I wandered to the cabin's rear. A lean-to storage cabinet clung to its back. The padlock had been clipped off, probably by the sheriff. I opened it. Two tall, white PVC cylinders—razor-clam guns—and a rusted portable barbecue were shoved against the back.

Would a chef leave his barbecue in such decrepit

condition? Not likely. I lifted its lid and poked in the ashes with a stick. Bingo. A key. This was too easy.

"Stella, I think I found it."

"Good." Stella's voice came from around the corner. "The bathroom window was open a crack, but I wasn't looking forward to squeezing through it."

Around front again, we surveyed the door. If Miles's construction techniques were standard—no guarantee—the door should open in. Then all we'd have to do is duck under the police tape. The key turned smoothly in the lock. I pushed the door and heard a ripping sound as the door hit resistance, then swung open.

"What was that?" Stella said.

A thick strip of shiny tape dangled from the wall. Shoot. "They must have sealed the door from the inside and left through another door." Inside, I pulled my sleeve over my hand again and tried to press the seal flat against the doorjamb.

"Well, we're in now. It won't hurt to look around." Stella stood next to me as we took in the cabin's layout. She looked as blatantly curious as I was.

It didn't take Margaret Mead to figure out that a bachelor had inhabited the cabin. The room was simply furnished with a sagging leather club chair in one corner and a side table stacked with books and a lamp shaped like a horse's head. Shelves bulging with books lined the walls on the side of the room. Against the opposite wall was a desk with a computer mouse sitting forlornly at its edge. The sheriff must have taken the laptop. Above the desk hung a seascape.

"I'll check the kitchen," Stella said.

"All right."

I examined the painting. Thick brushstrokes sculpted each wave with shades of charcoal and smoke. This was definitely Stella's work, although it looked simpler, maybe earlier. On instinct, I lifted it from the wall and flipped it over. I'd seen movies where people hid things on the backs of paintings. Nothing was hidden here, but Stella had inscribed the painting to Miles personally. "May this painting live in your home as you have lived in my memory." Thoughtfully, I returned the painting to the wall. "Memory," it had read. What did that mean?

"Stella," I said, testing the waters. "Miles has one of your paintings in here. Did you know that?"

"Oh, sure," she said from the kitchen. "I think I gave it to him at some point."

Her cavalier manner didn't match the inscription's emotion. Curious. I filed that away and moved on to the desk. It was fairly orderly, with the state parks and clamming permits tidily pinned to a bulletin board. Fishing poles leaned in the corner. The sheriff had undoubtedly searched all this, and if he found anything interesting—my gut clenched at the thought of Miles's calendar—he took it with him.

The already-weak light filtering into the cabin was fading now. I wondered if we dared turn on a lamp. Maybe Sheriff Koppen would somehow be able to get records from the electric company showing power had been used tonight, and we'd be nailed. I decided not to risk it.

I was curious to see the kitchen. What kind of kitchen would the chef keep at home?

"Find anything in here?" I asked Stella.

Of course the Airstream's kitchen was too small for him, so he'd built another kitchen around the trailer's nose. He used its metallic shell as a sort of wall-sized bulletin board with magnets holding up drawings and photos. I leaned closer. There was a snapshot of Avery at the beach, her hair blowing around her head. From its central location, I could tell it would have been the first thing he'd seen as he turned from the stove. I removed it from under its magnet.

"That's Avery, isn't it?" Stella said. "She looks happy."

"So strange." I held my breath a moment before releasing it. "He put this photo in such a prominent spot. Now she's being held for his murder."

"It's not right."

Reluctantly, I left the photo and continued my search. Against the cabin's outer wall was the stove, with a well-used cast-iron skillet on top, and a waist-high refrigerator. Beyond that was a small bathroom and the cabin's back door.

"Nothing here," Stella said. "He was working on a few mushroom recipes, but that's all. Nothing points to a motive."

"Mushrooms again," I said. "I can't help but think of the pickers who threatened Miles."

"Oh, Emmy. You don't want to get involved with that. Let the sheriff take that one. I'm serious."

"If they're that dangerous, it's all the more reason to follow up," I said.

"For the sheriff to follow up, you mean." Hands on hips, Stella surveyed the kitchen. "I want to check the drawers before we're through here. Why don't you take the trailer?"

"All right."

I ducked back into the cabin's main room and through the Airstream's open door. I stepped up into a small kitchen, now unused, next to a dining room table that looked to be put into service as another desk, only messier than the one in the main room. The sheriff would have searched the desk thoroughly, and he would have taken anything interesting with him. Still I poked through the papers. Mostly menu planning and food magazines.

Beyond that—the rear of the trailer—was a tiny bedroom wall to wall with mattress and pillows. The window at the trailer's rear opened to the outdoors. Miles was a reader, as shown by his armchair and yards of books in the main room. He would have read in bed, too, I was sure. Might he have stashed notes there? Feeling self-conscious, I stepped up to his mattress and settled myself as if I were him. The clove-and-leather scent of a man rose from the quilt around me. It was cozy in here—a nest. A small lamp hung from the wall near my head. His reading light. Tiny cabinets, almost like the storage compartments in an airline, sat snug against the upper inside wall. Their bottoms curved in typical Airstream style.

I unclipped a cabinet and found an extra quilt and pillow. For a brief moment, I'd wondered if Avery had ever used it, and felt a mixture of sadness and shame at my intrusion. I groped the bottom of the cabinet. My fingers touched paper. Working by feel, I extracted the paper from the bottom of the cabinet and pulled it forward.

Electricity records be damned—I needed to know what it was that Miles kept here, so close to where he slept. I clicked on the lamp and unfolded the papers.

"Stella, I think I found something."

She was at the bedroom door in a second. "What?"

"Look here."

The papers looked to be some sort of floor plan. I put my fingers at what must have been the front door and moved through the rooms. A restaurant—plans for a restaurant. And it was attached to a larger sort of complex, although only the edges showed. Avery had said Miles had dreams of his own restaurant. Perhaps this was it.

"Restaurant plans," Stella said.

"Yes. Does it mean anything?"

"Can't say. I don't know why anyone would kill him because he wanted his own restaurant."

"True." Maybe he looked at them from time to time when he was discouraged and needed that dream to give him a lift. In his cozy house within a house, he might have clicked on the lamp like I just did and pulled the plans from the cabinet. He would have spread them across the bed and dreamt of the world he planned to create with food and hospitality.

I returned the plans to the cabinet and turned off the light. The space's intimacy reminded me again that I wasn't supposed to be here. I smoothed the quilt behind me and slipped off the bed. Although the sun hadn't yet set, the cabin, surrounded by fir trees, was dark.

"What do you think?" I asked Stella.

"I don't think we're going to find anything. I'm glad we came, though. It gives us a better idea of who he was, and that should help."

Help what, she didn't say. But I knew what she meant. Anything that helped us understand Miles might illuminate why he was killed.

"Let's leave by the rear door, like the sheriff did." We took the back door through the kitchen, circling to the cabin's front, where the Corvette was parked.

I slipped the key into my pocket. I wasn't sure what we'd found—or not found—in the cabin, but it might be worth looking into again.

chapter twelve

THE HOUSE'S DARKENED WINDOWS AS I DROVE UP ONLY depressed me further. Bear was happy to see me and danced around my feet as I clicked on lamps here and there, but Avery's empty bedroom only drilled home what a dire situation she faced. I thought of Jack Sullivan's accusations, and my chest tightened. He wasn't right, of course he wasn't, but I knew he wasn't alone in his opinion of Avery. The whole town wondered—or would soon.

I wasn't sure what I'd learned by breaking into Miles's cabin, either, except that I think I would have liked him. The goofy way he built around the Airstream, the piles of books, how he lived his life the way he wanted—I admired all that. But I'd never met him in the flesh. I swallowed. Well, not alive, anyway.

"What next?" I asked no one in particular. "What should I do?" Bear, who thought that whenever I talked, whether on the phone or alone, it had to be to him, wagged his tail. I heaved a sigh and headed toward the kitchen. We still had some of Mom's casserole left.

The phone rang. "Mamma Mia" again. I groaned.

"Emmy," my mother said. "I have a bad feeling."

She couldn't have heard about Avery unless the Portland papers had picked up the news, which was all too possible by now.

"Indigestion again?" I asked. "Don't you have a special tea for that?" There was no way I was going to tell her about Avery and finding Miles. Her fretting would only worsen things. Surely within a day or two the sheriff would see he'd been wrong, Avery would be released, and things would go back to normal.

"Not about me. About you," Mom said. "I was just telling your father that you girls shouldn't be alone up in that old house."

I was more alone than she realized. I took the phone to the front porch and pulled a blanket over my knees while Bear trotted to the yard to do his business. "But we have Bear."

"You've had a very protected life, honey."

And whose fault was that? I added silently.

"Emmy. Are you listening?"

"Yeah, Mom. Why are you worrying about me now?"

"A mother's sixth sense, I guess."

"In this case, you have nothing to get excited about. Everything here is just fine." I hated lying to my mother.

A moment passed, then two. "I just worry that if anything happened, you might make foolish choices that could come back to haunt you later."

I hesitated, then asked, "Are you thinking of anything in particular?"

"No. Nothing special. But that's how life is. Things come up, and you have to deal with them."

If she only knew. "Mom, I'm not fifteen anymore. You have to let me live my life."

"You've been living on your own since college."

"Maybe technically, but when I was in Portland, a day didn't go by when you weren't around." The strain of the murder and Avery's arrest had found an outlet at last. Anger gathered in my chest. "You checked my refrigerator to see if I was eating all right. You talked to my neighbors when I wasn't home and asked them where I was. You wouldn't even let me buy my own sheets."

"Those were unbleached, organic cotton sheets I brought you, honey—"

"Why not just stitch together sandpaper? It would have been more comfortable."

"I'm not talking about little things like that. I mean bigger things. You've moved away and started your own business. You went to art school, not business school. How are you going to make it through the winter when you don't have all those tourists for street traffic?"

She'd struck a nerve. I had a vague idea of trying to set up Internet sales and exploring the indoor-kite market, but I'd only begun researching where to advertise and which kite clubs to contact. Then I thought of Frank Hopkins, my landlord. Frank had said he'd help me flesh out my marketing plan. "I have a good business plan, plus I'm getting marketing advice from a successful businessman, Mom. Now, would you leave me alone? Can't we have a normal mother-daughter thing?"

The silence on Mom's end pierced more deeply than any words she might have chosen. I softened my voice. "I have to make my own choices. Maybe I'll make a mistake from time to time, but that's part of learning, right?"

"Honey, I worry. I can't help it. You know it comes from love."

"I know."

"But you will tell me if you need our help, won't you? It's not a sign of failure to ask for help."

I rose and opened the front door. Bear charged into the house and waited expectantly by his bowl in the kitchen. With my free hand, I dumped in some kibble.

"Sure. Of course. But for now things are fine. I have to go, Mom. Was there a reason you called other than to tell me how to live my life?" I had to leave soon if I'd make it to the Astoria jail in time to visit Avery.

"Don't take that tone with me, Emmy."

Of course, she was right. I was being awful. My anger deflated like a balloon. "I'm sorry. I guess the stress of— the stress of opening Strings Attached and all is getting to me."

"Take care of yourself, hon. I mean it. Just take things a day at a time." Lord, she was irritating, but I did love my mom. "Anyway, I called to give you a few names of attorneys your father recommended."

"Thanks." I grabbed a pen.

"He said your friend better have deep pockets. A good defense could set him back a hundred thousand dollars, easily." Mom threw in one last piece of advice about how to make homemade toilet-bowl cleanser, and we said good-bye.

I set the phone on the kitchen table and heaved a monumental sigh. A hundred thousand dollars? Where would

Avery get that kind of money? As I gathered my keys and purse to visit Avery, I repeated Mom's advice aloud. "Take it a day at a time." If only it were that easy.

THE COUNTY JAIL IN ASTORIA LOOKED FROM THE OUTSIDE like a relic from a Dickens novel with its fortresslike walls and solid turrets. Fortunately, the inside was more up to date. I got on the list for the eight o'clock visiting session and sat uneasily in the waiting room, filling out paperwork. Around me, mothers shushed children, and other visitors browsed magazines or stared at the jabbering television hanging in the corner.

At last, a warden called my name and led me into a small room. Avery sat on the other side of a thick slab of foggy plexiglass. Other than a table, two chairs, and a clock audibly ticking on the wall, the room was bare.

"Avery," I said. "How are you?" What a stupid question to ask someone wrongly jailed for homicide. Besides, the shadows under her eyes told me clearly that she wasn't well.

"All right, I guess. Considering."

"Mom says hi," I said.

"You didn't—?"

"Not a chance," I said. We looked at each other uncomfortably for a moment.

Avery abruptly broke into a cheerful smile. "I'd offer you something to drink, but . . ." She lifted her palms in a *What can I do?* position and faked a search of the institutional green walls for cocktail makings.

"All right. I'd like a Brandy Alexander." This was one

of our old jokes from the first *Mary Tyler Moore* episode, one her mother forced us to watch whenever she caught it on television. I started to laugh, just a little, and then suddenly I was laughing so hard that I was crying, too. So was Avery. My throat hurt. "Have you thought about a lawyer? I got some names from Dad."

Avery's smile faded, and the shadows under her eyes darkened. "They assigned me a public defender. She's okay, I guess."

"Just okay? That's all?"

"She seems to know what she's doing."

I folded my arms in front of my chest. "If you're not out of jail soon, you need to consider hiring a real shark. I know it's expensive, but it's worth it."

"I'm not guilty. It's the guilty people who hire those guys. I—"

"I know, I know. I'm just saying." The clock ticked as the minute hand advanced. "What happens next?"

"I'll go in front of the judge, and he'll set bail. If he decides to set bail, that is. Then at some point a grand jury decides if there's enough evidence for it to go to court."

"Oh, Avery." I imagined the courthouse, the photographers, the judge. "I want you home."

"The Brew House—"

"Don't worry about the Brew House. I told Trudy you'd be away for a few days, and she's taking care of things." Avery looked at me. I knew she wanted to ask if I'd told Trudy the truth. "I didn't see the point of telling her where you were."

"I suppose she'll know soon enough."

"Not if you come home. Not if the judge sees how flimsy the case against you is."

"Is it flimsy? They found blood on the boat. The knife. I feel like this is someone else's life I'm living, a big joke. The house lights will come up, and we'll go home, and everything will go back to normal."

Just a few days ago, everything was normal. My biggest worry was running out of half-and-half for coffee. What I'd give to have the same old frustrations of daily life now. "I know."

"The sheriff thinks I did it. He keeps asking me the same questions over and over again. Like I'm going to have new answers."

"What does he want to know?"

"Where I was the night Miles was killed. If I was down at the docks. Things like that."

"You were home."

"I guess."

She guessed? Of course she was home. "I told him you were in bed."

She ignored me. "He asked a lot of questions about me and Miles. If we fought, what he was like. What we did together. You know."

I didn't know. Besides the day I found his body, she'd kept her relationship with him to herself. "You've never really talked much about Miles."

She looked at her hands, clasped in front of her on the table. "I just—I just didn't want to. That's all."

"I thought maybe you were going to say something about him; then you found the knife." The knife with its rust-hued stains. I shut it out of my brain.

Silence. Just like before. I couldn't tell what she was hiding or why.

"Did they find anything out about the knife?" I tried again.

"My lawyer says all they can tell is that it's from a restaurant-supply store."

"So it could be from the Tidal Basin," I said.

"Or the Brew House."

Damn it. This was infuriating. I leaned toward the plexi-glass barrier and lowered my voice. "I went to Miles's cabin today. Just to check it out."

"You did what?" Her forehead nearly touched the bar-rier between us.

"Avery, keep your voice down."

"You went to Miles's cabin?"

"Calm down. I went just to check it out. That's all."

She leaned back. "That cabin. Isn't it crazy? He built it all around that trailer. That was so like him." And so unlike Dave, I thought. Her gaze had lost focus, turned wistful. She turned it to me again. "Why did you go?" Her eyes widened. "You didn't go inside, did you? Tell me you didn't go inside."

"I had to do something. You shouldn't be here."

Her shoulders slumped. She knew. "Oh, Emmy. Leave it alone. I appreciate you trying to help me, but the inves-tigation is up to the sheriff. Don't mess it up for both of us."

"But I—"

"I don't need Sheriff Koppen saying I'm interfering with the investigation by having you stirring things up."

"I haven't stirred anything up; I just want to give him some helpful information. That's all."

"I appreciate it, Em. I just don't think he would, and that could come back to hurt me. Besides, what if you did find something? Maybe the sheriff wouldn't be able to use it. The prosecution would say you tampered with it."

"What if the sheriff has decided he's found the murderer and stops looking?"

Avery leaned forward. "You think I haven't thought of that?"

Satisfied she understood, I opened my mouth to reply, but she held up a hand.

"Drop it. Whatever you think of Sheriff Koppen, he's fair," she said.

I flattened my palm on the cold table, then drew it back. "All I want to do is see if I can point him in the right direction. It's not like I'm setting out to bag a murderer on my own. Besides, Stella went with me." I hesitated before going on with the story. "You know her, right?"

"Stella Hart? Sure. The hostess at the Tidal Basin. She was willing to break into his house?"

"We didn't really break in. We found a key."

"The one in the barbecue?"

I nodded. Maybe she knew Miles a little better than she'd let on.

"Stella and Miles had an interesting relationship," she said thoughtfully. "They saw something in each other . . . I've known you a long time."

"Yes?" I was wary.

"I know how you get obsessed with things. That's fine when it's a new kite design. In fact, it's what makes you such an artist. But in this case, you'd better leave it to professionals. I don't want to see you in here with me."

"But I can't just—"

"No 'buts,' Emmy."

Of course she was right. I just couldn't agree with her right then, so I changed the subject. "Speaking of which, what's it like in here?"

She looked at me with suspicion. "All right, I guess. A couple of the other girls are nice, and the food isn't as bad as you'd think."

"But no Brandy Alexanders." There. At least I'd made her smile. "Sit tight. You won't be in for long. I can feel it." Or so I wanted her to think.

chapter thirteen

FIRST THING THE NEXT MORNING, I WHEELED MY BICYCLE to the post office. Stella had said that the postmistress, Jeanette, had her finger on Rock Point's pulse. I wondered what she might know about people who had an interest in Miles Logan. Besides, I really did need to square away my mail. I hadn't received anything at Avery's house, and I kept getting mail at Strings Attached for the shop's former occupant, Mildred's Treasures.

The tiny post office was on the main drag. Inside was a wall of aluminum post-office boxes on the right and a short counter straight ahead. The left wall bore various notices, including the FBI's most-wanted list and a local bulletin board, filled mostly with ads for vacation rentals. A woman stood behind the counter, tossing envelopes into different bins.

I knew about people like Jeanette. They loved gossip, and with a little flattery they'd speculate on anyone in town.

"May I help you?" the woman said. Her name tag read simply "Jeanette." Yes, this was her. She was small and thin and probably well past retirement age. She must have some major clout with the postal-workers union to be hanging on to her job. Despite her thin face, her cheeks puffed like a squirrel's full of nuts.

"Please. I'm Emmy Adler, and I've just moved to town."

"At the Cook house," she said promptly.

"Yes." Wow. She really did know everyone's business.

"Why haven't you filed your change-of-address form?" she asked. She pushed aside the stack of envelopes she was sorting and put on the glasses hanging around her neck to examine me better.

"Well, I—that's why I'm here now."

She slid a form across the counter. "Here you go. Don't forget to sign the bottom."

"I also wanted to clear up the mail for my business, Strings Attached."

She sniffed. "You're receiving mail for Mildred's Treasures, aren't you?"

"Yes, I am."

"I knew it. Mildred moved out last summer. If you could see the garbage she called 'treasures,' you'd understand. Made-in-China ship models, imported seashells, ancient postcards . . ."

"If you knew she'd moved out, why are you delivering her mail to me?"

Jeanette looked at me as if my low IQ merited special attention. "That's the rules. If you don't fill out the forms, I can't change the delivery."

"Better give me a form for my shop, too."

She slapped another on the counter and returned to her

sorting. I waited for something—some hint that she knew I'd found Miles's body or that I lived with the prime suspect for his murder. Surely she'd want to pump me for information. Isn't that what everyone said? But she didn't make a peep.

"Uh," I said, struggling for something to say. "You sure have your work cut out for you, taking care of all of Rock Point's mail."

"Indeed I do." Envelopes sliced the air as they settled expertly into their bins.

"You probably know just about everything that happens in town."

I noticed a minute pause in her sorting. A vague smile played on her lips. "At the United States Postal Service, we're sworn to protect our customers' privacy. If I did know anything, I couldn't share it freely."

The "freely" stood out. So that's the way it was, was it? "If you knew anything about a murder case, you'd surely share information about that."

"A murder case? Whatever do you mean?" Jeanette wouldn't win any Academy Awards for her performance.

"Come on. I mean Miles Logan. You know Avery is being held for his murder. Wrongly. What can you tell me about him? Did he have enemies? Did he receive strange mail or bills?"

Jeanette focused on her sorting. "I have no idea what you mean. I don't go around and speculate like that. I don't know who you think I am, but you're mistaken."

I clenched my pen, then tossed it to the side. Flip-flip-flip went the envelopes. I softened my voice. "I found his body, you know." I stared to the side. "Yes, it was me. I'm the one who saw him washed up on the rocks. And what I saw—well, I wouldn't repeat it to just anyone."

Jeanette's eyes tripled in size. "What did you see?"

I sucked in a dramatic breath. "I don't feel comfortable talking about it."

"But you can't just keep it all bottled up." Jeannette tossed her envelopes aside and leaned over the counter. "You need to talk to someone. Get it all out."

"I don't know. I'm not sure I'm talking to someone sympathetic. Someone who understands how important it is to identify real suspects, not just the chef's ex-girlfriend." I did my best to appear tortured.

"Sam Anderson, Miles's boss, is getting some 'urgent' mail," she offered.

"Urgent?"

"You know, the special envelopes? Sometimes they're blue or stamped with a message? Running a restaurant is a thin-margined business."

So, the Tidal Basin had financial challenges. I let that soak in. Jeanette trained her gaze on me with laser precision. Time to uphold my end of the deal, the gaze said.

"Finding Miles was an awful shock. I didn't even know who he was." I wracked my mind for something to tell her that would be true, but not prurient. "It was my dog, Bear, who discovered the body. I had no idea what he was barking at until I—" The memory of Miles's sea-bleached body stopped me cold. I caught my breath and turned away.

Jeanette nodded. Slowly, she picked up her envelopes again. "Don't forget to sign the forms."

LEAVING MY BICYCLE AT STRINGS ATTACHED, I WALKED down toward the bay. I figured the Tidal Basin's owner and

Miles's old boss, Sam Anderson, would be at the restaurant taking care of business before the lunch rush. Thanks to Jeanette's hints, I wanted to talk to him before I opened Strings Attached for the day. I'd even concocted an excuse on the way down.

The Tidal Basin looked different in daylight. More bustling, less glamorous. At the rear entrance, trucks unloaded produce and seafood, and the restaurant's employees came and went. I tried that door—practical metal rather than the ornate wooden door at the front—and it opened into a short hall that, in turn, let into a workroom. Past a Latina woman chopping onions and a man pulling the legs off of a Dungeness crab was yet another entrance, this one to the main kitchen that opened onto the restaurant itself.

The door I wanted looked to be just to the right of the one I'd entered. It simply said "Office." I'd raised my fist to knock when the door burst open.

"For Christ's sake," Sam Anderson said. "Get out of the way." Thin strands of faded red hair mixed with gray stretched over his scalp. His freckled redhead's complexion seemed unusually pink.

I backed up a step. "I'm sorry."

"What are you doing back here?"

"I wanted to talk to you about catering Strings Attached's opening reception."

He seemed somewhat mollified. Dollar-bill signs didn't exactly light up his eyeballs, but at least I had his attention. "The new kite shop, right? I met you the other night. Isn't it already open?"

"Sure. A soft opening. But I wanted to have something more formal once tourist season really heats up." Of course,

I hadn't planned any sort of opening party at all, and if I did, it would be more along the lines of a few deli platters rather than the sort of spread the Tidal Basin put out.

"Listen, I'm busy now. You heard about our chef—"

"Yes. We talked about it, remember? Awful. At least the sheriff must have finished his work here by now."

Sam narrowed his eyes. "Oh yes. Of course. I can give you ten minutes; then I've got to get back to work. The wine vendor will be here at ten thirty." He stepped back into his office and invited me to follow. If anything, the office was smaller than Sheriff Koppen's and infinitely more cluttered. "However, we like to make a presence in Rock Point. Tell me about your event." As he spoke, he dipped his fingers into a bowl of sunflower seeds. He shoveled a few into his mouth and expertly divested them of their shells.

"Well." I hadn't thought this far ahead. "I'm anticipating about fifty people"—who those people were, I had no idea, unless Dad invited his Watergate-reenactment club—"and I'd like to serve hors d'oeuvres made with local ingredients."

"Naturally. That's what we do. Any ideas?"

"I was thinking about wild mushrooms. Lots of them. I adore wild mushrooms, especially morels."

Sam's pulse ticked in his temple, but his expression remained unchanged. "Sure. No problem. Won't be cheap, but if that's what you want—"

No problem? "I'd hoped you would say that. I remember hearing about some kind of dustup with mushroom hunters last week."

"Oh, that." He flipped his hand in a dismissive motion. "That's over."

"I heard they really got into it with Miles. You told me about it. Why would mushroom hunters threaten a chef?" I was pushing my luck, I knew it. While I talked, I examined Sam's office for hints of unpaid bills. A shopping-mall-issue family photo—short-haired wife and three kids—sat next to his phone. A stack of invoices was at his right hand. Sunflower-seed shells littered the linoleum floor.

"Miles had some idea for a wild-mushroom ragout with a morel duxelles base," Sam said. "You know how many pounds of mushrooms you need for a good duxelles?"

I shook my head. Truth was, I didn't even know what a duxelles was. Training my gaze toward Sam, I tried to get a better look at the invoices.

"Pounds and pounds. Ridiculous. I told him to forget it, too expensive. Heck, it'd be cheaper to use truffles."

"And the mushroom hunters were incensed because you didn't want to buy their goods?"

"No. That wasn't it. You have no idea how mushroom hunters get about their territory." He picked up his coffee mug and, finding it empty, set it down again on a stack of packing slips. "When I told Miles it was a no-go on the morels, he went out and collected his own. Pigheaded, that man. Now if it was crab, well, I do a little crabbing. No problem there. But, no, he wanted morels."

"And since Miles collected his own, the mushroom hunters were mad? Was it the lost sales?" A few pages down, the red ink of a "Last Notice" stamp stood out on an invoice. Jeanette would definitely have made a note of that.

Sam leaned forward, near enough that I could smell the soap he'd showered with that morning. "It would if he picked his morels on a plot they considered their own."

"Oh. And he was picking someone else's."

"You got it."

The situation began to crystallize. Miles had gathered mushrooms on someone else's turf, and they were angry. Angry enough to threaten him. "I had no idea people had private mushroom farms here."

Sam laughed to the point that he choked a bit. He picked a morsel of sunflower seed from inside his cheek. "Nope. You can't farm morels. They grow where they grow, and nine times out of ten it ain't in your backyard."

I felt stupid, but pressed on. "They're your regular mushroom hunters, then? I bet the sheriff was very interested in finding out more about them." He'd better be.

"They'd supplied us a few pounds here and there over the past few weeks, but to tell the truth, I can't even tell you their last names."

I waved at the dog-eared invoices on his desk. "But you have to pay them." Other than noting that the stack was fat, and at least one was overdue, I couldn't make anything else from what I could see.

"Sure. I pay them. Cash. And all I need to know is that they're Ron and Monica, and that's all they want me to know. And no, the sheriff hasn't asked me a thing about them, and I haven't offered anything up."

Got it. The Tidal Basin did a little under-the-table business with suppliers. That would explain why Sam didn't advertise the mushroom hunters' threats. "But if they had anything to do with Miles's death—"

"They don't. Feuds over mushrooming territory are old hat. There are lots of threats, lots of yelling, but nothing ever comes of it. Like anyone with any smarts, I let them battle it out and stay out of the way. Now, do you want a buffet, or will you pass the hors d'oeuvres?"

So, Sam hadn't said anything to the sheriff about the mushroom hunters and their threats. This was a real lead he could work with. "I—uh." I bit my lip in pretend worry. "I don't want to get into any kind of mushroom war or anything. Are you sure morels are the right way to go? I mean, what about the threats?"

Sam sighed and pushed back from the desk. "All right. Look. Here's what happened. This shaggy couple showed up at the kitchen door demanding to see Miles, right in the middle of dinner. I told them he was busy, but they busted in and started yelling at him."

"Yelling?" This was getting juicier by the second.

"Saying he'd stolen their mushrooms, that it was their spot, not his." He shook his head.

"What did you do?"

"Miles couldn't shut them up. People in the dining room could hear them yelling. The dishwasher had to kick them out. You can bet he got extra tips that night."

"You know them?"

"Nah." His gaze wandered to his phone. "Not really. Like I said, just their first names."

The ancient desk phone buzzed. One of its buttons flashed. A voice said, "Sam, it's Vino Variety at the bar. I set him at table twelve."

Sam punched the button. "Tell him I'll be right out." Then, to me, "Got to run, but let's talk soon about your event." He pushed his business card across the table. "Give me a call."

"Will do." Not. My next call would be on Sheriff Koppen. Now I had something solid to share.

* * *

STRINGS ATTACHED WAS SUPPOSED TO OPEN IN TWENTY minutes, but I didn't care. Sheriff Koppen had to know about the mushroom hunters. Avery had no motive to kill Miles. They did. Plus, Sam Anderson clearly had a few unpaid bills. If he suspected Miles was planning to open a new restaurant, who knew what he'd do?

I burst into the shop front that housed the sheriff's office and silently groaned. Deputy Goff looked up with a frown, as if she could hear my dread at seeing her. "Sheriff Koppen, please," I said.

"He's out." Deputy Goff sat among a stack of file folders at the desk behind the counter. She returned her attention to her computer screen.

"I need to talk to him. It's superimportant."

"Uh-huh. I'll be sure to let him know."

"Tell him it's me," I said. "Tell him it's about the murder."

"What else would it be about?" She rolled her eyes. "He's up in Astoria with the suspect now. Do you want to leave a message with me?"

"She's not 'the suspect.' She has a name, you know." The thought of Avery in jail, badgered by Koppen, galled me. "Look. I might know who killed Miles, and it wasn't Avery."

The deputy raised her eyebrows. "Naturally."

"I'm serious."

"So am I. We're following up on some leads ourselves."

"And do any of those leads have to do with some mushroom hunters, Ron and Monica, who threatened Miles just last week?" I posed a hand on my hip. Take that, Deputy Goff.

"The sheriff knows all about the mushroomers."

Her calm demeanor only fueled my frustration. "Then why hasn't he asked Sam Anderson about them? Speaking of Sam, what about the Tidal Basin's unpaid bills?" My heart beat a little erratically. It wasn't every day that I challenged a police officer.

"What have you got against Sam Anderson?" Her voice became cold, focused.

"What have you got against Avery?" I countered.

The deputy grabbed a handful of her short hair and pulled. "Good lord." She pointed to the dingy side chair across the desk. "Sit. Let's cover the mushroom gatherers first. Do you have any idea how many people hunt mushrooms this time of year? The morels are coming up, and they can get fifty bucks a pound if they know where to market them."

I wasn't sure if her question was rhetorical or not. "But they must get permits. Plus, I have names. All you have to do is track them down."

"The state park issued more than seventy permits this month alone. That doesn't even touch the number of people who gather without a permit. Or who gather morels on private property."

"Sam Anderson said they threatened Miles. To his face. Said he'd be sorry. As far as they were concerned, Miles was stealing their business. That's a reason to kill someone. And it's more of a reason than Avery has."

"I know she's your friend and you're concerned. Do you have any reason to think Avery knows the mushroom hunters?"

"Absolutely not." Once the words left my mouth, I saw where the deputy was headed.

"So they wouldn't know to hide a knife under her bed, would they?"

"Not so fast." I stood up.

"Sit," the deputy commanded.

I sat. "Word gets around fast in this town. Once they heard that Avery was under suspicion, all they had to do to seal the deal was to hide the knife under her bed."

The deputy shook her head. "Doesn't matter. But mushroom hunters have been threatening each other over territory for decades now, and no one's been killed."

"And people have been dating and breaking up for millennia, and no one has been murdered because of it." I thought again. "Well, not that many people."

"Look, I'll make a note of the mushroom hunters' names. Ron and Monica, you said?" She jotted their names on a notepad, but I had the clear idea she was doing it simply to pacify me.

"None of this leaves Sam Anderson off the hook," I said.

The deputy seemed to choke a bit. "Sam. Yes. I'm getting to him."

"That's what I said. Sam Anderson. Say the Tidal Basin had some financial challenges, and Sam learned that Miles was going to open a competing restaurant. What then?"

"We've questioned Mr. Anderson. It's none of your concern." Goff's face was curiously red.

"What do you mean? Of course I'm concerned. I found the body, remember? And it's my friend you've locked up for no good reason." Damn her. Would she listen to me?

The deputy turned her attention to a stack of papers. "I'll let Sheriff Koppen know you came by. And don't worry—we're doing everything we can to find the murderer."

"You're not going to find him sitting around the office," I shot off.

Fuming, I left. I could only hope Martino's was planning a batch of garlicky, anchovy-ridden pies for the day. The sheriff's office deserved some odor therapy.

chapter fourteen

ONCE STRINGS ATTACHED WAS OPEN, I CALLED DAVE. I knew I could count on him as an ally. "Could you come see me sometime today? I can't leave the shop, but I want to talk to you. It has to do with Avery." That would get him.

He showed up less than an hour later. "What's going on? Have you heard from her?" Dave's tall, sober figure contrasted with the fanciful kites around him.

"I saw Avery last night. She's holding up."

"I'm going to visit, too. I'm leading a kayak tour in the state park, but after that I'm driving to Astoria."

"I thought you had guides for that." Dave would have preferred to spend his time outdoors, but as the kayak store's owner, he'd explained that he felt he should be around the shop.

"Pete decided to go to school in New Mexico, and Robbie didn't show up yesterday. Didn't even call. I had to let him go. It's not easy finding someone who knows the terrain around here, especially on the water." He stepped closer to the counter. "How did she look to you?"

I remembered Avery's tissue-thin skin under the fluorescent lights, her fatalistic attitude. "Not good. Strangely resigned, actually. It worries me."

"What do you mean?"

"Just a sec," I said. A customer with a grade-school-aged boy in tow had just come in the shop. "Is there anything special you're looking for?"

"Nathan is begging me to get him a kite. He saw some others on the beach, and—"

"Mom, look at this one." The boy held one of my favorites, a kite shaped like an owl.

"Have you flown kites before?" I asked.

"No," both the mother and son said at the same time. "I thought something, you know, not superexpensive would be nice."

I wasn't kidding when I told Stella the diamond kites sold the fastest. I'd have to order some more and soon. "You might be interested in one of these. They're the classic diamond shape and have flown for centuries. Maybe a blue one?" I held up a robin's-egg-blue diamond kite with a darker blue tail.

"Mom. Cool. Can I have it?" He kept a hand on the owl kite. "Unless I can have this one."

"The owl kite is one of our easiest to fly. The wind is great today. Just let out the string slowly but consistently, and if it starts to dive side to side, reel it in a bit."

The mother examined the owl. A slight smile lit her face as she touched its beak. "It's a little more expensive, but not much. You say it's all right for a boy new to kites?"

"Absolutely," I said. The boy was practically holding his breath, willing his mother to choose the owl.

She glanced at him and smiled. "We'll take it," she said, and the boy gripped the kite tight.

After they left, Dave returned to the counter. Hands in pockets, he'd been examining the room's moldings, but his tapping toe belied his anxiety. "What did you want to talk to me about?"

"Mushrooms," I said.

"What kind?"

I nearly laughed. "Don't you even want to know why?"

"Well, yes. I guess so," Dave said.

"The week before Miles was killed, some mushroom hunters came to the Tidal Basin's back door and threatened him. I told the sheriff's office about it, and the deputy I talked to said it would be impossible to chase them down, that fighting over mushroom territory is pretty common."

"True enough."

"If I could give the sheriff names, maybe they'd follow up."

"Yes. I can see that. Did Sam have their names?"

"No, they're on a first-name basis only. So I thought I'd try to find them."

Dave dropped a hand to the counter. "And how are you going to do that?"

"If I knew where morels were growing right now, I could lurk, see who's picking lots of them, see if I find people matching Sam's description of them."

"It's high morel season now. There'll be dozens of people out."

"I have their first names. Ron and Monica."

"And then what? You find a couple that matches Sam's description and say, 'Hey, Ron and Monica, kill anyone lately?' Not a great plan. Plus, what if they think you're poaching on their territory?"

"I have a plan. I'll pretend I'm sketching, and they'll be able to see I don't have any mushrooms with me. Once I see them, I'll follow them back to their car and get their license-plate number."

Dave walked to the front door and looked out the window. Beyond the stoop he'd see the beach and a slice of ocean. I knew he was thinking of Avery.

Finally he turned to me. "I want to help find Avery's killer, but your plan isn't well thought out. For one thing, morels could be growing just about anywhere."

"Which is why I wanted to talk to you. Where do they grow?"

"Different spots every year. Morels love natural disasters. Flooded areas, land after a forest fire, places like that."

"So where around here would there be a place where a lot of morels grow? Enough to make it worth a picker's time?"

He returned to the counter. "There is one place along the river that flooded pretty badly last fall. I kayaked past a few days ago, and the riverbank was covered with morels. I wouldn't be surprised if it's been popular with pickers."

"Anywhere else?"

"Maybe. Probably. That's where you'd find the most in one area, though."

My pulse quickened. "Yes. I bet that's it. Where is it?"

A hand reached to his beard. I'd come to recognize this as Dave's sign of deep thought. Or worry. "I'll tell you, but only because it's popular enough that you won't be isolated." His hand dropped to the counter. "Do you have paper?"

I rushed to the workroom and brought out my sketch pad. With his concise, even hand, Dave drew a map.

"You won't approach anyone, right?"

"No. Scout's honor." I held up two fingers and avoided telling Dave that I was kicked out of Brownies for having a loud mouth. "In fact, I'll bring a friend." Stella would go with me, I was sure. "All I want to do is get a license-plate number and let the sheriff take it from there."

"When are you going?"

There was no reason to wait. "Tomorrow morning."

"I expect a call by noon, then."

I didn't know why Avery didn't jump all over Dave. He was quiet and methodical—not exactly bursting with spontaneity—but he was a solid, caring guy.

"Remember," he said. "Noon. And who is this friend who's going with you?"

"Stella. She's totally on board."

"ABSOLUTELY NOT," STELLA SAID OVER THE PHONE.

"But," I said, "this is our perfect chance to find the person who might have killed Miles."

"And get ourselves killed in the process? I know you care about Avery, but in this case you really do need to leave it to the sheriff."

"He won't follow up on it. I talked to the deputy. Besides, why are morel-mushroom pickers so much more dangerous than anyone else? And if they are, isn't that even more of a reason to find out who they are?"

I could almost see Stella shaking her elegant head as she replied. "Picking and selling morels is quick cash and doesn't require a lot of skill."

"And?"

"That means you get an unpredictable bunch doing it. People who can't hold jobs or who skirt the law. It's common knowledge that if you want to pick morels out here, you do it on your own land or at your own peril."

I couldn't believe it. Stella was bailing on me. "So you're just going to give up."

"No. I'm not giving up." She paused long enough that I noticed the falling dusk outside. "But I just don't think it's for us to follow up that lead. Leave it to the professionals. We don't need to get into the middle of a mushroom-territory dispute and get our tires slashed, or worse."

"I told you. The deputy basically told me, 'Tough luck.'"

A sigh. "Listen. What else happened when you talked with Sam? Anything else interesting?"

"No, but I talked to Jeanette down at the post office. She hinted that the Tidal Basin has a few unpaid bills, but she wouldn't tell me much more. I saw a 'Final Notice' bill on Sam's desk when I visited. Maybe he was threatened by Miles's idea of opening a new restaurant."

"Jeanette's a tough number, isn't she?"

"She definitely believes in the tit-for-tat method of information exchange."

"Hmm. Let me work on her. I might be able to squeeze out something more," Stella said. "As for Miles's restaurant, we don't even know how old that idea was."

"True." I balled up a piece of paper and squeezed it in my palm so hard that my thumb cramped for a moment before I released it. So much promise with leads, but so little opportunity to follow up. Meanwhile Avery rotted in jail.

"I can tell you're upset," Stella said.

"I just don't know what to do. Avery even told me to lay off, that I should just leave it alone. But how can I when she's in jail and shouldn't be there? Every day that goes by the harder it'll be to find evidence that points away from her."

"And Miles's murderer is still free."

"Exactly."

The tick of the mantel clock mocked me. Time was wasting, and I was useless.

"What are you doing tonight?" Stella asked.

"Nothing." Nothing but burnt pizza at home.

"Why don't we meet later at the docks? The old docks. The sheriff said they found bloodstains on the boat, right? Plus, Miles had a note in his calendar about meeting Avery there."

"True." I liked this idea, even if I had no idea what exactly we were looking for. But was that so different from searching Miles's cabin?

"Do you know what time they were to meet?"

"No, but it had to have been later on, about the time Dave and I were at the bonfire."

"How about if we meet at eight? We'll check it out, get an idea of what it was like down there the night Miles was killed. Maybe we'll notice something the sheriff missed. It's not much, but it's something."

"It's a plan."

SO FAR I HAD TWO POSSIBLE MURDER SUSPECTS. THE mushroom hunters might have killed Miles for revenge, or to stop him from poaching their mushrooms. Perhaps they also had a boat at the dock. Or maybe they "borrowed" Avery's. The blood might have come from Miles after he was killed elsewhere and hauled to the boat. Once they figured out the boat belonged to Avery, they hid the knife at her house. That didn't explain the calendar entry, though.

Miles's boss, Sam, might have killed him to make sure he didn't open a competing restaurant. Or maybe he simply got mad at Miles for not turning up for work, or for ordering a lot of expensive seafood, and stabbed him in a fit of passion. Miles was tall but thin. Sam could have loaded him into a wheelbarrow or something and wheeled him to the docks. Of course, he risked being seen. That's what I was counting on.

I parked the Prius near the Tidal Basin and walked the short distance to the docks. A light drizzle dampened its planked surface. Stella, right on time, came down the hill toward me. She wore European-styled flats and had wrapped an embroidered black cotton scarf around her neck, letting its fringed edges hang down her chest. Honestly, that woman would look refined shoveling cow manure.

"Ready?" she asked.

"As I'll ever be," I said. "Should we make a plan?"

"How about this? You'll say you were just having a bite at the Tidal Basin, and you decided to check Avery's boat, to make sure it's secure."

I buttoned my jacket up one more notch. The evening was chilly. "I just—the sheriff should have done all this questioning already."

"I'm sure he did. Our job is to make something fresh from the information, then give him something to follow up on. We might see something he didn't. Besides, sometimes people will tell things to an attractive woman they won't tell to the police."

"People probably do tell you a lot," I said.

"I meant you, silly," Stella said. We reached the dock. The mist had turned to a light rain. "Do you know which boat is Avery's?"

I didn't. Strangely enough, for all the time I'd spent in Rock Point, we'd never gone out on her family's boat.

Stella took my expression for the "no" it was. "Well, I guess we can fake it."

It's true that the old docks were close to the Tidal Basin, but they felt like a different town altogether. The new marina, where the cruising yachts and weekenders' boats were kept, was solid and well lit. A security guard kept tabs on comings and goings. Not so for the old dock. The relative lack of light and double row of boat slips between the old and new docks gave the old dock a seedy air. Especially after dark.

"I guess we'd better check it out," I said.

"What are we looking for, exactly?" Stella said.

"What do you mean? It was your idea to come down here."

She took in the dark pier and pulled her scarf closer. "Yes, but now I'm not sure it was a good one."

I scanned the boardwalk. This late at night it was deserted. The air smelled of seawater and tarred fir. We were on the opposite side of town from the rental cottages, but a few of the town's residents lived on the block above the docks.

"Do you think anyone saw Miles and—well, you know—that night?"

Stella squinted. "The dock's so dark. And they'd need binoculars. If the murderer pulled in with their lights on and made a lot of noise, I guess it's possible."

"I'll make sure the sheriff talked to them."

We both faced the dock and looked at each other as if willing the other to go first.

"All right, let's do it," Stella said. She strode down the pier and slowed as the light faded and footing became less sure.

I was right behind her. I nearly tripped on an uneven board but righted myself with only a quick yelp. "Sorry. Clumsy," I whispered.

"Careful, there's no railing," Stella said.

"Believe me, I know."

The dock had about a dozen slips on each side. I knew from an earlier, daytime visit that the boats were mostly old—some better cared for than others—along with a few better-maintained fishing craft. Now they all just looked like darkened hulks.

"So, Miles came down to the dock to meet Avery. Or so he thought." There was no one around, but I still felt I had to keep my voice low, yet firm enough to be heard over the bay lapping on the pier. "He would have waited at the entrance to the dock, don't you think?"

"Unless he expected Avery to be in the boat already."

Too bad I didn't know which boat was Avery's. It was too dark even to read their names.

"True. So he might have come up the dock."

"Someone might have been waiting in the shadows near a pier—"

Just then a rat scurried across the dock's old wood.

Stella grabbed my shoulder. We both stood a second and caught our breath. The rat disappeared beneath the pier.

"Someone could have stabbed Miles then," Stella finished.

"Then they'd have to drag him to the boat and take him out to sea." I shook my head. My heart rate began to return to normal. "That seems like too much trouble. Wouldn't it be easier to lure him on board, then kill him? Less messy, too."

"So someone lured Miles onto Avery's boat."

"I thought of that. Anyone could have retied the boat. Maybe the blood wasn't even Miles's."

We pondered. I wasn't sure where this line of reasoning led. The rain had picked up, and I wiped a damp strand of hair from my eyes. How could the mushroom hunters have found out about Avery and set up the whole boat business? Unless they were in cahoots with someone. Like Sam. The facts kept returning to him. The dark, the rain, the cold bay. No one was here at night. It was the perfect place for a murder.

"What are you girls doing?" a voice slurred from one of the boats.

Stella nearly fell over, and my pulse pounded so hard I could barely hear. "What?" I managed to get out.

"I said, what are you girls doing? Come in. Out of the rain."

I saw him now, a little guy holding a beer can on the wooden boat to our left. "Thank you, but we're just leaving," I said.

"Actually—" Stella shot me a glance. "If you don't mind, it would be nice to dry off a moment."

What was she thinking? Get on some strange guy's boat? "I'm not—"

"You're not fond of the rain, are you?" Stella finished. "It's so nice that this gentleman is offering us shelter for a few minutes." Stella's pointed stare said, *Get in here, dummy.*

Yes. Yes, Stella was right. The man might have seen something. But should we really risk it? Stella didn't even look at me for confirmation. She'd refused to go with me to find the mushroom hunters, but she'd get on a stranger's boat? Apparently so. She stepped off the dock onto his small boat, and after a moment's hesitation, I followed. I ducked my head to enter and raised it to a small cabin lit by a handful of pillar candles. It smelled of incense, beer, and—this was odd—litter box.

"I'm meditating," the man said. "Name's Ace." Ace did resemble a Buddha, in fact. A Buddha with a gray-streaked ponytail and beer belly.

"Oh, Ace Plumbing," Stella said, gracious to a fault. "You installed my dishwasher. I almost didn't recognize you. Nice work you did."

"After all that working the body, I find it a relief to get away from the missus and center my mind."

And consume a few gallons of beer, I thought, taking in the box of empty bottles near the door.

"Yes," Ace continued. "It's all about balance, the yin and the yang." A gray tabby, apparently deciding we were all right, leapt from behind his chair and butted Ace's head. "That's Yin," he said. "Yang's probably hiding under the bed."

"I adore cats." Stella reached to scratch Yin's head. I

didn't think Madame Lucy would hang out with these low-class boat cats, but maybe she shared her owner's sense of adventure.

"Me, too. In my line of work I find more than my share of strays and kittens. These two I spotted under the jiffy mart when I was snaking a drain. Their mother had abandoned them. I had to bottle-feed them the first few weeks." He stroked Yin under the chin, and the tabby lifted his head for a better angle.

"They clearly love you," Stella said. "Spend a lot of time here?"

Ace laughed, a broad ha-ha-ha. "Couple of nosey ones, are you? Come down to see where the chef was murdered?" He cracked open a beer. "Thirsty?"

No and no, I thought, but Stella had other plans. Rain pattered on the boat's roof as Ace dug in his cooler and retrieved another can.

"Why, I'd love a beer, Ace. Thank you," Stella said. "And I do admit to being a bit curious. I imagine the sheriff questioned you thoroughly."

Ace erupted into laughter again. When he caught his breath, he said, "That's a good one."

"So you didn't see anything that night," I said. "Or maybe you weren't here." Or maybe you weren't sober enough to care.

Yin had settled himself into Ace's lap and purred like a lawnmower.

"I was here all right. If I thought I had something the sheriff needed to know, I'd tell him."

"Maybe you don't think much of him?" Stella asked.

"He's all right. I put low-flow toilets throughout his

house. Paid me on time and didn't stand around trying to tell me how to do my job."

Unlike me, trying to tell the sheriff how to do his. I bit my lip.

"Sometimes even the smallest things can offer a lot of information."

Yin stretched a paw toward Stella, then circled to settle again.

"You're an attractive lady, uh—"

"Stella Hart. How's your wife?"

"Sorry, with so many customers, I can't keep track." He set his beer on the floor. "Mrs. Ace is fine, thank you. Her scrapbooking club meets tonight."

Stella smiled benignly. "So you didn't hear or see anything the night Miles was killed?"

"It's not like I keep an eagle eye on the dock, you know. People can come or go, and it's none of my business."

"Of course." Stella's voice was soothing. She hadn't touched the beer he gave her, and his voice was suddenly surprisingly sober. I had to wonder if his drunkenness was all a show. The bottles might have been piling up for weeks instead of days. "Still," she continued, "you might have a story or two."

One hand in Yin's scruff and another on his beer, he examined us. "Not about that night, I don't. Just the usual. Sam and—"

"Sam Anderson?" I nearly leapt from my chair.

"Yeah. And another lady—"

"Sam was here?" I repeated.

Ace squinted at me. "Didn't know he was so exciting."

"He was Miles's boss," I said.

"And a crabber," Ace said. "It was slack tide then, a good time to go out, although crabbing's not so great in the spring."

"He has a boat on this dock?" Stella said.

"Sure. Didn't I say he crabs?" He looked around as if someone else might be in the claustrophobic cabin and leaned forward. "He might be doing a few other things, too."

"Like what?" I said.

"Not telling." He tossed his empty can in the box. "Ace ain't no tattletale."

"You said he was with a lady. Did you get a good look at her?" I asked. A lady could have been Annabelle. Or someone else.

"Did I say lady? I didn't mean that."

"What did you mean, Ace?" Stella asked in a satiny voice.

Ace smiled and shook his head. "You are a charmer. I swear, if my old lady and I hadn't been together so long, I might make a play for you myself." He chuckled. "How do you feel about a man who meditates a bit in his boat?"

Lord, he was irritating. "You saw someone," I said. "Now you're trying to cover it up."

Ace's smile turned to a frown. "Your friend doesn't have your finesse, Stella."

"She gets edgy in tight spaces, that's all," Stella said. She turned away from him and mouthed to me, "Calm down."

"He clearly saw something," I couldn't help saying. "The sheriff should know."

Ace set his can on the floor and rose. "I'll see you out."

On the dock, the rain pounded. Stella and I, each of us

with our heads bent against the downpour, made our way back to the parking lot.

"What got into you back there?" Stella asked once we were clear of the dock.

I'd blown it. I was too anxious, and I'd blown it. "He knows something."

"And he might have told us if we'd handled it right. You know what they say about bees and honey."

"You're right." Just then I felt a lot more bitter than honey.

chapter fifteen

EARLY THE NEXT MORNING, I PARKED THE PRIUS ON AN old logging road just past the turnoff where Dave had said morels were growing. Avery's words came to me. I should leave the case alone, because "it could do more harm than good," she'd said. I wasn't interfering, though. I was trying to find more information—information that I'd give the sheriff to help him. Not get in his way. I was doing this for Avery's own good.

Figuring that the most serious morel gatherers worked early, I'd set my alarm for 5:00 a.m. It had been dark out when I left the house, but now the sky was turning pink, and the air smelled damp and sweet with cottonwood trees. I'd filled my daypack with a couple of sandwiches and a thermos of coffee, and my sketch pad and pencils were zipped into an outer pocket. Private investigators sometimes had to stake out apartments all day in their cars. I was ready to do the same.

The autumn before, Dave had told me, torrential rain had swollen the river to the point that it had washed over its banks in the state park northeast of town, where I was now. After a week, the river had returned to its bed, but the film of silt it left in its wake was fertile ground for morels. Although thanks to Dave I felt up to speed with morel-growing conditions, honestly, I couldn't tell you what a morel mushroom looked like. The terrain around me was covered with small growing things: tiny ferns, slugs, baby-sized firs, and, yes, all sorts of fungi.

I chose a fallen log at the edge of the clearing and settled in. From here I'd be able to see most of the bend where the river had flooded. I set my sketch pad next to me on the log and took out the thermos. To me, the clearing looked about as dangerous as an Ansel Adams photograph. In other words, I wasn't exactly shaking in my boots.

A few hours later, the sun was up, my thermos was empty, and I'd seen no one. No one but a doe and two fawns, that is, that picked their way over branches to drink from the river. I sketched one of the fawns with her gangly legs and blond spots. Beautiful. But my hind end hurt from sitting so long. Plus, the sky was thickening, and it looked like last night's rain would be returning.

Thudding car doors from the turnout warned me that someone was coming. I grabbed my sketch pad and made like I was absorbed. A couple dressed in matching navy waterproof jackets trudged into the clearing.

"Jonathan," the woman said. "Why can't we go back to the picnic benches? I think it's going to rain."

"Too many people. Come on. The guy at the hotel said we should be able to find a trailhead somewhere around here." He strode through the clearing, stepping over logs, the woman trailing behind. They didn't see me. "This way. I think I see it."

Not long after came the day's first mushroom pickers. Stella's warning rang in my ears, and my pulse quickened. Then they came into full view, a couple of elderly women garbed for the elements in chin-strapped sun hats and cotton gloves. Each woman had a plastic milk jug with a hole cut away in it and the handle looped through a canvas belt around her waist. They spotted me immediately and waved a cheerful hello. Honestly? These were the "dangerous" mushroom hunters I'd been warned about?

"Oh, now isn't that nice. Sketching, are you, dear? Well, don't mind us," one of them said.

"Just gathering mushrooms," the other said.

"That's nice," I said. "I hear you can turn a nice profit with those."

"When you live on a fixed income you learn to get crafty," the taller woman replied. "This is a popular spot. It's best to get here early."

"Before the meth heads wake up," the shorter woman added.

"Oh." Good grief. I set aside the egg-salad sandwich I'd intended for breakfast. "Meth heads?"

"Drug addicts, dear. They have great focus, but aren't always the most polite."

"Oh no. Think they own the place. Take my advice. You see them, just keep to your sketching and don't mind them any. As long as you're not taking morels, you should be fine."

"Should be," the taller woman said. "Personally, I wouldn't risk it. Not without this." She scanned the clearing, then lifted her jacket to reveal a steel gray handgun tucked in her belt.

Should be? I swallowed. "All right. Thank you."

I spent the next hour or so working on my comet-kite design. Jack had been right. The area for the wind's up-thrust was small, and that coupled with its asymmetrical design doomed its flightworthiness. Once the ladies had filled their pails and left, I was alone again. But it was peaceful. Stella and Dave were full of baloney. It was perfectly safe to be out here.

It was looking like the day might be a bust when a couple of rough-looking guys carrying ten-gallon white plastic buckets, the kind restaurants get supplies in, strode into the clearing. Could one of them be Ron? These men were not the easygoing ladies or the determined kayakers. They meant business. The skin on my neck prickled.

I glanced behind me to see if I could ease out of sight. It was too risky. I'd have to stand up, and they'd see me for sure. By keeping still I stood the best chance of going un-noticed. The men barely talked to each other and kept their eyes to the ground, yanking mushrooms from the silt and tossing them into their buckets. They seemed to focus mostly around logs and washed-up branches. On one man's hip was a worn leather holster holding a hunting knife. I barely breathed.

"I'll get the edge," one of the men said. He lifted his head, then stopped. *Damn.* "Chet. Look here." He tossed his head in my direction. Both men headed toward me.

Panicked, I stood. "Nice day for sketching." I waved my sketchbook as proof.

Despite the chill in the air, the men were dressed only in jeans and sour-smelling T-shirts. The one called Chet was heavier, and it took a moment for his breathing to slow from the effort of crossing the clearing. The other one's

T-shirt prominently featured SpongeBob dressed like a mad scientist saying "Get yer nerd on."

"Sketching? Here?" The one with the SpongeBob shirt squinted over the nature-ravaged clearing. He was right. It wasn't particularly scenic.

"Let me see." Chet pulled my sketchbook from my hands.

"Hey," I said.

"That don't look like no landscape," the other man— Ron?—said. He was dark haired and stocky like Sam had described him.

"It's a design for a kite," I said, my voice climbing toward a squeak.

"Why are you here to draw kites?"

"I do my best thinking outdoors," I improvised. "Fresh air. You know." And rain. A gentle patter began to fall around us. "I sketched a fawn, too—look."

The other man lifted my backpack. "Put that down," I said. "That's not yours." Panic had me by the throat now. I searched the clearing, hoping someone else had shown up, but it was just us. With the worsening weather, it would likely stay that way. Why hadn't I listened to the warnings?

"Could be mine. Depends on what I find." He pulled my other sandwich from the pack and dropped it in his bucket. "No citations."

Citations. Realization dawned. He thought I was inspecting permits. "No. No, I'm just sketching. That's all. Looks like it's raining now." I forced a laugh. "Time to go home."

The men looked at each other. "What should we do with her?"

Do with me?

"Hmm." Chet looked me up and down. "We might—"

I bolted. Blood pounded in my ears. I made it a full three yards before I hit a branch and fell facedown into the mud. I groaned. The men lifted me, one on each arm.

"Well, would you look at that," Chet said. "She's scared of us. Tried to make a run for it." He tossed me back on the log next to my daypack. I wiped silt from my eyes.

"Go figure." SpongeBob laughed until it became a wheeze and then a cough. "Relax. We're not gonna hurt you. Are we?" He looked to Chet.

"Nah," Chet said. "Just having some fun. That's all. One thing for sure, you aren't a mushroom picker."

"Ha-ha-ha." I felt like crying in frustration but plastered a fake smile on my face. "Nope. I hate mushrooms." This was beginning to be the truth.

"No mushroom gatherer would have missed these." Chet stooped to my feet and chucked five mushrooms in his half-full bucket. "They're growing all around you."

"You know, you might hate mushrooms, but you'd love morels," SpongeBob said. He leered at his partner, who nodded in return.

"Maybe she'd like to buy these from us," Chet said.

I scanned the clearing again. Still no one. I was alone with these guys. "Oh no, I'm not sure when I'd get around to—"

"Yeah. You'll love morels so much. How much money you got on you?"

"Let's check," Chet said. He pulled two twenties and a couple of ones from my wallet. "Not much. Maybe enough for a pound."

Forty dollars a pound? I yanked my wallet from his hands and slipped it into my inside pocket. I stepped back but hit the log and nearly fell again. *Think, Emmy, think.* "Ron and Monica don't charge that much."

"Ron and Monica." Chet glanced at his friend. "You hear that? Ron and Monica. Where'd you hear about them?"

"Down at the Tidal Basin," I said. I held my breath.

"Losers," SpongeBob said.

"I wonder if they'll be out picking today." I tried to keep my voice casual, but my voice was climbing back into soprano territory.

"They're down at the burnout left by that big fire last summer," Chet said. "I don't mind telling you. Go pick their lot dry before they get there."

"Come on, let's get back to work," SpongeBob said. "We'll let our artist friend go home. She don't want to get wet."

"I don't know. Looks like she could use a shower. Got a bit dirty making her big escape." They laughed at their joke.

Relief flooded over me as I brushed a twig from my jacket. They were letting me go. "Yes. I'd better be getting on."

"I guess you'd better. And why aren't you?"

"You still have my daypack," I said, torn between needing my stuff and wanting to hightail it out of there.

He laughed again. His back molars were riddled with fillings. "We'll keep it." He tossed me my keys and slung the pack over his shoulder. "Those morels by rights are fifty a pound."

The rain had built to a shower pattering around us. I glanced toward the opening to the old highway. My car was not quite a quarter mile up the road, and my rain poncho was in the daypack.

"Don't forget your mushrooms." SpongeBob handed me the bucket. "You bought them fair and square."

I RAN ALL THE WAY BACK TO THE CAR, TOSSED THE MO-rels on the passenger-side seat, and locked myself in. Dave and Stella had been right. What was I thinking to go down there alone? I was lucky simply to be robbed. I glanced at the mushrooms. Kind of robbed, anyway. At least I'd come away with solid intelligence. And mushrooms.

After a few deep breaths, I collected myself and drove to the sheriff's office.

"I know where the mushroom hunters are," I said after bursting into the small office.

Deputy Goff again. Would I ever catch a break? The deputy was on the phone and motioned for me to sit. I was too antsy, though, so I paced the front room.

At last she set the receiver in its cradle. "Now, what are you saying?"

"I found out where the mushroom hunters are. The ones who threatened Miles before he was killed." I cocked my head at her. "Don't you start rolling your eyes."

She looked toward the ceiling, and her lips formed a silent growl. "I'm not rolling my eyes. I don't understand you. Slow down. Start at the beginning." She pulled a pad from her desk and brought it to the counter.

I felt like I was explaining things to a six-year-old, but I slowed down. "Remember how I came in yesterday and told you that some mushroom hunters had threatened Miles Logan?"

The deputy nodded. "Sure."

"Well, through—uh—through a series of events I found

out where they pick morels. If you want to find them, question them about Miles, it'll be easy."

"And where is that?"

"Down at the burnout." As soon as I said it, I realized that I didn't know where that was. Maybe I should have checked with Dave first.

"The burnout from the Fetzger fire, on the other side of Highway 101?" She jotted a few notes.

"Are there any other burnouts you know?" I said this as if the answer were obvious, since I had no idea.

"Not this year," she said, and continued jotting. "How did you get this information?"

"I was talking to some other morel gatherers," I said casually. "They told me about Ron and Monica. Knew them well."

"Last names?"

Damn. "I'm not sure."

"Next time you're sleuthing, you might want to pick up some useful evidence like the suspects' names."

"It's more than you came up with," I said. "It's a start."

The deputy set down her pad. "What are you implying?"

"Look, I'm here with some potentially useful information for you. I know you don't believe me, but you have the wrong person in jail. Meanwhile, someone is going scot-free for a murder." Didn't she get it?

"I can't believe you—"

"There's one other thing. I wonder if the mushroom hunters might have been working with Sam Anderson to kill Miles."

The deputy's jaw dropped. "What?"

"Sam may have had his own reasons to want Miles out of the way. Miles was thinking of opening a restaurant. It would have competed with Sam's, and the Tidal Basin is already operating on a slim financial margin. Remember? I already told you this."

"I don't believe it. Sit," the deputy said. I sat. "You are way off track, and I want you to butt out now. Understand?" She leaned forward for emphasis. "You'll mess everything up."

What was she talking about? "Where's the sheriff, anyway? I want to talk to him."

"In Astoria. Did you hear me?"

"If he's in Astoria, does that mean Avery might come home?"

"Ms. Adler, listen. We have procedures and the benefit of a skilled group of crime-scene investigators. You can be sure that the sheriff is looking into every possible angle. Understand?" I nodded. "Good. Now, thank you for this information. I want you to go home now and let us do our job."

I nodded again. "And Avery might come home?" The judge must be setting her bail.

"That's not for me to say." The deputy slid the notebook into a desk drawer. "Good-bye, Ms. Adler."

chapter sixteen

I LOADED BEAR INTO THE CAR AND STOPPED BY THE SHOP.
The scare from talking to the thugs by the river had been
replaced in part with the thought that the sheriff would carry
on from here and that Avery might be home soon. The judge
would set her bail and release her. Maybe I'd finally have
the chance to open that bottle of champagne I'd intended
for Strings Attached's opening day. Once the sheriff tracked
down the mysterious Ron and Monica, once the judge looked
at the evidence, we'd be in the clear for good.

When I arrived at Strings Attached, Stella was reading
an Isabel Allende novel behind the counter. "Did you have
a good day today?" she asked. She set the novel down.

"Yes. Thanks for filling in for me today. I spent some
time sketching out a new kite design." Those schoolteacher
eyes seemed to read my mind. I averted my gaze. She didn't
need to know about my forays to the morel grounds or

sheriff's office. Bear slipped past me into the kitchen work-shop. I heard him lapping at his water bowl. "How's business?"

"Sold three more diamond kites, some line, and one of those lovely lotus kites."

The lotus kite was one of my favorites. I'd designed it as a soft tube and wrapped it in filmy petals of pink ripstop nylon and a gray fine-weave net with green and mauve woven through it. Maybe whoever bought it was down at the beach flying it now.

"Do you want to take over here?" Stella asked. "I've been enjoying it—relaxing, talking to the people who come through. I even came up with an idea for a kite. But if you'd rather—"

"No, I promised you the full day, and I wouldn't mind working a bit in the workshop."

"Maybe you'd let me watch? We'll hear the doorbell if someone comes in. I'd love to learn a little more about how kites are made."

"Sure. Come on in. I'm trying something new with the comet design, and I thought I'd cut out the pattern."

Stella followed me into the workshop and sat in one of the chairs at the small kitchen table. We kept the door open so we could hear the front door's bell ring if a customer came in. I pulled a roll of tissue from a side cabinet and cut a piece large enough to span the gridded mat that lined my drafting table.

"Do you draw the pattern freehand?" Stella asked.

"For this one I will. For a more symmetrical kite, I'd probably design it on the computer or even draw on graph paper, then project it onto a sheet of tissue on the wall." The process of transferring my ideas to paper always absorbed me, and a touch of anxiety melted away as I secured the corners of the tissue.

"What are those?" Stella pointed at the fabric weights, which I'd made from mustard jars full of lead shot.

"They hold down the nylon while I cut a pattern. This tissue wants to curl up, so I'll use them now." I'd sketch the pattern on the tissue, using the gridlines underneath as a loose guide. Then I'd cut the pattern into a rigid paper with the weight of a file folder. That would be the pattern I'd use directly on nylon.

"I love being in here surrounded by art supplies," Stella said. "Early in my career I taught third grade. The tissue, colorful fabric, pens, and scissors—it reminds me of art time." She laughed.

"Did you ever want kids of your own?" I asked absently. My fingers traced the comet's head, big and round, like an elongated bulb. I hoped by giving it more surface area it would catch the wind.

Stella didn't respond. For a moment I wondered if she'd heard me. I was just about to ask again when she said, "My schoolchildren were my children. I was nearly forty when I married. A little old for having my own."

"I see." I only half heard her words as the comet's curves transferred from my brain to paper. Kites were such an escape for me. They always had been, from watching their shapes ripple in the wind as a kid, to later, when I learned how to design them. Other people read to escape, or listened to music or hiked. I had kites.

I wondered what Avery had. Especially now, in jail. I set down my pencil. My hand dropped to my side.

"Thinking about Avery, aren't you." Stella said it more as a statement than a question.

"Yes. She goes before the judge today." It wasn't all about me, I reminded myself. "Miles. You must be missing him." She gave a noncommittal shrug. "You worked together. You love talking to people, Stella. I know you said you didn't really know him well, but I can't help but think his death has affected you, too."

She opened her novel and smoothed the page before pushing it away again. "You're right." She met my eyes. "I do miss him. When I first came to Rock Point last summer, we spent a little time together. He liked my paintings. You know, he was an artist, too, but not with paint. I'd thought— well, it doesn't matter what I thought." She must have caught a shift in my expression, because she hurriedly said, "We were friendly, but that was all. I mean, you wouldn't get any ideas that—" She broke off her thought with a laugh.

I didn't know what to think.

AFTER I'D FINISHED MY INITIAL SKETCH OF THE PATTERN, I called for Bear and walked down to the beach. Maybe I'd see the lotus kite that sold earlier. In any case, it would do me some good to gather my thoughts. The anxiety of not knowing Avery's fate with the judge, plus the melee earlier with the mushroom pickers—and my tiff with Deputy Goff—well, I needed to walk off some of this energy.

Only a few people were on the beach. Bear ran ahead to chase a patch of sandpipers trotting near the water's edge. The rain had cleared, and the sky reflected blue on the wash left by the surf.

Just like with Avery, I wasn't sure Stella was telling me the full story about Miles. They clearly had a connection she wasn't willing to talk about. She had a lot of allure about her. Although she was old enough to be his mother, it crossed my mind that maybe they'd had a romance. It wasn't out of the question.

I certainly wasn't telling the full truth about Miles—how we'd searched his cabin, for instance. Tomorrow morning before the shop opened, I planned to visit the burnout the mushroom hunters had told me about. This time I'd come better prepared, and this time I'd leave with something more substantial to tell the sheriff. I'd better.

I eyed a bleached log that had obviously been tumbled many times by the sea. The perfect perch for the next quarter hour of calming my brain. But where was the dog? "Bear!" I called. He was playing with a man farther down the beach. I only saw his back, but he was throwing a ball into the surf, and Bear was running after it and returning, wet bellied, to drop the ball at his feet.

I hurried over. "Sorry about—"

The man turned. It was Jack Sullivan. Shoot. "That's your dog?"

I quickly looked away. Something about him made me self-conscious. My hair had dried from my earlier shower, but I knew I was no beauty queen in my fleece hoodie and T-shirt advertising a natural-foods co-op in Portland. Thanks, Mom.

"Bear!" I called again to hide my agitation. Tongue lolling, he ran up. "Yep, he's mine. My family's dog, really, but I have custody."

"He's great," Jack said. His voice was soft, friendly. I tugged at my T-shirt, willing it not to bunch up like it always did.

Bear shifted his attention to Jack and sat at his feet,

staring, the tennis ball still in his mouth. "Sorry, boy. No more ball for you."

The dog dropped the ball at his feet and stared up. "Not now, Bear," I said. "Jack doesn't want to touch that disgusting thing." The ball was covered in sand and dog spit.

"I don't mind. I grew up with a black Lab. Talk about droolers."

Who was this man? Where was the Jack with DNA straight from cranky old man Sullivan? "You're awfully nice to humor him."

"I'm glad I ran into you," Jack said.

My face warmed. "Oh, I—"

"I've been thinking about your kite, the one shaped like a comet."

My heart fell. Of course. "I know you're convinced it will never fly."

"Actually, I think the problem was that there wasn't enough surface area. But what if you shaped the body as a tube? Or a cup? Then it would catch the wind."

He'd mentioned it earlier, and it wasn't a bad idea. Like my lotus kite. "I cut out another pattern today. The problem I'm having now is the tail. I want it to be substantial, like a real comet's tail." Of course, if I fashioned the kite as a tube, or cup, I could do whatever I wanted with the tail.

He echoed my thoughts. "A tube design would take care of that."

"I like it." I patted my pockets, but I'd left my sketchbook back at the shop.

Jack drew his gaze from the bay toward me. "I also wanted to apologize for what I said about Avery. It's no excuse, but I was upset about Miles, and I'm afraid I took it out on you. That wasn't right." He caught a wave of hair that had blown into his face and pushed it back. He had such long fingers. Just right for a tall guy.

Still, I was wary. "She didn't do it, you know."

"I believe you."

"What changed your mind?" I asked.

"I realized I was being one of those jerks around town who based his opinion on hearsay. That's not fair. You and Dave said Avery was home when Miles was killed. I believe you over rumor. It doesn't matter if they found blood on the boat or whatever. If Avery wasn't there, she couldn't have done it."

A moment passed. "Thank you," I said finally. "People in town have been looking at me funny."

"Rock Point is small. People talk for entertainment. Don't pay any attention. I'm sorry I did."

By some unspoken agreement, we slowed our pace to walk up the beach together. Jack really cared about Miles. "I always—"

"Always what?"

"I've wondered about Miles. What he was like. You knew him. Maybe you don't want to talk about him now, though." We wandered nearer the waves, where the sand was packed tight.

"Didn't Avery tell you about him? I thought women talked about those things."

"Avery and I are like sisters, it's true. But for some reason she never told me much about him. But you grew up together, right?"

Jack picked up Bear's tennis ball in one hand. He threw it ahead of us, and Bear shot off like a rocket after it. Jack could have played baseball with that arm. "We spent a lot of time in Rock Point when I was a kid, but I didn't grow up here, no. We lived in Salem. My dad worked for the state."

"But you ended up here."

"I got an engineering degree and thought I'd get a job at Boeing or someplace like that, but when Grandpa started declining . . ." His voice faded. "Anyway, once I was back, I didn't want to leave. It was natural to take over the shop."

He was easy to walk next to. Our strides found a natural sync. "Sullivan's Kites is the reason I took up kite making—and selling—to start with," I said.

"Really?" He stopped and turned to me. He smiled.

A rush of warmth poured over me. "Definitely. My family came here every summer when I was kid. My parents were big friends of the Cooks. That's how I met Avery."

"You went to art school together, too."

We'd started walking again, but I looked up in surprise.

"Dave told me," he said.

"Oh." Dave might have told Jack a lot of things about Avery. Maybe they were closer than I'd thought. "Every summer, my dad let me choose one new kite from old man Sullivan's—" I blanched at the words.

Jack laughed. "Don't worry. Everyone called him that."

"Well, I couldn't wait to see him every year. One year I bought a box kite. I'd been dreaming of that kite since the Christmas before and how I'd sail it on the beach." My mind shifted back in time, remembering how Dad and I put the kite together and took it to the car to drive to the beach. Maybe it was the excitement, or just the pollen, but I had an asthma attack. My father tossed the kite in the driveway and took me to the emergency room.

"How'd it do?"

"Dad drove over it on accident. I cried until I hiccuped,

so we bought a new one, and somehow my baby sister, Sunny, dragged it into her playpen and jumped on it. Busted the spars. I ended up with another diamond kite that year."

Bear had given up on the ball and trotted along with us, sniffing at clumps of seaweed and half-buried crab shells. Every once in a while he darted back to Jack for a scratch between the ears. Traitor. By now we must have walked a quarter mile up the beach. The beach here was nearly empty. Trails led up through the beach grass to small wood houses here and there. The old lighthouse stood tall on the cliff ahead.

"Miles never got the kite thing," Jack said. "Cooking was his outlet. I liked him, though."

"What did you do together?"

"Guy things. We hiked. Usually enjoyed a great meal at the end of it."

I thought of the jumble of books in Miles's cabin, of Stella's description of him as "his own man." "What was he like?"

"He was curious, always interested in the next thing."

"He did well at the Tidal Basin," I said.

"But I wouldn't have called him ambitious. It was more like he wanted to try something new, learn about something new. Last year he took off on a solo tour of Asia just to eat. He was gone a month. Came back with notebooks full of recipes."

"Did you . . . did you ever talk about Avery?"

"Emmy, we're guys. We don't talk about that stuff."

My heart skipped a beat at the sound of my name from his mouth. "You must have a sister—or a serious girlfriend. That sounds like the voice of experience."

He kicked a rock up the beach, but his voice was light. "A twin sister, actually. She sets me straight."

I noted he'd ignored the girlfriend part. But a sister—she'd be a real looker if she had his height and thick hair. Not to mention eyes. I imagined them on visits to their grandfather's kite shop, playing in the sand near the bay. "But you liked Miles."

"I did. He was his own guy, that's for sure. He built a crazy cabin around an old Airstream trailer, if you can believe it. He'd spend his evenings reading, or taking midnight hikes, or researching historical seafood recipes. He could talk about anything."

"Except women."

He laughed again. I liked the sound of it. "Miles really cared about Avery, and I thought she felt the same. I was surprised they broke up."

"I wonder why they did."

"Don't know. Can't say."

Clouds were beginning to thicken again, and not much daylight remained. I glanced at the sky and then at my cell phone. No call yet from Avery saying she was coming home.

Jack picked up his pace. "I guess we'd better be getting back."

chapter seventeen

AS JACK AND I WANDERED BACK TOWARD TOWN, I MAR-
veled at how easy it was to talk with him. We covered
conversational ground on kites, of course—Jack seemed
more interested in flightworthiness, while I focused on their
beauty—but before long we were talking about all sorts of
things: our childhoods, favorite books, grandparents. I can't
say Jack was exactly loquacious, but he was thoughtful.

At one point, engrossed in a discussion about the best
karaoke songs, I tripped on a branch of driftwood. Jack
caught my arm and set me straight, all while extolling the
virtues of Willie Nelson versus David Bowie. I felt the
ghost of his hand on my arm the rest of the walk. He finally
split off as we approached Strings Attached.

When I entered the shop, Bear ran ahead to Stella, who
waved his favorite stuffed hedgehog toy back and forth for
him to growl at and play. I vowed to be Stella when I grew up.

She set down the toy and smoothed her denim skirt. "Did you have a nice walk?"

"I went down to the beach and walked a bit with Jack Sullivan—" I began.

"Have you ever noticed his eyes? They are like pearl gray velvet. They're what the French must mean when they speak of a sky as 'grisaille.' Just like a Monet winter canvas."

"Oh," I said. Of course I'd noticed. All at once I felt self-conscious. As we talked, I flipped the door sign to "Closed" and clicked off the lights in the shop. Stella and I moved to the workshop-slash-kitchen. I sat at the dinette table and laid my arms over its linoleum top.

Stella seemed cheerful, even forcefully so. "Your friend Dave's a sleeper, but Jack has got it going on."

"He does, doesn't he? But—" The day's weight—Avery in jail, the mushroom hunters, Jack's surprising comfort—hit me square between the shoulders. "Everything is too much right now."

"I know, darling." She leaned forward. "The poet Robert Burns said that time is measured in heartbeats. Real time only happens when you feel something, good or bad."

"With your husband's death, you've certainly had the opportunity to think about that." I sighed. It seemed like I'd been sighing a lot lately.

"Think about it. In the past week, you moved, opened a new business, found a body, and now—"

"Now my best friend has been arrested for murder." I fished my cell phone out of my bag and checked it again. Still no call from Avery. "Shouldn't the judge have posted bail by now?"

"Honey," Stella said. "I have something to tell you."

I raised my head. This couldn't be good.

"The news is reporting that the judge is holding Avery without bail."

"Oh," I said. I couldn't think of anything else to say. My throat closed. "I thought she might have called . . ." I laid my head on the table. "It's on the news, huh?"

"The radio, at least. Probably in tomorrow's paper, too."

"Oh, Stella."

"Sheriff Koppen is a smart man. He doesn't give up easily. He'll get to the truth, I know it."

"But he did give up. He let the judge keep her in jail."

"There hasn't been a trial. Not even an indictment. It doesn't mean she'll stay there forever."

The morning's fight had gone out of me. Avery was stuck in jail. Home would be cold and empty—again.

"I'm sorry," Stella whispered.

I reached across the table and put my hand over hers. "Thank you, Stella. I just don't know what to think right now. I stopped by the sheriff's office earlier, and they didn't seem too interested in what I had to say."

"Don't give up yet, darling," she said.

Easy for her to say. My chest felt heavy, but I didn't want to cry in front of Stella. I tried the only thing I knew might ward the tears off—anger. "I thought you were going to help me find evidence to give the sheriff. Now everyone thinks Avery is guilty, and you say just to let the sheriff do his job? Why should he?"

Stella backed up a step. "I didn't—"

"The sheriff won't listen, either. I told Deputy Goff about the mushroom hunters, and she brushed me off. Then I went back with a solid lead, plus the fact that Sam Anderson was on the old dock the night Miles was killed, and—"

"What do you mean, 'solid lead' on the mushroom hunters? Don't tell me you—"

Uh-oh. Stella wasn't supposed to know I'd gone to the morel patch.

"You went to find the morel hunters, didn't you?" She smacked a palm on the table. "Damn it, Emmy. I warned you about that."

I'd never seen Stella angry. The self-pity drained right out of me. "I had to do something."

"Like get yourself shot at?"

I wasn't about to admit to the robbery. "It was fine. I'm safe. Nothing happened."

"You promised me you wouldn't go." I kept my lips pursed. "Did you go alone?" she asked. I looked at my shoes. "Oh, Emmy. Remember that story I told you. You could have—"

Bear barked at a rap at the back door. Frank's face appeared in the door's window. I rose to answer it.

Frank stepped inside. "Is it too late to drop in? I know the shop is closed, but I saw you two in here."

"No," I said. "We were just chatting." I glanced at Stella, who folded her arms in front of her chest and refused to look at me.

"I saw the news about Avery, Emmy. I'm sorry." He shifted on his feet. "Maybe you two would like to join me at the Tidal Basin for a bite."

"I need to get home," Stella said. "Madame Lucy will be expecting her dinner." She rose and plucked her cardigan from the back of her chair.

"And you, Emmy? I have a few ideas for your marketing plan. We could talk them through. Take your mind off things."

I thought of the dark house and the burnt pizza in the refrigerator. "I don't know."

"Oh, honey," Stella said, finally meeting my eyes. "You've had a rough day of it. Why not end the day with a decent dinner, at least?"

"And good company," Frank added.

"Absolutely," Stella said.

I looked around the workshop. There was nothing I had to do here. At home, I'd end up going to bed early just to avoid thinking. It was too late to make it to Astoria in time for the last shift of visiting hours.

"I'm afraid I won't be very good company," I said finally. I looked at Stella to see if she was still mad, but she'd transferred her attention to Frank.

"Nonsense. It will boost my reputation to be seen with a lovely lady like you."

"Your reputation is solid in that area," Stella said.

Frank laughed. "Touché. And next time I hope you'll bolster that reputation by accepting my dinner invitation."

"We'll see," she said.

Their flirtatious banter had managed to squeeze a smile from me. I glanced at Stella again, hoping to see signs of forgiveness. "How about if I drop off Bear at home and see you at the Tidal Basin in half an hour?"

"It's a date." Frank waved and headed up the outside stairs to his apartment.

Shrugging on her cardigan, Stella fastened her eyes on me. "Well?" she said.

"Stella, I'm sorry for my attitude. I shouldn't have spoken to you like that."

She ignored me. "Details on the mushroom hunters, please."

I sighed and gave her a recap of my morning, skimming past the bit with Chet and Mr. SpongeBob. "I did get good information, though. I found out where Ron and Monica pick morels, and it sounds like they do it mornings." Before Stella could reply, I added, "All I want to do is get their license-plate number. That's it. I'll give it to the sheriff and let him deal with it." Maybe I'd put it in a note this time so I wouldn't get another dressing down by Goff.

Stella slowly shook her head. "Fine. I don't like it, mind you, but you're not doing this alone. I'll be at your place tomorrow morning at seven." She left as if the matter were settled.

I WAS A FEW MINUTES LATE TO THE TIDAL BASIN, BECAUSE I'd passed a mirror at home and realized that there was no way I could show up at a nice restaurant looking like I'd crawled through a swamp and followed it up with a tumble on a wet beach, so I pulled back my hair and tossed on a cotton dress. I winced a bit, guessing what Jack must have thought of my bedraggled state. Well, he'd been friendly enough. Maybe even friendly enough to call. I hoped.

As I pushed open the Tidal Basin's oak door, I looked forward to countering the day's drama with some relaxation. Stella had been replaced as hostess by a sullen teenager, hopefully just temporarily pressed into service until Sam Anderson found a worthy replacement. Frank had his usual table in the corner. He tore his attention from the bar's TV when he saw me.

"Have a seat," he said. "I ordered us a nice pinot noir. Figured it would go well with whatever we chose for dinner."

A glass of wine sounded good. The day had been an emotional roller coaster—one I was ready to get off. "Thank you."

A waiter approached and handed me a menu, but not Frank. "The usual?" he asked Frank.

"Since you don't have the mushroom ragout, I'd like the crab risotto."

I set down the menu. My brain was fried, and even making a decision about dinner was too much to handle. "I'll have the same, please," I said.

"I know I said it once, but I really am sorry about Avery. I know how hard this is on you."

"It's a lot harder on her, stuck in jail."

"I'm sure justice will be served, whatever it is."

"It's not Avery. She didn't do it," I said, irritated at his hint that she was guilty. "There's no way. Apparently I'm the only one who believes it."

Frank pushed his dinner roll around the bread plate. In places like this, you had to order bread separate. He must be a traditional guy. "Emmy, sometimes people aren't what you expect."

"But, Avery—"

"I'm not talking just about Avery. In my line of work, I've dealt with a lot of different types of people, and—"

My phone began to chirp from my purse, and the thought that it might be Jack flashed through my mind. Then I recognized the unmistakable tones of "Mamma Mia." The news must have reached Portland.

"My mother," I said. "I'll just let it ring through."

"Well, all I wanted to say is to be careful. It doesn't pay to get too emotional about things."

I trained my gaze on his. "Life isn't all business, Frank.

I can't help it if I care, and life wouldn't be worth it without making attachments to people." I might have said that last bit a little louder than I'd intended.

As if on cue, Annabelle materialized at our table. "Care about what?" she said.

"Annabelle." Frank laid a hand on her arm. "Emmy just heard they're holding Avery without bail, and Avery won't be coming home—"

"Not right away. But soon," I added.

"And I didn't want her to be home alone. I thought the neighborly thing to do would be to buy her some dinner. Besides, I have a few marketing ideas to share."

I looked from Frank to Annabelle. Frank seemed to be overexplaining. Annabelle wasn't jealous, was she?

Her expression softened. "Of course. You're right, and I'm so sorry, Emmy."

"Would you like to join us? We can have another chair brought over," Frank said.

"Thanks, but no. I'm here with a friend." She nodded toward a man by the hostess's station. My heart dropped. Jack. He was looking right at me. I smiled, but he turned away. Annabelle gestured for Jack to follow her to a table. My phone again erupted into "Mamma Mia." This time I silenced it.

Luckily, their table was out of sight. Our dinners arrived, followed by two snifters of pear brandy. "Compliments of Annabelle," the waiter said.

"So, Emmy, I've been thinking about Strings Attached and how you can boost business."

"Business hasn't been bad." Just because Jack and Annabelle were at the Tidal Basin together didn't mean anything romantic was happening. They might just be friends.

"No, but there's Jack."

"Jack?" Now he had my attention.

"Sullivan's Kites. You have to make sure you're offering something different. You'll do best to complement, not compete."

"Strings Attached and Jack's store do sell some similar kites." I thought of the basic diamond kites and supplies. "But I sell my designs, too. They're less about doing tricks in the sky and more about the fun of flying something beautiful."

Frank nodded. "Your advertising needs to focus on that. You might think about adding a few wind-related items that aren't kites, too. Like those things people stake outside their beach houses. You know."

"Wind socks?" Not a bad idea. In fact, my lotus kite would make a gorgeous wind sock. Wind socks weren't seasonal, either, unlike kites, whose sales dropped in bad weather. "I could definitely make wind socks. Custom designs, too."

I'd lost Frank's attention. He was riveted to the television, and in a glance I understood why. The screen, on mute, showed a woman on the steps of the Astoria courthouse. The banner read, "Breaking News: Avery Cook held without bail. Attorney has no comment." It took me a moment to realize what I was seeing. Then it all became too real. I clasped my hands to stop them from shivering. She might never be free. The TV switched to the baseball game in progress.

"I can't believe it," was all I could say.

Frank studied me a moment. "People are going to have a lot of questions. Have you thought about how you'll handle this?"

"Handle this?" That people would be looking at me seemed a lot less important than finding Miles's killer. I was sick and tired of all this "The sheriff is a good man" BS. Somebody had to do something.

Frank pushed his risotto bowl away, leaving a thin slice of mushroom at its edge. Mushrooms. Since Avery had been charged with Miles's murder, how likely was it that the sheriff would follow up with the mushroom hunters—or with Sam? He already had his suspect. Who cared about my shop's business? If Avery were convicted, I'd never want to see Rock Point again.

"I see your mind is somewhere else," Frank said.

"What? Yes. Avery, of course."

"It's awful. I know you don't like to think of your friend in jail."

There was really no response to this. I put down my fork and pushed my bowl away, too. I was done eating.

"I hate to bring it up—maybe it seems insensitive, but I feel I should mention it—but have you thought about where you might move?"

"You mean, away from Rock Point?"

"I mean out of the Cook house. With legal fees, and Avery not being able to work, she probably won't be keeping up her part of the house's expenses. She might even need to sell."

"Sell?" The possibility of Avery losing her home hadn't even crossed my mind. I knew that keeping the Brew House running was a concern, but Trudy was a competent manager. I'd have to see her tomorrow, fill her in. I took a gulp of the pear brandy and coughed at its burn.

"Don't worry, Emmy. If you want, you can rent my place upstairs through the winter until you figure something out." He paused. "I mean, if it comes to that, of course. I own the small green building on Main, too, and there's an apartment upstairs—"

"You mean the building with Martino's?"

"It's a cute place once you get used to the garlic smell."

"It's not going to happen. Avery is innocent." I felt like I'd already said that a dozen times today. "She'll be home soon." I remembered my outburst at Stella earlier and quieted my voice. "But thank you for thinking of me."

Frank looked at me with what I hope wasn't pity. "I'm happy to help if I can."

The dining room was lively with conversation. The hostess led a couple to a nearby table, and she gave me a curious look as she returned to her station. Had she heard about Avery, too? I'd have to get used to the stares. Deep in the restaurant near the bar, a flash of pasty skin and red hair, rose then disappeared.

"Do you know much about Sam Anderson?" I asked.

"A little. Not much. Why?"

"I just wondered if he was from Rock Point."

"Not sure. I doubt it, though. I think he saw a nice opportunity for a gastropub and relocated his family here."

"So it was a business decision."

Frank shrugged. "Probably more than that. Living by the ocean is wonderful for kids, and I know Sam loves to crab. But, yes, in the end, business probably had a bit to do with his decision."

"A restaurant like the Tidal Basin would be an expensive proposition. I can't imagine he's making a fortune," I ventured. No matter what Deputy Goff said, I wasn't letting Sam off the hook that easily. He had a motive for killing Miles, even if it was a weak one. And he'd been on the dock.

"These restaurants always keep tight margins. The smart thing would be to factor in more stable income, through a hotel or something like that."

"But you don't know if he's having money trouble."

"No. I don't have any business dealings with him." Frank drew his eyebrows together. "Why do you ask? Do you think he has something to do with Miles's death?"

"Someone has." Attitude, Emmy.

Raised voices near the restaurant's front door drew our attention. "Before he was killed, chef Miles Logan—"

"You can't come in," the teenaged host told the reporters we'd overheard.

Diners' heads swiveled as Sam Anderson rushed past them. "Put down the camera. This is private property."

A small woman in navy blue waved the cameraman to point toward Sam. "May I have your name?"

"You'll have to leave. Now," Sam said. He turned toward the bar. "Luis?"

A meaty guy with a dirty apron and a towel slung over his shoulder had been lurking near the divider separating the bar from the dining room. He had to be the dishwasher who'd tossed out Ron and Monica, the mushroom hunters. The reporter and cameraman didn't need a second invitation to leave.

"It's starting," Frank said, his expression grim. "It'll only get worse when it goes to trial."

I couldn't take any more. So much for a relaxing evening. "I appreciate your goodwill gesture, but I should go home." I reached into my purse for my wallet and saw that my mother had left eight messages on my cell phone.

"Let me take care of the bill. And don't worry about Avery. Justice is on its way. Just let it unroll like it should."

Justice was rolling along all right. Right down a hill and off a cliff. I would not let that happen, not to Avery.

In the parking lot, the news van occupied a spot under

a light. Annabelle stood nearby, the reporter's microphone stuck under her mouth. "Rock Point isn't that kind of town," she said. "We're peaceful here. Happy. What happened to Miles was all a mistake."

ALL NIGHT I TOSSED AND TURNED. THE HOUSE GROANED in the wind, and rain battered against the windows. I felt so alone, so far from anyone else. Avery was sleeping in some cold cell. Frank's words about not trusting anyone still rang in my brain. Could we really lose the house? The fear I'd felt standing face-to-face with the mushroom hunters rose again. What should I do?

Bear, immersed in his own dreams, growled from his bed.

Deep, deep from some recess of my brain that only sleep pierced, I remembered, too, my asthma attack and being in the hospital with my mother and father around me and a mask clamped to my mouth. I'd felt so small—I *was* so small. But that was a long time ago. I was an adult now. This was my life, these were my problems to solve alone.

When I woke, it was still dark.

chapter eighteen

I CLENCHED MY COFFEE CUP AS DAWN STAINED THE HO-
RIZON apricot. Stella wouldn't arrive for at least another
half hour. My thoughts careened to Avery once again.
She'd warned me—rightly—that I could screw up her case
by getting in the sheriff's way or collecting evidence il-
legally. But what was I supposed to do? I couldn't sit while
nothing happened. Besides, this morning's plan was
straightforward: get Ron and Monica's license-plate number and hand it to the sheriff. That's all. I plopped on the
couch and let my head roll against its back as I waited for
the purr of Stella's Corvette.

We decided to take my old Prius so as not to attract attention. I wasn't sure whether it was the early hour or Stella's
reluctance to have anything to do with the mushroom hunters, but we drove to the burnout in silence. No joyriding this

morning—not that the Prius was much of a powerhouse on the roads.

"We should park out of the way," I said.

"Good idea," she replied, but that was all.

The sun had come up by now, but there wasn't much traffic. I pulled the Prius onto a side road a few hundred yards past the burnout and parked, figuring that anyone headed for the burnout would have parked at an earlier turnoff. I'd brought the same tools I had yesterday—a couple of sandwiches and my sketching things—but I'd emptied my wallet this time. No use tempting fate.

"We'll have to hike from here." My eyes ached from lack of sleep, but at the same time I felt good to be doing something to help Avery.

"That sounds good to me," Stella said. "We watch; we take notes; we get out of there."

I let a moment pass before replying. "You seem awfully quiet this morning. I hope you're not still mad."

She looked toward the woods. "I'm not angry. It's just that this is dangerous. We shouldn't be messing in someone's morel territory."

"We won't be picking them."

"They won't know that."

"They will if we don't have any mushrooms with us."

"If they take the time to check, sure," Stella said.

"Should we go home?" This was frustrating. I paused, not sure if I should take the keys from the ignition.

"No. We're so close. Let's get it over with. Besides, I know you'd come right back without me."

She was right. I slung my tote bag over my shoulder, and Stella led the way down a path through the woods that

I never would have found on my own. The forest's pine-needle floor smelled fresh and damp. We tramped through the woods for a few minutes before Stella lifted an arm to stop me.

"Through there," she said.

In a clearing where a wildfire had flattened the underbrush and seared the lower branches from the trees, new undergrowth pushed through. Dampened patches that might hold morel mushrooms peppered the Douglas-fir seedlings.

"Let's stay here," Stella said. "We can see into the burnout, but we're out of the way. As long as they park in the closest spot"—the spot we'd passed—"they'll come from the other direction." She was already settling in to wait.

I took a thermos from my pack and sat on a log. The damp seeped through my jeans.

"We want to find out their license-plate number, and we aren't going to see it from here," I said.

"We can't go any closer. We don't want them seeing us."

"True." Stella was clearly nervous about our expedition, which was funny given how brave she'd been on the dock.

"How about this?" I proposed. "When we find someone who fits the bill of Ron and Monica, I'll hike out to the road until I find their car. Then we'll get out of here."

"That sounds safest to me." After scanning the burnout once more, Stella slid an issue of *ARTnews* from her pack and settled in to wait.

I leaned against a fir and took out my sketch pad. Might as well dream up some new kites. Half an hour went by with both of us engrossed in our pursuits. No one entered the burnout.

When Stella put down the magazine, I spoke. "Do you know Jack Sullivan very well?" I'd been wanting to ask her but was embarrassed to bring it up, especially if he and Annabelle were an item.

"A bit, I guess. I know he was good friends with Miles. Why?"

"No reason. Just wondered." I let a moment pass. "Do you think he has a thing for Annabelle Black?"

"Why?" The hint of a smile played on her mouth.

"Last night I was at the Tidal Basin and saw them together. That's all."

"I wouldn't read too much into that," she said.

It was a frustratingly inadequate answer. "Oh," I said.

"You like him, don't you? Miles once told me—"

Just then, faint voices drifted our way. I set down my pad, and Stella and I exchanged glances. A man and woman came into the burnout, each carrying plastic buckets. From behind them, a little girl, not much older than kindergarten age, charged from behind a fallen log.

"Boo!" she yelled.

Her parents seemed unimpressed. "Honey, don't run. You'll trip on something," the mother said. The adults picked methodically, only exchanging words every few minutes. The girl amused herself by chucking rocks into the woods in our direction. Thankfully, she was too far away to hit us.

"Ron, keep an eye on her," the woman said.

Ron. "I think that's them," I whispered. Ron and Monica. I leaned toward Stella, close enough to smell her lily-of-the-valley perfume. "I'm going to find their car. You stay here, and come after me if they leave." It seemed safe to hurry off now, while they were still busy.

Stella glanced at them, then turned to me and nodded once.

I crept through the underbrush, my tote bag still slung over my shoulder. Within a few minutes, I reached the road. I kicked the pine needles and dirt with my shoes so I'd know where to turn again, then I headed down the road, expecting I'd run into a car pulled over close to the burn.

The mushroom hunters would surely still be picking morels for a while. After all, they'd only just arrived.

At the turnoff we'd passed earlier, an older Subaru wagon was parked at the side of the road. It had to be theirs. I looked up and down the road and didn't see any other reason someone would be there. I slipped my bag from my shoulder and reached for my pad to jot down the car's license-plate number.

"What are you doing?" a small voice asked.

I spun around. The morel hunters' daughter stood behind me. She wore a stained pink sweatshirt and denim pants. Her mousy hair was pulled into a ponytail.

"Where are your mom and dad?" I answered as a knee-jerk reaction.

"Where are *your* mom and dad?" she said.

"What's it to you?"

"What's it to you?" she repeated. "Are you supposed to be out here?"

"Are you?" I said quickly. We stared at each other.

"I asked you first."

This was getting nowhere fast. I jotted down the Subaru's license-plate number and returned the pad to my bag. "My name is Emmy. What's yours?"

"I'm not allowed to talk to strangers," the girl said.

I nodded. "Uh-huh. And I bet you're not supposed to leave your parents, either."

She edged toward the car a few steps, then leapt to the door, jerked it open, and locked herself inside. She pressed her nose against the glass and stuck out her tongue for good measure.

Shoot. I had the information I needed, but I couldn't leave the girl alone. It wasn't safe. At the same time, I could hardly wait around until the mushroom hunters returned and found me. I glanced down the road, then back at the car. The girl pressed a coloring book to the window. It showed a scrawled pink house with orange smoke billowing from its chimney. She tossed the coloring book aside and hung her head.

The girl was in the car, waiting for her parents. Her parents, who had threatened Miles—and maybe worse. I had the license-plate number. I could simply return to Stella, but I hesitated.

"Hannah?" a woman's voice shouted. "Hannah, where are you?"

Twigs cracking in the woods made up my mind. As quietly as I could, I jogged out of sight into the trees and along the road. Up where I'd initially emerged from the woods, Stella was already standing on the shoulder.

"They left," she said as we walked toward the Prius. "They only picked for half an hour or so, then noticed their daughter had run off. I was just about ready to come after you."

"It's all right," I said as I caught my breath. "I got their information."

"Satisfied?" Stella asked. "This should give the sheriff

everything he needs to find the people who threatened Miles."

I unlocked the Prius. "Their daughter came back to the car. I didn't want to leave her there alone, but I heard her mom."

"Do you think she'll tell them about you?"

I hadn't thought of that. "She might. I hope she's known for her imagination." Somehow I guessed she was. I imagined the girl at dinner, telling her parents about me. Shoot. I'd told her my name, too.

"They probably rely on their mushroom sales to pay the bills," Stella said.

I wanted to find the person who'd killed Avery, not split a family apart. Seeing the girl made it all too real. I backed the Prius into the road. "Did you get a good look at them? Was it anyone you'd seen before?"

"I've seen Ron—if that's him—shopping at the grocery outlet. I don't think they live right in Rock Point. I'll ask Jeanette at the post office. I'll tell her about Ace's meditation hideaway in trade."

"Good idea. If anyone will know, she will."

When we arrived at the house, Stella refused my offer of a cup of tea and went straight to the Corvette. I did a double take at her bulging tote bag.

"Your bag," I said. "I didn't notice that you brought so much stuff."

"Stuff? I only brought my magazine." Stella opened the Corvette's door and bent to slide in.

"Are you sure?" She was being cagey. After her silence earlier that morning, it made me nervous. "Nothing's wrong, is it? I really do appreciate it that you came with me this morning. I know you didn't want to."

"You're right."

"But you came anyway. Thank you."

"No," she said. "You're right about the bag." With a guilty smile, she pulled it open and showed me. It was full of morels. "I picked them when you were down the road. Maybe this outing wasn't such a bad idea after all."

chapter nineteen

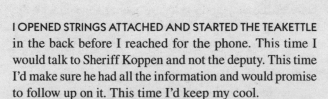

I OPENED STRINGS ATTACHED AND STARTED THE TEAKETTLE
in the back before I reached for the phone. This time I
would talk to Sheriff Koppen and not the deputy. This time
I'd make sure he had all the information and would promise
to follow up on it. This time I'd keep my cool.

"You again." As I'd feared, Deputy Goff had answered
the phone.

I ignored her icy tone. "May I speak to Sheriff Koppen?"

For a moment, I heard nothing, as if Goff were tempted
to hang up. Finally, the line buzzed. Miracle of miracles,
the sheriff was in. "Koppen here."

"What's with Deputy Goff? I know she's not wild about
me, but she's being downright rude."

"Thank you for letting me know," the sheriff said in a
tone indicating that he couldn't care less. "How can I help
you?"

I clutched the phone tightly. "I have some important information about the Miles Logan case. Can I come by?"

He let out a long breath. Whether it was from frustration or hope, I couldn't tell. "No. That's not a good idea at the moment. Are you at the shop?"

"Just got here."

"I'll come see you." He hung up without waiting for my good-bye. A few minutes later, Sheriff Koppen opened the front door, his body a khaki-clad pillar among the colorful kites rustling around him.

"Tea?" I asked, and felt a little foolish. This wasn't a social visit. Besides, the sheriff looked to be a coffee man. Black.

"No thanks. I understand you've been dropping by the office."

I went to the kitchen in the workshop but kept the door between the shop and workshop open. I fidgeted with the teapot and took a little more time than necessary setting up the mug and strainer. "You seem pretty certain you've found Miles's killer. I'm not so sure."

"I didn't say that." Again, that impassive expression.

"But you're holding Avery in jail and won't even let her out on bail. To me, that says you feel certain."

"Not necessarily. What it means is that the prosecutor convinced the judge not to take any chances. We're talking about a homicide."

"I know." I slammed the electric teakettle on its base and remembered my vow to rein in my temper. "I mean, I know how important this case is to Rock Point and to Avery. I simply want to make sure you're following up all your leads."

"You told me you had information for me. What is it?"

I brought the teapot and mug to the sales counter. Now for

the big reveal. "Have you checked out the morel hunters, the ones who threatened Miles in front of all those witnesses?"

"Deputy Goff said you were concerned about them."

"Well, I have their first names and license-plate number, so now you can follow up." I pushed a piece of paper across the counter.

"Ron and Monica. Sure. Ron was laid off at the lumber mill in Clatskanie and has been gathering morels to make a little income. Had to move to his mother-in-law's house with his wife and daughter."

The little girl. "So you know them."

"Uh-huh. I'm not surprised they're selling morels. They need the money."

"Do you know what he was doing the night Miles was killed?" I had a suspicion I sounded like a petulant kindergartner.

"Do you think he broke into the Tidal Basin and stole a knife, then tracked down Miles and killed him? Oh, then hid the knife at your house?"

"He might have." I took a long sip of tea. It scalded the inside of my mouth, but I didn't care. "He sounds pretty desperate. Maybe Sam Anderson had something to do with it."

"Deputy Goff says you're set on Sam Anderson for some reason. Why is that?"

"Well, he was down on the dock the night Miles was murdered, for one thing."

"Yes, he was. We know that." He stepped forward. "How about you? How do you know it?"

My gaze darted through the store as I pondered a suitable response. "Word gets around."

"I see." He wasn't convinced; I could tell.

"Look, Miles wanted to open his own restaurant. Maybe Sam didn't want the competition."

Somehow Sheriff Koppen conveyed rolling eyes even as his expression didn't change. "So he murdered his own chef, the chef that had earned his restaurant such a great reputation? He's somehow managing to run the Tidal Basin now without Miles."

Good grief, he was enraging. "Maybe he hired the morel pickers to do his dirty work for him; then he took the body out to sea."

This time the sheriff's face cracked. Into anger. I found myself wishing he'd go back to the same old impassive expression. "Ron has a bad temper, but he's not a murderer."

"And neither is Avery."

We stared at each other. A face-off.

I didn't know how the sheriff did this to me, but once again I was roiling mad and humiliated, all at the same time. "Fine," I managed to spit out. A moment passed. "I'm sorry," I said, this time sincerely.

The last two times I'd seen him, he'd softened at this point and let me off the hook. Today, no dice.

"All right," he said. "I'll question Ron about the scene at the Tidal Basin, and I'll find out what he was doing the evening Logan was killed. I'll question Sam Anderson again, too." A muscle ticked in his jaw. His breath came evenly, but almost too evenly. Forced. "Emmy. Promise me. Leave this alone."

I nodded, eyes wide.

"I don't want to be taking your body to the medical examiner any time soon."

* * *

I WAS UNEASY ALL MORNING AT STRINGS ATTACHED. AS soon as the sheriff left, I called Avery's lawyer, but I had to cut the call off when a customer came in. I was never able to get back in touch with her. Business was good, but not brisk enough to keep my mind from wandering back to Avery and the sheriff's warning. I recognized a few customers as locals, and they wanted to get a front-row view of the accused's roommate. Those "customers" I sent on their way as soon as it became clear they weren't really interested in the kites. Even my trusty sketch pad failed me as my few attempts at a new tail for the comet kite languished.

During an afternoon lull, I bit the bullet and called my mother.

"Finally," she said simply.

"Well, it's been superbusy here." How much had she heard? Maybe she'd called for another reason. To warn me that Saturn was in Libra or something.

"I guess. Superbusy now that Avery's in jail."

Damn. She was unusually calm. Too calm. I wasn't sure how to respond. "Well, like I said, it's been busy." I half wished someone would rush into the store demanding a kite so I could get off the phone, but the sidewalk outside was silent.

"Tell me what happened. All the newspaper said was that Avery was charged with killing the chef from the Tidal Basin and was being held without bail."

"It's all a huge mistake. Someone is setting her up. The sheriff thinks she was down at the docks when Miles Logan was murdered, but she was home. They say—"

"Honey, you don't have to explain. I know Avery is innocent."

Mom's reassurance brought a lump to my throat. Like a little girl, I felt like crying. "Thanks, Mom."

"This is why you called for the name of an attorney, right?"

I sighed. "Yes, Mom."

"Why didn't you tell us? We might have helped."

"There's nothing you could have done. It's just a matter of letting the sheriff do his work." Now I was sounding like Deputy Goff.

"The sheriff might take care of the evidence, but who's taking care of you and Avery?"

"Oh, Mom." I cleared my throat and pretended I was totally self-sufficient. "I'm fine. You keep forgetting that I'm adult, well beyond the years of needing someone watching my every move."

The phone whooshed with my mother's exhale. "I know that. You've been quite clear about it, and the croning circle agrees—"

The croning circle? "Mom—"

"But when your roommate and best friend is wrongly jailed for murder, a little support is in order. You can't argue with that."

"You're right. But that doesn't mean that it has to be you doing all the work. I'm just fine. I have friends here. People helping me."

"I can't just let you suffer, you know," she said.

"I know, I know." Here's the thing: if she came, I'd be in worse shape than if she stayed home. I'd end up stuffed with quinoa and herbal remedies, and I'd feel like I had to pacify her when she was supposed to be taking care of me.

I was supposed to be proving my independence. Instead, I was walking a fine line and risking falling back into my old pattern of letting her run my life.

Then an idea struck. "How about this?" I said. "How about if I call you once a day to give you an update?"

The other end of the line was quiet.

"Mom?"

"I'm thinking. You'll call me once a day, you say?"

"Every single day. I'll let you know what's going on. That way you can stay in touch, and you'll know I'm all right."

"I still don't really know what's going on, though."

"I can't talk much right now because I'm at the shop. But I'll call you tonight, all right? Then once a day."

I could tell she still wasn't completely satisfied, but she couldn't think of a reason to argue, either. "All right," she said at last. "Once a day, starting with tonight. But if I don't hear from you, I'm driving straight over."

"You'll hear from me. Things will be fine. You'll see."

I KNEW I COULDN'T PUT IT OFF ANY LONGER—I'D HAVE to stop by the Brew House and tell Trudy that Avery might be out for a while. Hopefully she'd understand why I wasn't completely honest about Avery the last time we spoke. I taped a "Back in 15 minutes" sign on the front door and hurried to the café.

The Brew House was busy with people scattered among the tables, sipping lattes and grazing on cookies and Avery's famed carrot cake. Trudy was stocking the pastry case with cookies. When she saw me, she closed the case and gestured for me to join her in the kitchen.

"Any news about Avery?" she asked.

"Oh, Trudy, I'm sorry I didn't tell you the truth earlier. I was hoping she'd be out again and I wouldn't have to stir up any drama."

"Don't worry about it. I understand." A timer dinged, and she opened the oven to stir a batch of granola, releasing a wave of cinnamon and coconut.

"What do you need to keep things running here?" I had no idea of how to run a café, but someone had to do the books and order the supplies at the very least. I assumed that had been Avery.

"I can manage the staff and run the café, no problem, as long as I can get someone to open so I can drop Kaylee at day care. But payroll's coming up. And we need to take care of some bills."

There was a reason I went to art school and not business school. I could do this, I told myself. It would be good for me. "Is there a place Avery keeps her paperwork?"

"Back here." She pointed to a locked cupboard in the corner with a folding chair nearby. "I've been putting the day's sales receipts and bills in there, too." She slipped a key from her ring and handed it to me.

"Thanks. If you don't mind, I'll take them with me and sort it out tonight."

"Emmy," Trudy said, "how's Avery? Have you seen her?"

"She's getting by. It's awful."

"She shouldn't be in there."

"No." I piled an envelope full of cash-register receipts and any paper that looked important into my arms. "I'm going to visit her tonight. I'll tell her you said hi."

"Do that." She reached out as I turned. "Keep in touch."

With my free hand I lifted the counter that gave access

to the kitchen, then hastily let it return to its place as I scooted back into the kitchen. Trudy jumped out of my way.

"What's wrong?" she said.

"That's Ron."

Standing in the café's door was Ron, the morel picker, surveying the room. He hesitated, then strode to the counter. My heart kicked into overdrive. *He doesn't know you*, I had to remind myself. *Relax.*

"I'd like a regular coffee," he told Trudy. I melted into the background.

"Sure, Ron," Trudy said. "On the house. It's the least I can do to thank you for fixing that gutter. I wouldn't have even noticed it was overflowing if you hadn't said anything. Here. Have some carrot cake, too."

He took his order to a table and glanced around again before taking a seat.

"Do you know him?" I asked Trudy when she stepped back into the kitchen, keeping my voice low. The music— an Eric Clapton album; Trudy liked her 1970s classics— made sure we wouldn't be overheard.

"Sure. He brings his daughter in sometimes, too. They've had a rough time of it, and I don't think it's going to get better any time soon."

"What do you mean?"

Trudy turned off the oven and pulled out a cookie sheet deep with granola. "About an hour ago, Sheriff Koppen came in. Ron was here, too. I'd hired him to do a few odd jobs around the building. Avery would have approved," she assured me. "The sheriff told him he had some questions for him and led him out."

"To his office, I bet."

"That'd be my guess." She hung her oven mitt above

the stove. "I'll let this cool." She glanced out at Ron. "He's brave to come back. I guess he wanted to show he had nothing to hide."

Ron methodically dug into the carrot cake, almost deliberately not looking up. "What do you mean?"

Trudy propped a hand on her hip. "It's a shame. The whole town will know he's been questioned about Miles Logan's murder. He'll be lucky if he ever gets a job now."

ONCE I'D CLOSED THE SHOP, IT WAS HARD TO REMEMBER why I'd been so eager for the day to end. Frank wasn't taking me to the Tidal Basin for a splurgy dinner. Jack hadn't seen fit to call. All I had waiting for me was a cold, empty house. And Bear. At least I had Bear.

I figured I had an hour or so to make dinner and take Bear to the beach before I had to leave for Astoria and the county jail.

Shaded by a group of fir trees, the side of the house facing the driveway was dark as I pulled up. It would be lighter at the front of the house, where the porch faced the ocean and the setting sun, but from the angle I arrived, the house might well have been abandoned. Frank's warning came back to me about losing the house. I clutched the steering wheel more tightly. Unease crept over me. Except for the ocean's steady grumble, it was quiet up here. Remote.

"Hey, Bear," I called as I unlocked the front door. Silence. "Bear?" Normally he'd be running in circles in the front hall at my arrival. My pulse leapt. "Bear!"

A few yips and scratching on wood told me he was somewhere near the kitchen. I dropped my purse and ran in, nearly blinded by adrenaline. "Bear!" I yelled again, my voice contorted with fear. His yips came from the laundry room. I opened the door, and he rushed into my arms and licked my face. "Bear, you're all right. How did you get in there?"

He backed out of my arms and started barking again. Then I saw it. The kitchen's cupboards were flung open, dishes smashed on the floor and counter. Broken jars of condiments made a minefield of the floor.

Someone had broken in. Someone had come into the house and ransacked it. My breathing tightened, and I stood, frozen, gasping tiny breaths. I looked toward the dog. He pranced from one leg to another in distress, but he didn't act like anyone else was still in the house. What else would I find?

I grabbed the cast-iron skillet from the stove to use as a weapon. Steadying myself, I passed back through the hall and into the living room. Avery's family photos had been swept to the ground as if an arm had wiped across the mantel in one swoop, and the vase of flowers had been upended. Otherwise, the living room was relatively unscathed.

Avery's bedroom was next. "Come on, Bear," I whispered, my voice cracking. I didn't want to be alone.

As I'd feared, Avery's bedroom had been deconstructed in pure anger. Usually, it was an oasis of calm with its cream walls, framed drawings, and ever-present vase of flowers on the bureau. Now the curtains were ripped from their rods, and the bureau tipped facedown. The closet suffered the worst of the violence. Every single item, from Avery's lovely pastel sundresses to the chambray shirts she wore around the house, was ripped from its hanger and shredded.

The fury the intruder must have felt still resonated through the house. It was palpable. I forced my breathing to slow. I hadn't had an asthma attack in years, but the tightening in my lungs warned me that my clean spell might be ending. I closed my eyes tight and opened them. *Deep breaths, Emmy. Deep.*

One more room to visit.

My bedroom door was ajar. This could not be good. Skillet held high, I gingerly pushed the door open with my foot. I groaned and fell back against the door frame. *Not here, too.* The covers on my bed had been pulled back, and some kind of toiletries—shampoo? soap?—were dumped all over the mattress. My oil paints had been squeezed from their tubes in viscous smears on the sheets. The closet's contents were strewn across the floor, and the curtains yanked from the windows. Every one of my dresser drawers had been pulled clean from the bureau, their contents dumped.

But the mirror above the dresser. A crack severed it diagonally, probably made with the fireplace's poker, which lay beside the bed. My blood ran to ice. Scrawled across the glass in the paint from a tube of oils read a single word: "KILLER." Next to it was a crude drawing of a hanging man.

chapter twenty

"YOU'RE NOT STAYING HERE TONIGHT," THE SHERIFF SAID hours later. He'd found me on the porch, staring at the blackened sea and swaddled in blankets. Inside, a few people still lingered, taking photographs and dusting for fingerprints. Curiously, Deputy Goff wasn't among them. Sheriff Koppen said she'd "taken a few days off the case."

"Did you hear me?" the sheriff said.

"Yes. I'll pack up a few things and leave." The fight had gone out of me. From below I heard the surf, but the sky was too cloudy for stars. I just wanted to sit, to not move, to not think.

Still staring toward the ocean, I felt the couch give next to me. I looked toward the sheriff. For once, he didn't have out his notepad.

"I'm sorry about all this. Rock Point's a small town. I wish I could say that everyone held to the belief that a person is innocent until proven guilty, but they don't. With the news about Avery being held—"

"I think it's the same person," I said.

"Pardon?"

"I think whoever broke in today is the same person who hid the knife in Avery's room." It was a campaign to frame her and to scare me off.

I returned to staring toward the ocean, and the sheriff was quiet. He shifted. "I didn't want to say anything—didn't see the need to—but we received a letter today."

I whipped my head toward him. "From whom?"

"Not signed. An anonymous letter. Someone said he—or she—saw Avery down by the docks the night Miles was killed."

"A setup. They're framing her."

"The letter writer wasn't the only witness, Emmy." I refused to reply. "People are talking, and they're coming up with their own conclusions."

"You think they'd carry out some kind of vigilante justice?"

"I wonder if they have," he said. "Tonight."

"There's one thing I wonder." Koppen didn't reply. "Why did they write the warning on my mirror and not Avery's?"

"That worries me, too. Maybe they mistook the bedrooms. Or maybe their anger is shifting focus to you."

I didn't even have the energy to feel afraid. I was emotionally wrung out. "Oh" was all I managed.

"It's a small comfort, but it looks like there was only one intruder."

"I guess it only takes one to . . ." I couldn't finish the sentence.

A crime-scene technician, camera case in hand, stuck his head out. "We're done here. I'll take this back to the lab."

"Gotcha. We'll catch up tomorrow." The sheriff stood. I was grateful he'd left the porch light off, because I didn't want to be blinking up at him. "I talked to the Brewsters this afternoon."

"Who?"

"The Brewsters. Ron and Monica."

Oh yes. The image of Ron sitting forlornly at the Brew House that afternoon seemed so far away. I'd ruined his chances of supporting his family. It was just another contribution to today's massive heap of failure. "Did you learn anything?" I asked, although I could guess what Sheriff Koppen would say.

"They couldn't have killed Miles. All that night they were at the emergency room with Ron's mother. She has heart trouble."

"I saw him at the Brew House today. He's doing some odd jobs there."

"Good thing he has some work, because I had to report him for gathering morels without a permit. He won't be getting any more income that way."

"Oh." I pulled the heaviest blanket up to my chin. If only I could shrink into a tiny speck and work my way into the sofa's fabric, where I could stay forever. Nothing would matter. I bit the inside of my mouth. When I was envying dust motes, I'd pretty much reached bottom.

"Where are you staying tonight?" he asked again.

"I called Stella. Stella Hart," I said. "She said I could stay with her."

He nodded. "Good. I'll send someone by your shop from time to time, and we'll put a regular patrol up here, too."

"Thanks." The last of the sheriff's crew were packing up to leave. I wasn't afraid of mob justice or whatever the sheriff was hinting at. It was Avery I feared for. She was being set up something good.

When the lights of the last car had trundled down the road, I turned to the mess in the house. It could wait.

The sheriff wanted me to give up, stay out of the way. He had a point. Up to now, I'd lost a family its livelihood, destroyed Avery's house, and tainted every bit of evidence I might have touched along the way, knowingly or unknowingly.

The ocean below roared and spilled and pulled back again, all at the force of the moon's gravity. The earth spun on a tilt, hugging the sun. I felt insignificant. Heck, I practically *was* a dust mote. Why was I even bothering? Why didn't I stick to Strings Attached and feel lucky to have my own shop and leave everything else alone? Everyone told me that justice would take care of itself. I made kites— I didn't solve murders.

Mom would welcome me home any time. I knew that. I could even open a kite store in Portland and save money by sleeping in my old room. Home was safe. Nothing bad could happen to me there. Why not do it? Why not call her right now?

Because that's not enough, a voice in my head told me. Avery was as close as a sister—closer, actually, than my blood sister. If I stopped now, the murderer had won. Avery might well end up in prison for the rest of her life. She'd lose the house. I'd lose my friend. It was wrong.

Bear whined from the house. The crime-scene people had leashed him in the kitchen while they worked and apparently forgotten to let him free. I untied him, and he explored the house, sniffing room by room.

If I was going to continue to explore who might have killed Miles, I couldn't do it alone, and Stella had her limits. I found my phone. After a glance at directory assistance, I punched in a number.

"Jack?" I said. "It's Emmy Adler."

"Is everything all right? It's so late."

Shoot. It was. I'd been so caught up in my drama that I'd completely forgotten about the time. "Sorry about that. The sheriff just left."

"Sheriff?" Jack cut in.

"Someone broke into the house and trashed it. Left a nasty note on the mirror."

"I can't believe it." He paused as if processing this. "You're all right, though. You weren't home?"

Jack's worry encouraged me. "I'm fine. A few things are wrecked—vases and pictures and things like that, and there's a real mess to clean up, but no one was hurt."

"That's a relief, at least. You're not staying there, are you?"

"No. I'm going to Stella's."

"Good."

"I don't think whoever broke in is returning, anyway. They made their point. They left a note accusing Avery of being a murderer."

"I see." A pause. And then in a distinctly cooler tone, "Was there something you wanted from me?"

Where was the warm, friendly Jack from the beach yesterday? "Well"—I chose my words carefully—"I know you want to figure out who killed Miles. So do I. Maybe you aren't as sure of Avery's innocence as I am, but you're open to the idea that it was someone else."

In the background, I heard jazz. Maybe Miles Davis. I didn't know if Jack had inherited his grandfather's house, or had his own apartment somewhere in town.

"Emmy, this is hard to say, but it's not looking good for Avery."

"What? You said—"

"I know. But I've been hearing that she was spotted at the dock. Dave admitted you two couldn't be sure she hadn't left the house."

"Those are lies. Someone wants to frame her, that's all."

"Could be true." The jazz faded. Either he'd turned it off or moved to another room. "We should leave it for the sheriff."

"That's just the point. The sheriff is at a dead end. He has Avery in jail, so why should he keep looking? Meanwhile, the court of public opinion has decided she's a murderer."

"Look. I don't believe in mob justice, but the evidence against Avery is piling up. We'd better leave it to the sheriff. I appreciate your loyalty to your friend, but I have to go. It's late."

"Fine." "We'd better leave it to the sheriff" seemed to be everyone's favorite line. My eyes burned with unshed tears. I clicked off my phone without saying good-bye. Another failure to add to the day's list.

Bear jumped next to me and rested his merled head in my lap. "Bear bear." I kissed him between the ears. My chest felt like it had been emptied then refilled with hot

lead. I was too emotionally drained even to cry. "Bear," I
whispered. "Let's go somewhere we have friends."

BY THE TIME I'D ARRIVED AT STELLA'S, SHE'D SET UP THE
guest room and even put out a bowl of water for Bear. Bear,
being the noble and fine creature he was, gave Madame
Lucy a wide berth. Madame Lucy barely deigned to look
at him, but Bear wasn't taking any chances.

"I'm so sorry to hear about the break-in," Stella said.
"How was the sheriff?"

"He was fine. He was Sheriff Koppen. He thinks it was
some outraged Rock Point citizen." The thought of the tiny
drawn hanging man shot shivers down my arms.

"Oh, darling. Do you want to take a bath?" she asked.
"Maybe some chamomile tea?"

"Tea would be nice." I followed her to the kitchen, Bear
on my heels. Bear plopped on the kitchen floor between
us, coincidentally safe from Madame Lucy's clutches
should she decide to show him who was boss.

Stella took two squat, wide-bowled porcelain teacups
from a cupboard. Each had dogwoods painted inside. "My
mother's," she said. "She bought them in the late nineteen
forties and always cherished them but never used them."

"But you do." She would. It would be part of Stella's
philosophy to savor life, not keep it locked up in a china
hutch. "Are you close to her?"

"She died several years ago, and, no, we weren't particularly close. It's too bad. I think we'd have a lot to talk
about now. We both lost our husbands, and both changed
our lives afterward."

I thought about Mom, then winced. Shoot. I was supposed to call her tonight. Too late now. She'd have finished her pre-bed yoga stretches by now. I'd call her first thing in the morning. She was an early riser.

"I love my mother, but it seems like we're constantly at odds," I said. "Part of the reason for my move to Rock Point was to get some separation."

"And you're doing it." She poured water into a teapot. The golden chamomile buds bobbed to the top. "Despite how topsy-turvy your life here has turned."

"It probably seems ridiculous to move hours away just for independence."

"Not really. Mothers form a strong bond," she said.

"You never had children," I said. "But you have a maternal streak for sure."

"I had all those students. Hundreds of them over the years."

"That's a lot of letting go."

"Yes." Her voice was barely a whisper.

I looked at Bear, his head on Stella's foot, at the serene home she'd created around her and decided to go for it. "Stella, I have to ask. You've downplayed your friendship with Miles, but I can't help but feel that he was more important to you than you admit."

A pause. "What makes you say that?"

"Well, there's the painting you inscribed to him. And you lost interest in working at the Tidal Basin when he died. His death seems personal to you. You're even willing to help me dig up information about his death."

Stella lifted the teapot's lid and stirred the chamomile buds. She seemed to make up her mind. "Let's sit down."

She put our tea things on a tray and carried it to the coffee table surrounded by the mishmash of chairs I loved so much in the living room. Bear gave Madame Lucy some distance and settled unusually close to the velvet slipper chair I'd chosen this time.

"I'm not sure how to start," Stella said. I waited. "You know I was a teacher, right?"

"Right."

"I married late."

"I see." She seemed to need to warm up to her subject. I gave her time by pouring each of us some tea.

"When I was still single in my late thirties, I had a relationship with another teacher. He kept to himself, mostly, but we met a few times by accident in the early morning. One morning I brought him coffee, and we talked. He was separated from his wife. They had a—"

"A child," I guessed.

"A three-year-old girl. He showed me pictures. She was beautiful." Stella's tea was untouched, and I held mine more for its warmth than to drink. "He loved that girl. Anyway, over the course of the next year, we fell in love. He was ready to divorce his wife—and then he wasn't. He couldn't leave his daughter. Just couldn't do it."

I could imagine Stella with her long, thick hair—then chestnut—and her kind, elegant way. My heart ached as I suspected I knew where this was going. "That's awful."

"At about the same time, I discovered I was pregnant." She absently raised the teacup to her lips but didn't drink. She set it in its saucer again. "I couldn't tell him, of course. I couldn't rip him up like that, make him choose between the children."

"So you just let him go?"

"Don't you see? I had to."

As if in sympathy, Bear sighed next to me on the rug. I dipped a hand into his fur. "I see. But you had the baby."

"I told the school I needed a sabbatical, and I came to the coast and rented a little house. That's when I really got serious about painting."

"When you were pregnant."

"Yes."

I couldn't even imagine the pain. "And you gave him up." Now it was coming together. I understood.

"A kind nurse let me hold him for a few minutes before they took him away." Stella rose and strode down the hall. She returned with a small framed photo and handed it to me.

The photo, a Polaroid, showed a pink-faced infant swaddled in a white blanket, with a black-sleeved arm holding him. "That's him," I said.

"The nurse gave me his photo. She wasn't supposed to do it."

"Then he was gone."

"Then he was gone," she repeated. "Not long after, I met and married Allen. But I never forgot my baby."

I waited for her to say it, for her to say his name. "No. You wouldn't. Did you register to find him?"

"I did, but he never got in touch with me."

"So you tracked him down." She'd said that once her husband had died, she'd changed her life. Part of that was to dedicate her time to painting, but part must have been to find her son.

"It wasn't easy, but yes. I don't have to tell you that Miles was my son. He's why I moved to Rock Point. You saw the painting I gave him?" I nodded. "I painted that when I was carrying him."

It made sense now. Miles was as much an artist as Stella was. They'd shared a singular approach to life. "I'm so sorry."

"He never knew," she said.

"Did you have much time together?"

"A few years, and I'm grateful for it. Going through Allen's illness and death taught me a lot about cherishing the time you have with someone, not taking it for granted." She smiled, a wistful smile. "He must have thought it odd that a woman old enough to be his mother"—she looked up to catch my smile in return—"would show so much interest in him. But he was his own man. He followed his own star."

"He got that from you," I said.

"We had a lot of deep conversations, especially in the summer while the crew was closing down the kitchen. He'd take a beer to unwind to a picnic table set up out back for staff. I feel like I really got to know him."

Anything I might say would sound cheap, so I stayed silent.

"I'm sorry for the earful. You've certainly had enough drama tonight. Would you like more tea? This has gone cold."

I set down my cup. "No. Thank you. But I have one more question. You got to know Miles pretty well. Do you think he cared about Avery?"

"There's no doubt in my mind he did. And she cared about him. No doubt at all. That's another reason I wanted to help you. I still do."

Stella's story settled into my brain. Her love and her loss. I shivered. "There has to be something we can do," I said.

"I did finally talk to Jeanette at the post office. She didn't have much to say about Ron and Monica, but she told me what she'd mentioned to you about the Tidal Basin's bills. She let something else drop, too."

The sheriff had cleared the mushroom hunters, and he said Sam Anderson had an alibi, although he wouldn't tell me what it was. As far as I was concerned, Sam wasn't off the hook yet. "What did she say?"

"Apparently Sam is having personal trouble. It sounds like a divorce is in the offing."

I wasn't sure what it all meant, but the sheriff probably knew less than that. I fixed my gaze on Stella. "Are you busy tomorrow night?"

chapter twenty-one

I LEFT STELLA'S EARLY THE NEXT MORNING. THANKS TO the break-in and the police's fingerprint powder, I had a fair amount of cleanup to do at the house before I opened the shop, and although Stella offered to come help me, I thought a morning of scrubbing and sorting might help start the kind of scrubbing and sorting my brain needed right then.

When the car made the last turn up the rutted drive, my foot slipped to the brake. A car was parked next to Avery's. I nearly shrieked in exasperation. It was my mom and dad's VW bus. Seated on the steps to the porch was my mother, looking, if possible, more irritated than I felt.

My car door wasn't even open before the barrage began. "You said you'd call last night."

"Things got busy. I forgot."

"I'll say they got busy."

"You scoped out the house, didn't you?" I could imagine her creeping from window to window.

"What did you expect me to do? You said you'd call, and you didn't. I thought something awful might have happened, that you might be—" Bear leapt into the front seat and pushed out the driver's-side door toward her, his whole hind end wagging.

My frustration melted away. "I'm sorry, Mom. I really did forget." I stepped up to the porch and sat next to her on the steps. She clutched me close. After a few minutes, her tears subsided.

"Emmy, I was so worried."

"I know. I'm sorry. I'm fine, though. I really am. After the break-in, I spent the night at a friend's house."

She took a deep breath that hitched on the inhale. "What happened in there?"

I rose. "Come in. You might as well see for yourself."

As my mother wandered from room to room, opening cupboards and peering around doors, I told her the story. She halted in front of the warning smeared on the mirror.

It was coming, I knew it. She turned to face me. Now she was going to tell me to pack my bags and return to Portland. Now she was going to pitch such a massive fit that I couldn't refuse but do what she said.

Instead, she stared at me. I waited for the deluge, but it didn't come. "Is there something you want to tell me?" Like, to pack my bags and get in the bus for home?

"No, honey. Except that we'd better clean this up."

It was too much. Avery in jail, the house wrecked, Stella's revelations, half the town hating me, and now my mother acting rationally?—it all hit at once. Now I was the one to burst into tears. My mother brought me a glass of water, which I downed in a few gulps. Choking, I handed her back the glass. "Thanks." She pressed a wad of tissues into my hand. I dried my eyes.

"Yeah," I said. "Let's get cleaning."

We spent the next few hours filling garbage bags, scrubbing surfaces, and doing laundry. Mom mixed up her usual batch of eco-friendly cleansers. Soon it was time to open Strings Attached.

"There's still a bit more to be done here," Mom said. "Why don't I take care of it?"

"If you don't mind," I said. "Do you want to stay? I could fix up a bed for you." She hesitated. "I don't think anyone will break in again. It was just a warning."

She touched my cheek. Her hand smelled of borax. "I'll stay. Let's talk tonight. Unless you have plans."

I did have plans—to visit Avery, and then to meet up with Stella. "Not until later on."

"I'll make us dinner."

"Thanks, Mom. I mean it."

IT WAS A SLOW DAY AT STRINGS ATTACHED, BUT THIS early in the season I didn't expect a lot of business, even on a Saturday. A real kite nerd stopped by, and we spent nearly an hour happily talking about the state of the kite industry and some of my newer designs. By lunch I was ready to close the store for half an hour and drop in to the Brew House. When I visited Avery that night—the break-in had preempted last night's planned visit—I wanted to be able to tell her everything was fine.

On the surface, it was. The Brew House bustled with conversation, punctuated by the hiss of the steamer. Someone had put an old Cat Stevens album on the turntable.

"Hi, Emmy." Trudy's smile looked forced.

I was on alert. "How are things?"

"Fine—and not so fine."

"Is the morning shift working out all right without Avery?"

"That's not it. The schedule isn't a problem." Trudy put down her rag and drew me into a corner. "Have you seen Avery since all that business on TV?"

"I'm going to see her tonight. Why?"

"It's been strange here. This morning a fight broke out between two of the regulars. One of them would barely talk to me, and I don't think she'll be here again. She only seemed to get her daily latte so she could make nasty comments about Avery. The other customer defended her, and—well, it got ugly."

"That can't last long," I said. "Avery will be out of jail just as soon as other evidence comes up." I was trying to convince myself as much as I convinced Trudy.

"That's not the worst," Trudy said. "When I came in this morning, someone had drawn a bloody knife on the back door in permanent marker."

"Oh, Trudy." I sank into a chair. I'd hoped it had ended with damage at the house. But now this. "I'll call the sheriff."

"I already did, and we painted over the door with some paint I had at home. It's pansy pink now." She looked at me with apology. "From doing the nursery."

I hugged her. "Thank you. Can you bear to keep going? You aren't afraid?"

"Oh no. We have a good security system. Plus, I know Avery's innocent. I've known her too long. Besides, business has been better than ever. Every Nosey Parker between Cannon Beach and Astoria has dropped in for a cappuccino."

Avery was so lucky to have Trudy on staff. "Call me if you need anything," I said. "In the meantime, how about a chicken-salad sandwich to go?"

On my way back to the shop, I ran into Stella. Her mind was somewhere else, and I was right next to her before she recognized me. I knew that expression. It was the same lost look Avery had. Or maybe, knowing what I did know about her relationship to Miles, I simply saw more deeply.

"Coming to see me?" I asked.

"Yes." She looked out toward the bay, then to me again. A long strand of white-gray hair blew over her face, and she pushed it behind her ear. "I just wanted to tell you that Miles's funeral is tomorrow morning."

"I knew it was coming up, but so soon?"

"It's been more than a week. The family is ready."

"Oh." No wonder Stella wore such a bewildered look. I'd seen Miles's body; she hadn't. I knew he was dead, but to Stella it was something her brain couldn't have fully processed. Tomorrow's service would change that.

"Are you going?" Stella asked.

"I don't know." A passerby—I recognized him as a clerk in the minimart—was so interested in looking at me, the purported murderer's roommate, that he nearly ran into a lamppost. "I don't know how people would feel about having me at the funeral. There's so much bad feeling about Avery out there."

"I understand."

It broke my heart to see such a vibrant woman so profoundly sad. "Unless you want me there."

"No. No, I think you're right, but thank you." She briefly rested a hand on my arm. "I made it through Allen's death. I have a pretty good idea of how grief works by now. I'll be fine."

I reluctantly let her go and continued to the shop.

And there I had my third surprise of the day. Annabelle Black was waiting on the stoop to see me. She was wearing yet another Laura Ashley–style dress, this one laced up the bodice, with the top lacing undone a few notches below manufacturer's recommendations. I couldn't imagine she was looking to buy a kite.

"Annabelle. What a surprise," I said.

"May I come in?"

"Of course." I unlocked Strings Attached. My sandwich could wait a few minutes.

"I wanted to say how sorry I am for how I've treated you. I've been downright rude."

I raised an eyebrow. Really? "Oh, please—"

"You're simply being polite, and it's more than I deserve. I've been a regular bitch to you, and it's inexcusable."

"I don't know what you mean." I totally knew what she meant, but it didn't seem worth it to go down that road.

"No. When we first met, and then again at the Morning Glory, I was less than polite, and I'm not proud of myself. You've been through a lot lately, and I understand. You don't deserve having to deal with my attitude, too."

"I appreciate that, Annabelle."

"And you've been through so much with Avery. I hope she's released soon. Neither you nor she deserves this. It can't be easy." The afternoon sun brought out slight dark circles under her eyes. I'd forgotten that beneath her melodrama lurked a genuine attachment to Miles.

"Thank you," I said, and I meant it. "I'm just looking forward to having a bath and going to bed tonight."

"The Morning Glory is hosting the reception after the funeral tomorrow. I hope you'll come."

I thought about the break-in, the baldly curious looks people had been giving me. "I don't know. I'm not sure the top suspect's roommate would be welcome."

"I'd welcome you. You did find him, and you need a chance to make peace with it. Besides, some people around town are always looking for an excuse to feel superior. Don't pay attention."

"Thank you for saying so," I said, but it didn't mean I planned to go. Miles's family might be less than happy to see me there, too.

"You're letting other people's opinions get to you, aren't you?"

"It's hard not to," I said, thinking of the break-in.

She browsed the shop's perimeter, touching a kite here and there. "I don't tell a lot of people this, but my family were real outcasts for years. Decades, really. I understand what you're going through."

"Did you grow up in Rock Point?"

"We moved here when I was a child. Our old family farm was in the valley east of here. Dad was a gambler, though, and we lost it." She laid out this information in a matter-of-fact way.

"That had to be tough. I'm sorry. "

"Don't be. It's simply the way it is. I've come to terms with it."

"It couldn't be easy, though, losing your home. Especially as a child."

Annabelle smiled shyly. "Thank you. It's not my heritage, though. My grandmother used to tell me stories about the Oregon Trail and how we came out here as pioneers. She taught me a real respect for the land and gave me confidence in what a Black can do."

I remembered her earlier stories. "That carries through in the inn and how you carry yourself."

"You mean this." She touched the cotton lace at her neck. Her prairie dresses fit her image. Still, my family had been railroad workers, and you wouldn't catch me in striped overalls and carrying a whistle. "People judge you by what they see or what they hear," she said. "I want visitors to see me and think of Annabelle Black, who symbolizes strength, graciousness, and the pioneer spirit."

"You're memorable. That's for sure."

"I didn't come here to talk about me, though. I just wanted to apologize for how I behaved earlier and say that it's not fair how people are treating you and Avery."

"Thank you," I repeated. "That means a lot to me."

She leaned on the counter. "I'm glad we were able to talk for a minute. I think we're both strong women—businesswomen—and we need to stick together. Rock Point is growing, and we can grow with it. I don't kid myself—" She smiled, and it seemed sincere, but I couldn't help being on guard. "Maybe we'll never be best friends, although I'd like it if we were. I do think we can be closer than we have been."

Warily, I stepped around the counter and hugged her. Wonders never cease.

* * *

AS PROMISED, MOM WAS WAITING FOR ME AT HOME. THE
kitchen smelled of lemons and cooking grains—the lemon
was probably part of Mom's cleaning up, and the grains
were certainly part of dinner. Mom wore one of Avery's
aprons, and her gray-streaked hair was pulled into a low
ponytail. I kissed her cheek.

She pulled a casserole dish from the oven. She must
have gone grocery shopping, because I knew for a fact that
as of that morning the refrigerator hadn't held more than
coffee grounds, an egg, and the bottle of champagne I'd
never opened.

"Smells good," I said.

"Mushroom barley casserole with chard." She set the
dish on the stove to cool. "You had some morels in the
crisper drawer. You girls couldn't have bought them. There
must have been a hundred dollars' worth in that bag."

"Fifty, actually." At my mother's raised eyebrow, I
quickly added, "I found a great spot to gather them just
outside of town."

She returned her attention to the casserole. "While I
was at the store, I got a few other things for the house, too.
I noticed that you don't have any arnica. What do you do
for muscle aches? I started a batch of kombucha, too—it's
fermenting on top of the water heater."

My warmth at seeing my mother was beginning to cool.
"Mom, I don't drink as much kombucha as you do—"

"Well, you should. You don't get enough fermented
foods in your diet." She busied herself in the kitchen as if
it were her own. I had a sneaking suspicion she might have
reorganized the cupboards, too.

On the kitchen table was the bookkeeping I'd brought from the Brew House. It was sorted with a list on top. "You found Avery's paperwork for the café."

"It was in a jumble by the front door. Honey, you shouldn't keep important papers like that."

"What did you do with them?"

"Not much. Just sorted income from accounts payable and tallied the hours for payroll." She opened a cupboard and pulled out a tumbler. Yep, she'd reorganized all right. Tumblers used to be stored nearer the sink. "You know I kept books for your father's law firm when he got started. We didn't have computers then, so I'm a pro at double-entry bookkeeping."

Mom's love, which had been so comforting this morning, was closing like a vise grip around me. "I appreciate everything you've done for me today, but—"

"I was really surprised that your garbage bags aren't biodegradable. So I picked up some of those. Your father's composting club can recommend a good countertop food bin."

"Stop!" I exploded. "Just stop."

"Honey." Mom froze, wooden spoon in hand. At last, she was still.

"Can you please let me do things my way?"

"All I did was a few helpful things around the house. I'm not questioning your life."

"It feels like it, though. You don't even approve of where I keep my drinking glasses."

"They were so far from the dishwasher." Mom's smile faltered. "And I cleaned up the rest of the mess from your break-in."

"I'm grateful for everything you've done, but I need to live my own life. I have to figure out things on my own, make my own choices. If that means that I use bleached toilet paper, so be it."

"I just thought—" She backed into a chair at the kitchen table.

"Oh, Mom, I'm sorry. I didn't mean to hurt your feelings. But we've been through this before."

She looked at me, eyes wide. "My feelings are fine."

"I'm not an asthmatic ten-year-old anymore who needs you to trail after me with an inhaler. You raised me. You fed me, got me to school, listened to my stories, cared for me. Now it's time to let me go."

"Oh, Emmy. It's just—"

"It's just what? Mom, it's just life."

"You're such a daydreamer. I worry for you. You need someone looking in on you."

"No, I don't. I don't need anyone. I have to figure it out on my own." I willed my lower lip to stop trembling.

My mother had no such compunction and burst into tears. We didn't seem to be able to see each other today without one of us boohooing. "Honey, I'm sorry."

"I'm sorry, too, Mom." I fell into her open hug. Dang it, she got me every time.

After a few moments of a barley-scented embrace, she released me. "I've been thinking about our talk this morning."

"Yeah?"

"You have so much direction. You know what you want in life. You love art and designing kites. Other than raising you and your sister, I never had that kind of focus. I guess now that you're away and Sunny is in college, I'm at a loss. I'm taking it out on you. You give me purpose."

I sat down next to her. Funny, I'd never thought that my

mother's protectiveness had to do with her own needs. I always figured it was because she thought I was somehow lacking.

"I love knowing that you're there if I need you," I said. "But you have to let go a little bit."

"You have everything figured out," she said. "Even your father has his composting group and Watergate-reenactment club. I envy you."

I envied her relationship with my father and her seemingly unending fount of energy. "Mom, you're the best. It's time for you to put yourself to work finding out what inspires you. Your herbal remedies, for instance. You have a real gift there. Or maybe you could write a cookbook of vegan casseroles." Okay, I might be casting wide.

"Carolyn—she's a gal in my croning circle; I don't believe you've met her—said my tincture worked wonders on her hot flashes."

"See? You should explore that."

I wasn't sure she even heard me. Her mind seemed somewhere else. "But I don't know. You're asking a lot of me, to leave you alone when Avery is accused of murder and the town seems convinced she's guilty."

"Not everyone in town," I said, hoping it was true.

"I just don't like the idea of you staying here alone. Not now. Unless you have a better alternative, I'm staying." She pretended to wipe up a spot on the spotless counter. "Or you could come back to Portland with me."

No way. Absolutely not. I'd wondered when this would come up. At the same time, she had a point. Staying at the house alone wasn't the best idea. "How about this? How about if I ask Dave to stay here with me?" He would do it for Avery's sake if nothing else.

"That nice man who helped you put together your furniture? Yes, I guess that would work."

"It won't be for long, anyway. I'm sure the sheriff will figure out who the real murderer is." I mentally crossed my fingers on that one. It seemed like I'd been repeating it a dozen times a day.

She sniffed and pulled a handkerchief from a pocket to blow her nose. "Okay. But you'll call me every day. No forgetting this time." I swore I would. Her shoulders relaxed a bit. "Other than Avery, do you have any idea who the sheriff is questioning?"

"He doesn't talk to me about it, Mom."

"Knowing you and how you get obsessed, I'm surprised you haven't given it more thought yourself." She raised an eyebrow. "Or have you?"

"Of course I've *thought* about it." I turned away so she wouldn't see my eyes.

"And?" She pulled two bowls from the cupboards and scooped casserole into each. "Follow me to the dining room. Or should we just eat here?" She bent her head toward the kitchen table.

"Here is good."

"So, the suspects," Mom said. "Who were the chef's enemies?"

"He made a lot of people mad, but not homicidally so. At least, not as far as I can tell."

"Like who?"

Steam rose from the casserole as I dipped in my fork. "Well, last summer he decided at the last minute to take a culinary tour of Asia. He was away for weeks, and his boss was mad. Plus, he had a habit of sometimes not showing up for work."

"The murder was premeditated, right? Not a crime of passion. I mean, someone planted evidence against Avery. That says 'forethought' to me."

Mom was right. "Miles might have also been picking morel mushrooms on someone else's territory, which is a big deal around here."

"Oh dear, yes. Last matsutake mushroom season, the Rileys had the misfortune to camp in the wrong area, and they were chased out at gunpoint. The sheriff said they were lucky it was only that."

"Exactly. Plus, some morel hunters had threatened him at the restaurant. The problem is that those mushroom hunters couldn't have killed him, the sheriff says. They were at the hospital the night he died."

Mom's bowl was already empty. At least I knew she wasn't still doing that thing where you chew forty times before swallowing. "You know what your father would say."

"What?"

"Follow the money." She grimaced. "So much swearing when he plays Dick Nixon. I just wish they'd let him be G. Gordon Liddy, like he keeps asking. They say he doesn't have the mustache for it, but I don't see why that's a problem."

"Follow the money," I repeated. Deep Throat's famous line. It made sense. "Miles had drawn up a design for a restaurant, but he didn't seem to have any immediate plans to start it up."

"Are you sure?"

"I could ask around."

"Maybe he owed someone. Took out a loan and couldn't pay it back."

"Killing someone who owes you money is hardly the smart way to get repaid."

"Maybe it's more complicated than that. It bears some thinking."

"Hmm." I didn't know what else or who else was involved in Miles's restaurant plans, or even if the plans were real enough to involve anyone. Surely he'd talked with someone about them.

"Eat up," Mom said. "Or you'll never make it to Astoria in time to visit Avery."

chapter twenty-two

MAYBE IT WAS THE FLUORESCENT LIGHTS, MAYBE THE puke-green uniform, or maybe the weight of a murder charge, but Avery looked awful.

"Hi," I said.

"Hi."

A minute passed. I couldn't think of anything to say that would cheer her up, and apparently she couldn't, either. I didn't want to lead with the break-in. Finally, I said, "Mom stopped by."

That made Avery smile. "She did?"

"She heard about the—the to-do on the news, so she drove out. She was sitting on the front steps the first thing this morning when I pulled up."

"At home? Where were you?"

Whoops. I hadn't intended to get into the break-in and

warnings so soon. "I'd promised to call her the night before, but I forgot, so she drove over from Portland."

"And you weren't home when she arrived?"

"How do you like your lawyer? I saw her on TV."

"She's all right, I guess. You're not answering me, though. I—"

"Have you given thought to hiring a lawyer who specializes in this? Remember, Dad gave me names."

"I can't afford one. Besides, the court-appointed attorney is all right. It's going to be fine. But—"

"Fine isn't good enough. I—"

"Emmy." Avery folded her arms in front of her chest. "You're not telling me something. Talking about my lawyer isn't going to distract me. Spit it out."

There was no way around it. I gave Avery a softened version of the break-in, but she took it hard.

"People are hounding you. Because of me," she said.

"They're wrong, and they'll find out. This is just a temporary thing."

"I feel awful." She was starting to drift into her depression again.

"It's not your fault." I lowered my voice so as not to attract the guard's attention. "Someone is framing you for Miles's death. The truth will come out. It has to." Another moment passed with no response from Avery. I tried again. "What does your attorney say? Does she have any insight?"

"She's doing the best she can. We'll see. If the grand jury indicts me, I'll consider hiring someone else. I'll worry about it when the time comes." She pulled in her wandering gaze and focused it on me. "When's the funeral? The sheriff must have released his body by now."

"Tomorrow." I wondered if television reporters would show up to that, too.

"I wish I could be there."

"I'm glad you won't be." I imagined the crowd, the gossip-hungry residents. No telling what they'd do if Avery showed up. As much as I hated to say it, she was better off under police protection.

"It probably wouldn't be smart, anyway. Not until my name is cleared. His parents must think I'm some kind of monster."

Every subject seemed rife with emotional minefields. I tried a different one. "I've been spending more time with Stella."

"Oh yes," she said, her mind clearly still on the funeral.

"She and Miles were close—"

"They used to talk after his shifts," she said. "He told me about it. Once I stopped by when he was closing up, and he and Stella were sitting out back chatting like long-lost friends. She's such a lovely woman."

Stella hadn't told me not to share her secrets, and I didn't plan to broadcast them. Still, Avery was my best friend, and I felt like she should know what I knew about Miles. "You asked why Stella was willing to break into Miles's cabin, and well—"

"Well, what?" Her jaw dropped. "Don't tell me they were lovers."

"No. No. She was Miles's birth mother."

Avery sat back. Her eyes widened. "No kidding."

"For real."

"He was adopted. I knew that." She tilted her head to the side, thinking. "She used to come into the Brew House and chat from time to time. I always kind of wondered if she was sizing me up. But his mother. Wow."

"I know."

"Now that you've told me, I can see it. They have similar eyes—wide set. Blue. And come to think of it, they both gesture a lot with their hands." She met my gaze. "She must be taking this hard."

"She is, but she's remarkably philosophical about it, too. People always say to appreciate what you have, but she actually seems to have done that. More than missing Miles, I think she's grateful for the time she spent with him."

I'd lost Avery's attention. Either that, or she needed to think. She worried at a hangnail.

"When we talked about Miles before," I said, "you sounded so casual about him. I can't help but think he meant more to you than that."

She slowly lifted her eyes to mine. "He did."

"For some reason you don't like to talk about it," I coaxed. "I sense it. But I'm not sure why."

Her voice dropped. "There's something I need to tell you. I should have said something earlier, but I couldn't."

This was it. I knew she'd been hiding something from me. "Yes?" I glanced toward the clock. I didn't want our time to run out.

"I've wanted to tell you, but it's just been too hard." She wouldn't look at me. "I started to say something the last night I was home, but the knife . . ." She let her words fall off.

I leaned closer to the plexiglass barrier. It clouded with my breath. "You can tell me anything, Avery. You know that."

"Well." She swallowed. "The sheriff was right. I was down at the dock the night Miles died." She glanced at me, then quickly down at her hands.

"What? But you said—" All those times I'd defended her, told people she was at home in bed. And now she was saying she wasn't?

"Nothing. I said nothing. Nothing afterward, anyway." Avery's anguish was real. "I let you believe I'd stayed home because it was too painful to tell you the truth. I'm sorry."

"What about the headache? The tea?"

She bit her lip. "That was for real. I made your mom's tea, but when I decided to leave, I dumped it down the drain and closed my bedroom door so you'd think I was asleep."

She'd lied to me. "I've been telling everyone you were home—the sheriff, Jack."

"I know." Her words were barely audible.

"You must have had a good reason."

She nodded but didn't reply. I tried again. "So Miles did have a meeting planned with you."

"He did. But I didn't kill him. I swear."

Again, I waited for more. I knew from experience that Avery had to take things in her own time. But finally I couldn't wait any longer. "Why were you there?"

"It's hard to talk about it."

"You've lost a lot in the past few years with your parents' accident."

She shook her head. "Let me start at the beginning. I should have told you to begin with."

I nodded. The minute hand on the wall clock clicked as it advanced. We didn't have all night, but I'd stay until she was finished explaining, even if they had to drag me out by the armpits.

"When we dated, I really started to care for Miles. He was such an odd guy—but so seductive at the same time. He did his own thing, and I loved that. I could have sworn he cared about me, too. I could have sworn it, but—" She broke with my gaze and looked toward her lap. "He stopped calling. All at once. We talked every day, saw each other all the time, and then—nothing."

"For no reason?"

"None that I could tell."

"He didn't explain? At all?"

"I asked, but he made excuses. I didn't understand."

"Nothing happened between you? No arguments or anything like that?"

Her voice shrank to a whisper. "No. I couldn't figure it out. He seemed troubled the last few times we got together, and then he quit seeing me. That was all." I could tell by her choked voice that her throat was tightening with emotion.

"Something was off. I know he cared about you. Stella says so, too. Something was wrong." I pondered this a moment. "But what about the other night at the dock?"

She took a breath. "He called, said he wanted to meet privately. I didn't know what it meant, and I hoped"—she looked away—"I hoped maybe he'd missed me. But I couldn't admit it, even to myself."

"Why the dock?"

"It was his suggestion. He said he had a surprise. It suited me, because I knew you'd be at the house, and I didn't want to explain everything if nothing came of it. Oh, Emmy." She closed her eyes a moment.

"I understand." And yet I didn't understand. Yes, I felt Avery's pain, but I still couldn't believe she didn't tell me earlier. "Did you see him?"

"No. I'd decided that I wouldn't go through with it after all. After how he treated me, why should I drop everything and see him? That's when I told you I had a headache and went up to the house."

"But you did go."

She nodded. "Finally, I did. I wanted to see him so badly." She looked at me to see that I understood. I nodded. My heart ached for her. "I was late. I waited at the top of the dock and even checked the family boat, just in case. It was dark. He wasn't there."

Or he was there, but dead. From the tension on her brow and jaw, I knew Avery was thinking the same thing.

"Maybe I could have saved him," she whispered.

"Or maybe you'd be dead, too," I said. "Does your lawyer know?"

She nodded. "And Koppen. It'll come out."

I wanted to clasp her hands across the table, but the barrier made that impossible. "I'm sorry."

"Will you go to the funeral?" Avery asked. "Will you go for me?"

I WENT STRAIGHT FROM VISITING AVERY TO STELLA'S. AS we'd planned, Stella was dressed all in black, including a black scarf wrapped fashionably around her hair headband-style and dangling down her back. Her somber clothing matched my mood.

We walked toward the center of town, and she filled me in. "Like I told you, Jeanette at the post office says that Sam's marriage is on the rocks."

"Alimony and child support would definitely bite into his finances. If the Tidal Basin was already challenged—"

"My thoughts exactly."

"There's something I need to tell you, too." I told Stella about my visit to Avery and that she'd been on the dock the night Miles died. "I was sure she was at home all night."

"Oh" was all Stella said for a moment. "It doesn't look good for her."

"But you believe she's innocent?"

"Yes. She really cared about Miles, I know. She wouldn't have killed him," she said. "He'd wanted to see her. I wonder what about?"

"Avery didn't know. I think she'd hoped he wanted to get back together."

"Maybe he did."

It was nearly midnight, and a cold wind blew off the bay. We kept our voices low so as not to attract the attention of the few Rock Point residents who might still be awake. As we came down the hill, I saw a small light still on in the back of the Morning Glory Inn, Annabelle's bed-and-breakfast. It had to be a tourist, I told myself. Not Jack.

"Sam should be closing up the Tidal Basin any minute," Stella said.

"Where does he live?"

"Jeanette said his wife kicked him out, and now he's getting his mail at the post office. That's all she knows."

"I guess we'll know more soon." Our plan was to follow him each night after the Tidal Basin closed until he went to the old dock. Ace the plumber might not be willing to tell us what Sam did there at night, but that didn't mean we couldn't find it out ourselves. Although I didn't relish another middle-of-the-night visit.

"Sam usually walks to work and leaves through the

rear. If we wait in the alley by the bookstore, we should be able to see him."

After a few minutes, we arrived at the street behind the Tidal Basin. As Stella suggested, we stood in the dark alley between the bookstore and the ice cream store next door. As was true for most of downtown's buildings, the top floors held apartments, some of which were occupied year-round. We'd have to stay silent.

Stella was right about the timing. On schedule, Sam left the Tidal Basin, locking the rear door behind him. He zipped his coat to his neck and strode in our direction. We plastered ourselves flat against the wall. I closed my eyes, as if that would make me less visible.

"He's headed north," Stella whispered.

We waited a moment, then stepped out of the alley to see Sam's back receding down the street. A block up, he turned left. We followed.

I'd never followed anyone before. In movies, the detective always had to pretend to read a newspaper or look at a store display if the suspect turned his way. Here, it was midnight, and besides at the tavern, no one was out. Pretending to read a newspaper would get us nowhere.

As I pondered this, my foot hit a crack in the sidewalk, and I stumbled. Stella grabbed my arm and threw us both behind a parked car. Sam's steps ceased. Keep walking, keep walking, I prayed. At last, his steps up the block continued.

When it seemed safe, we rose from our crouched positions behind the sedan and followed. Sam had turned again. Stella spotted him up a side street, pulling his keys from his pocket. We ducked around the corner and waited until we heard the door open, then close.

"Come on," I whispered. A light appeared in an upper window of the dingy apartment building. Sam was home. I jotted down the address so we could return later if need be. "Look," Stella said. As suddenly as it had turned on, the upstairs light shut off. Sam could hardly have had time to get in bed already. "Step back," she said.

Sure enough, just as we retreated into the shadows, Sam was on the street again, locking his front door. He strode down the hill, whistling "Strangers in the Night." Unbelievable.

We were in luck, though. He looked to be going straight to the dock. Judging by his pressed pants and button-down shirt, it wasn't to go crabbing, either, unless he kept another set of clothes on his boat. He'd even slicked back his few strands of hair.

If he took the boat out tonight, there was no way we'd be able to follow him, of course. If he didn't take out the boat—well, that was even stranger.

He was definitely headed toward the dock. We lingered near the Tidal Basin until he was well down the dock. He stepped onto a beat-up fiberglass cruiser and disappeared below deck. The mercury lamp buzzed in the night. After a few minutes, it became clear that Sam wasn't going to untie the boat from the pier.

"Should we follow him?" Stella asked.

It was a risk. If he came up when we were on the dock, we'd be spotted immediately. But then again, why were we there if we weren't going to investigate?

"I'm game if you are," I replied.

We crept up the dock. The sound of lapping waves and the occasional groan of the dock hid any noise we might have made. Ace's boat was dark. Hopefully he was home

dreaming of pipe fittings while Yin and Yang snoozed below deck.

"Let's watch from there," Stella said, pointing toward
Ace's boat. "If we lie on the deck on our bellies, we should
be able to see if anyone else comes or goes."

"We could lie there all night," I whispered.

"For a little while, at least," Stella said.

After a nervous glance up toward Sam's boat, I stepped
to Ace's deck and lowered myself.

Sam was up to something on the boat. Maybe he was
selling drugs or dealing in stolen boat parts. Miles might
have accidentally caught him when he went to meet Avery
and been killed. I glanced at Stella, who somehow managed to look graceful even while lying prone on a dirty
boat. We were in the same situation Miles had been. If we
discovered Sam's secret, what might happen to us?

"Thank goodness for my morning yoga practice," Stella
whispered as she shifted on her elbows.

No sooner did we lie down than new steps hit the dock.
They became louder as they approached. I raised my head
just barely and could make out a woman's legs—in pants
and boots, but definitely a woman's—and swinging arms,
one of which seemed to be holding a wine bottle.

A wine bottle? Sam had a rendezvous. As the figure
passed, I raised my head higher. My jaw dropped.

"What?" Stella said, noticing my shock.

"It's Deputy Goff," I said. She leapt onto Sam's boat as
if she'd been there a dozen times already and let herself
below deck. I sat full up. "It's Deputy Goff, and she's visiting Sam. And she brought a bottle of wine."

"No joke." Stella looked just as surprised as I was.
"Who'd have thought?" She swallowed a chuckle.

"It looks like she even put on lipstick."

"We should wait a few minutes to make sure they're, uh, you know."

Sam wouldn't have killed Miles because he'd stumbled over Sam's love nest. As for Deputy Goff—nah. I couldn't see that, either.

"Now we know why the sheriff is so sure of Sam's alibi," I said. Then I remembered pressuring the sheriff to question Sam, the deputy's insistence that he was innocent, and her "break" from the case. No wonder Goff hated me. I'd forced her to reveal her affair. With a divorce in the works, likely neither of them wanted to go public just yet.

Stella sat up, too. "Listen. Is that Sam's voice?"

A voice drifted across the dock. "Well, if it isn't my sweet cup of Goffee," it said.

Even under the dock's thin light I made out Stella's grin.

chapter twenty-three

I WAS WARY AS I PULLED INTO THE SMALL CHURCH PARK-
ing lot for Miles's funeral. I wore a black dress—the same
dress I'd worn to Avery's parents' funeral a few years
earlier—and planned to sit near the back, where I hoped I
wouldn't be noticed. Miles's family might not be keen on
having the roommate of the woman jailed for murdering him
present at his funeral. Had it only been me, I would have
stayed home. But I was there as Avery's proxy. I would be
her eyes and ears, and I would send her best thoughts. Besides, I'd found Miles's body. Being with him as his friends
and family said good-bye would bring some closure.

I hesitated before signing the register just inside the
door but went ahead and wrote my name clearly. A one-
sheet program showed a photo of Miles, smiling. I pulled
it closer for a better look. I'd heard so much about him,
been in his cabin, sat in his bed, even. But I realized that

I'd never seen what he looked like animated with life. It was a candid shot, showing Miles's head and shoulders with firs in the background, as if it had been taken when he was hiking. At first glance, I wouldn't have said he was handsome. But the intelligence in his eyes and the seed of a smile on his lips showed me he could have been a heart-breaker. The bottom of the program announced a post-funeral reception at Annabelle's Morning Glory Inn.

I found an empty chair toward the edge, eight or nine rows back, that gave me a good view of the room. An older man held his wife at the front row. Miles's parents. Stella sat across the room, her eyes on them, her face solemn. She'd been such a good sport last night, even if our outing only knocked another suspect off the list. Today she was a grieving mother.

A few rows behind Stella sat Dave and Jack. Dave turned to me and nodded. He'd told me last night that he'd pack a few things and take them straight from the church to my house. Jack didn't turn, but I had a good view of his profile. He wore a suit and looked particularly fine, damn him. He'd been right, too: Avery had been at the dock the night Miles was killed. But that didn't excuse him from jumping to conclusions about her.

Annabelle swept up the aisle. Somehow she'd got her hands on a black gown complete with underskirt and a laced bodice that hugged her torso. She looked like a cross between Laura Ingalls Wilder and Morticia Addams, but that didn't keep several of the men's heads from swiveling in her direction. She stopped at the aisle where Dave and Jack were seated and asked people to shift their seats so she could claim a spot next to Jack. Frank entered a moment later, and Annabelle repeated her orchestrations so

Frank could sit on her other side. In front of me a few rows was Sam Anderson. Sweet cup of Goffee. Ha.

The pastor, a plump, older woman with gray-streaked hair twisted into a large bun, took the lectern as the soprano finished her hymn. "Welcome," she said. "I've presided over many funerals, and each of them carried a singular feeling of loss. But this service is particularly difficult. Our Holy Father took Miles Logan, with his youth and his talent, from us so early, leaving us a deep grief to bear. We can't deny that grief, but we can remember that just as God took Miles, he also gave us Miles's gifts. This afternoon will celebrate his memory."

Stella discreetly dabbed her eyes. I longed to put my arm around her, but I knew it would bring little comfort. She'd lost Miles so many years ago, then found him only for a short time before losing him again. For a mother to lose her son twice was so unfair.

A few rows behind her, Annabelle's sobs started up. Jack awkwardly patted her arm but seemed unsure of what to do next. Frank, on her other side, pulled a handkerchief from inside his sport coat and handed it to her. Dave kept his eyes trained on the pastor. Poor Annabelle. For all her irritating characteristics, she was a decent person. I thought of her apology a few days ago and her suggestion that we support each other. Maybe her way of being in the world wasn't the same as mine, but it didn't mean we couldn't be friends. Of a sort, anyway.

Mom was convinced the murder had to do with money. Now that the question of the morel hunters had been solved—I winced a bit—it seemed a logical deduction. Who would be threatened by a new restaurant? I looked at the back of Sam Anderson's head. He certainly had had a lot to lose. Miles would not only have left the Tidal Basin without a chef, but he would have become a fierce competitor. Media attention and customers would have followed him, and the Tidal Basin would have lost some of its cachet. My landlord, Frank, was the only other money-related possibility I knew, but only because he invested in Rock Point. I couldn't come up with a reason he might have killed Miles. If anything, Frank would have helped Miles raise the money for the restaurant; then he would have wanted a stake in it. From launching Strings Attached, I had some idea of how to start a business, but a restaurant— with all its employees, suppliers, and the vagaries of tourism—would be a whole different beast.

When the service ended, the pastor indicated where we could line up at the edge of the church and file past the casket. I was tempted to slip out to my car, but for Avery's sake I wanted to touch the casket and thank Miles for the depth of emotion he'd raised in her, even though if he were alive I would have slapped him for disappearing like he did.

As we formed a slow-moving line, I glanced back and saw Sheriff Koppen toward the rear of the church, his hair pulled back into its sleek ponytail. Without his sheriff's uniform, his Native American features stood out. He nodded toward me. Not far behind him were Ron, Monica, and their daughter. As far as I knew, they weren't aware that I was responsible for their losing their mushroom income. I quickly turned and faced the front of the room. The daughter wouldn't call me out, would she? I relaxed. Even if she recognized me, it didn't mean her parents would connect me with the sheriff. Unless the sheriff made the connection for them.

Miles's parents stood, heads bowed, near their son's

casket. I approached and knelt for a moment on the prayer bench and said a few clumsy words in my mind. They had less to do with Miles finding his way to heaven than with justice finding its way in Rock Point.

When I rose, Miles's mother made eye contact. Her eyes were red and faced lined with grief. "You found him," she said quietly, without accusation.

A potent surge of pain pierced my heart. "Yes," I mouthed. Her gaze was unbearable. I dropped my eyes for a moment but couldn't resist looking up again.

"Sorry," she said, her eyes filling with tears.

"No, I'm sorry. I'm so sorry." Someone behind me nudged me away from the prayer bench, and I moved on.

THE STREETS AROUND THE MORNING GLORY INN WERE bumper to bumper with cars. Annabelle had hung black streamers around the inn's porch. I opened the door to a hall packed with mourners and the low murmur of voices.

Dave had said he'd pass on the reception and go straight to my house, unless I wanted him along. I'd told him he was free to go. Surrounded by strangers, though, some of whom undoubtedly resented my presence, I had a sudden urge to find a friend. *Stella*, I thought. I'll find Stella.

Now that I had a purpose, I plunged into the crowded hall. People made way for me, some doing a double take, and at least one elderly man pointed and whispered to a younger man standing with him. A teenaged girl offered me a cucumber sandwich from a platter. I smiled and shook my head and scanned the crowd for Stella.

Off to the side, Jeanette huddled with a couple of Rock Point's longtime residents. Her plump cheeks jiggled, and her eyes darted through the room as she talked. She'd undoubtedly come away from the reception with plenty of dirt to feed the town's gossip mill.

At last I found Stella. She was standing alone near the buffet table in the dining room where I'd talked with Annabelle the week before. As elegant as ever in her thick gray chignon, simple but stylish black dress, and swipe of nude lipstick, she was a soothing sight next to the almost-Victorian array of sandwiches and petit fours towering on footed platters on the buffet. Despite the crowd milling around her, she was still, her gaze softened toward the window.

"Stella." I put a hand on her arm.

"Oh." I'd interrupted some faraway thoughts. Up close, she looked older than usual. Tired. "Hello, Emmy."

"It's awful for you, isn't it?" I said.

"I thought I'd gotten used to it, the idea that Miles had died. Today . . ." She let the sentence drift off.

"I suppose that's part of the function of a funeral, to bring everything home."

"And force you to deal with it your own way," she said. "I know. Allen's funeral was only a few years ago."

I'd been so lucky, I realized. My parents were healthy, and death wasn't something I'd had to deal with on an up-close-and-personal basis. Except with Miles, of course. "Can I get you something? Maybe some tea or one of the sandwiches? There's one trimmed like a star." It might make a nice kite shape, actually.

Stella smiled. "No, thank you, darling."

Miles's parents huddled together on a loveseat across the room. People approached them, said a few words, then left.

"Have you talked to the Logans?" I asked.

"I gave my respects, of course. But really talk? No. This isn't the right time."

I felt ashamed for mentioning it. It wasn't the right time to complicate things emotionally. "You're right. I don't know what I was thinking."

Now it was her turn to comfort me. "You're a sweet girl, Emmy. You have a good heart, and it shows in your dedication to Avery—and in your caring for me. Thank you." She touched my arm.

"It's nothing. Anyone would do the same."

"I wish that were true, but it's not so. Be careful of that tender heart." Compassion softened her expression, but it couldn't smooth away the sadness. "It's time for me to get home. I need to spend some time alone."

"Are you sure? If you want company—"

"Thank you, but I'm sure. I need some time by myself."

I watched Stella's head weave into the crowd toward the hall. I ached for her. I'd check in on her tomorrow, see how she felt. Maybe she'd like a walk on the beach.

"Why did Stella leave so soon?" Annabelle asked. She'd materialized out of nowhere, an apron over her dress and a tray in hand. She transferred the few smoked-salmon canapés left on a platter to another and cleared the spot for a tray of tiny cupcakes.

"She needed to get home." Then, because I didn't want to talk about it, I said, "Quite a crowd this afternoon. You've put together a wonderful reception."

"It was the least I could do." Her gaze swept the room, taking in the crowd, the half-finished plates, even lifting to the crazy fish-detailed moldings. "Work helps me get through this. It's the one thing I know I do well."

"This can't be easy for you."

"I won't lie. It's not." Only when we looked each other straight in the eyes did I realize I'd usually avoided talking directly to her. She looked softer, more vulnerable than I'd remembered. "I'm not the only one, though. Stella, for instance." She nodded toward the hall through which Stella had just left. What did she know? "Stella worked with him. It's clearly taking a toll on her."

"Yes," I said with relief. Stella's secret was my secret, too.

"And Ron and Monica," she said. I hadn't seen them earlier, but they and their little girl stood in the dining room's doorway.

Shoot. I still felt awful about messing things up for them. "What about them?"

"You may not know, but the sheriff questioned them about Miles's death. I guess they thought Miles was picking on their morel turf, and they made a stink at the Tidal Basin. Now they can't pick at all. Ron's out of work, too. They're broke."

"Oh." As if I didn't know.

"I feel awful for them. Since they were murder suspects, no one will offer him a job. Rock Point is so petty that way. Maybe I'll offer Ron some work taking care of the garden. It's the least I can do."

"Annabelle," I said suddenly. Maybe it was my pain in seeing Stella so upset, or the funeral, or regret over Ron and Monica, but emotion surged. "I'm sorry for your loss. I truly am."

In that moment, I felt we made a real connection. "Thank you," she whispered.

"Annabelle?" a voice from behind her asked. "Do we have any more napkins?"

"Excuse me," she said, and hurried toward the kitchen.

That was it. I'd had enough, felt bad enough. I was going home.

"Hey, little miss," came a familiar voice. Where had I heard it before? I turned to face Ace the plumber. His hair was in a loose ponytail, and he was accompanied by a woman who could have been his double, but for her voluptuous figure. "Meet my old lady, Michelle."

Michelle had constructed a tower of tiny snacks that the builders of the Empire State Building would have admired. She popped a cheese puff into her mouth. "Pleased to meet you," she might have said. Her mouth was too full for clarity.

"I didn't know you knew Miles," I said.

"Sure. Helped him plumb out the kitchen and bathroom at his cabin. Man, that's some crazy stuff he had going down there. Built the whole thing around a trailer. Genius." He looked around, then leaned forward. "I hear you have a special relationship with the deceased, too. Found his body."

"Yes."

"Some people been saying your roommate did it."

"She didn't." Ace's wackiness was getting on my nerves now. To make things worse, Deputy Goff, wearing a dark pantsuit, bumped past me on her way to the buffet table. She curled her lip and didn't even apologize.

"Relax," he said. "Why's that one so rude?" He jerked a thumb toward Goff, who was now jockeying for position with Michelle near the cupcakes.

"Long story," I said. "I raised some questions that revealed she was on the dock the night Miles was killed. As surely you know."

Ace chuckled. "Yeah. The sheriff questioned me about

that, too. Turns out he doesn't exactly have a bead on everything that happens in Rock Point—or in his own office."

"You did see someone besides Goff on the dock, didn't you?"

"What?"

"Someone else. Not just Goff." I knew Avery had been there. "I know you did, Ace. I know it. Whether you told Sheriff Koppen or not."

He raised an eyebrow.

"You saw Avery."

"I don't know any Avery."

"You know, the owner of the Brew House?"

He still looked stumped.

"A blond?"

A smile of understanding spread over his face. "Oh, I saw a blond all right. And that's all I'm saying. Don't worry, I won't blab on your friend."

Before I could ask him what he was talking about, he turned his back and grabbed Michelle by the arm. She tipped her plate into her tote bag, and they headed for the door.

ON THE STREET, I HEARD A GIRL'S VOICE. "I KNOW YOU," she said.

Standing near the rear of the car was the little girl I'd seen at the burnout. Ron and Monica's daughter.

"Come on, Hannah," said the woman I now knew as Monica.

The girl ignored her mother. "What are you doing here?"

"What are *you* doing here?" I countered. Good grief. We were at it again.

Monica approached and took the girl by the arm. "I'm sorry. She needs to know everyone."

"No apologies necessary," I said. Worry lines trimmed Monica's eyes and mouth. "In fact, I was just about to see if she'd like a kite."

Monica stepped back, but Hannah clapped her hands together. "A kite!"

"Yes, I own a kite store in Rock Point. I have an old diamond kite I keep in the trunk, and it occurred to me it was perfect for a little girl."

The girl turned to her mother. "Can I?"

I popped the hatch and pulled out an old red kite I kept for testing the wind. It was worn from years of test flights, and normally I would have been too ashamed of its condition to offer it to a stranger. But instinct—and maybe guilt—convinced me offer it up now.

"No. We can't accept a gift like that," Monica said.

"Honey?" Ron asked from their old Suburu across the lot. His steps crunched on the gravel as he approached.

"I was just saying that I have an old kite in my trunk, and I'd love to give it to your daughter."

"Can I, Dad?" Hannah asked.

"I feel kind of embarrassed offering it really," I said. "It's in such bad shape. But I thought if your daughter needed an extra kite, you know, one for when you don't want to be too careful—"

"We can't accept it, but thank you," Ron said. He drew his daughter close. Looking from mother to father I could see these were decent people down on their luck. Thanks to me, they were really, really down on their luck.

"Oh well. I guess I'll just leave it for the garbage truck." I pulled the kite from the truck and wound its long tail around my hand. "It's in awful shape. Part of the tail is ripped away."

Monica glanced at Ron. He bit his lower lip, then released it. "Well, if you were going to throw it away anyway, we might be able to use it a few times."

"Hurray!" the girl said.

"I'd feel much better about it getting a few final sails in the sky rather than seeing the Dumpster," I said.

Hannah held the kite and smiled so wide I thought her lips would crack. "Can we fly it? Can we take it to the beach?"

"I was just going to the beach myself for a walk. Would you like me to show you how to fly it?"

Monica's expression softened as she watched her daughter. "Oh, Ron, could we?"

"She'll have it in the air in a few minutes," I added. "I'd love to watch. It would be great marketing for Strings Attached, in fact. You'd be doing me a favor."

"Thank you," Ron said.

Hannah skipped to their car, laughing. I wished the kite were so much more than a few hours of entertainment. But if it could be just that, it was still something valuable. Now more than ever I felt the importance of making the most of every day.

chapter twenty-four

"YOU'RE THE ONE WHO FOUND CHEF MILES, AREN'T YOU?" Monica asked, breathing quickly as we stepped down from the boardwalk and trudged across the sand. Hannah had run ahead. "Jeanette at the post office told us."

"Yes," I said. No surprise there. "Up north." I hoped she didn't ask more. Like about their being busted for picking morels without a permit, for example, and about my insistence they might be his murderers. "Did you know him?"

"A bit." She looked up the beach toward her husband and daughter. Hannah was pointing toward a blue stunt kite, the kind Sullivan's Kites sold by the dozen.

"Of course. You wouldn't be at the funeral otherwise."

"We did business with him. Used to sell him mushrooms," she said. "Your roommate, she was . . . ?" The rest of the question, although unspoken, was clear.

"She's innocent." I watched Monica for signs of the blame I'd seen in some other people's eyes.

Her expression was unchanged. "A shame. People are so quick to point fingers. I hope it's all worked out soon, for your friend's sake."

We'd reached Ron and Hannah. The girl jumped up and down at the prospect of flying the kite.

"Ready?" I asked.

"Yes," she said breathlessly.

I remembered my first time flying a kite, here at this very beach, and felt a surge of joy for the girl.

"Okay, here's what you do. First we make sure there aren't any electrical lines or trees the kite can get stuck in." I knew full well we were clear, but it was a good habit for Hannah to get in.

Hannah's eyes widened as she scanned the sky. "Nothing up there."

"Good. Now we get an idea of the wind. Sometimes it feels more still down here, but the wind is really blowing up high. We need wind."

The wind on the beach was almost always strong. Hannah's sandy hair blew in her face, and a flag on the boardwalk thwacked against its pole. "Let me see." She licked her finger and held it up. "Yep. Wind."

"So, it's time to get the kite into the air. It's windy enough down here that the kite will take off the second we let go, so let's make sure the line is reeled up with a few feet of give"—I showed her the full spindle of line—"and that it's centered." I handed the red kite to Hannah but kept one hand on it until we were ready to launch.

"What do we do now?" Her voice had leapt a few notes in pitch.

"You hold the kite up high and let go. Keep a firm grip on your line."

She trembled with excitement, and my heart flooded with warmth. I knew this thrill. She looked to her parents, then to the tattered kite and let it go with a yelp. The wind greedily yanked it above Hannah's head, where it met the end of the line.

Hannah let out a rip of laughter. "Can I make it go higher?"

"Just a few feet at a time. Watch the wind pull it up. If you start to see it dive back and forth, that means it doesn't have enough wind. When that happens, just reel it in a bit."

With a profound smile, Monica watched her daughter grip the spindle in both hands. Ron stood a few feet away, head tilted up, legs a few feet apart. The kite climbed and climbed, its tail whipping.

"Thank you," Monica said.

"My pleasure," I said. It really was. "Did you fly kites as a kid?"

"Not me," Monica said. "Ron did. He grew up around here."

The man nodded, his face wind chapped. "Kites weren't so much my thing. Hiking, boating, hunting. I was more into that."

"You must know the country around here well." I thought of the mushroom patch at the burnout. Not everyone would stumble over it.

"I love it here. We didn't move back under the best of circumstances—"

"The mill closed," Monica added.

"—but one of the blessings was coming home."

The kite had climbed a few hundred feet above the beach, a bobbing speck of red in the sky.

"I hope the blessings keep coming," I said.

chapter twenty-five

I'D GIVEN DAVE A KEY TO THE HOUSE, BUT I DIDN'T WANT to return right away. Instead, I went to Strings Attached and settled in the workshop to stitch up my latest prototype for the comet kite, this one bowl-shaped with a pocket for the wind. The hum of the sewing machine, the careful cutting of the nylon, the searing of the kite's rounded corners—all were meditative to me.

Maybe as I sewed my brain would work free some important detail about Miles's death. The old saying claimed that the murderer always returned to the scene of the crime. Could someone at the funeral have killed him? Every day that passed was another strike against Avery.

My mind shifted gears, and I smiled again at the thought of Hannah's delighted face when her kite took off. I hoped that she would find some of the joy in kites that I'd found as a girl. It was the least I could do. Then a thought occurred to me. Dave said he was down a wilderness guide, and Ron said he loved to hike and knew the area well. Maybe he'd be a good candidate for the job. I'd ask Dave.

I stretched my back. Floorboards creaked as Frank moved in his apartment above me, walking back and forth as if he was taking something to a spot above the shop, then pacing back to get more. Packing, maybe. Half an hour later or so, I saw him pass by the kitchen window on the way to his Land Rover. I waved. He came to the back door with an overnight bag.

"I'm off to Bandon Dunes for some golf. Everything okay down here?"

"Yes. Got a kite design I'm working on. I'll be leaving in a few minutes, though."

"Good, good. It was a nice service today for Miles."

Frank was dressed casually, and his silver hair sat thick around his ears. "It was. You want to come in for a minute?" I asked.

"Just a minute," he said. He glanced around the kitchen-slash-workshop. "I like seeing it so well lived-in down here."

"It's the perfect setup for me," I said. "After the service, well, I wanted to think about something else."

He nodded. "I understand."

"I just don't understand how or who—"

He nodded again. "None of us do."

I looked at him for a moment, remembering that Stella said he'd invested in the Tidal Basin. If anyone would understand restaurant financing, it would be him. Of course, if anyone financed Miles's restaurant, it could well be him, too. I'd have to be cautious. "They say Miles wanted to start his own restaurant."

"I'd heard the same, and after the success of the Tidal Basin, I'm not surprised," Frank said.

"How would that work? I mean, if he wanted to start a restaurant, what would he do?"

Frank pulled out the chair across the table from me and sat. "Well, he'd need a business plan, of course, like you had."

"Oh, I know. But a restaurant is a whole different thing."

"True. A lot would depend on if he wanted to build or renovate a building or if he was simply taking over another space. Why do you ask?"

"I can't help but keep thinking about motive. I mean, Avery can't have killed Miles. It simply isn't possible."

"But, the sheriff—"

"I know she's in jail, but I'm telling you, it isn't possible."

Frank looked at the tabletop, as if its age-old linoleum were more fascinating than the Rosetta stone. "I understand. You know Avery, and you don't want to think she's capable of something like that."

"She's not," I emphasized.

"So naturally you think about motive. And you wonder if Miles wanted his own restaurant, and if maybe that factored into his death."

"Exactly."

His smile was kind. "I'll tell you, but I do want you to have faith in the sheriff. I know Avery is your friend, but you can't solve all the world's problems."

"You would do the same in my place, Frank. You would. At the very least, you'd think about it, wonder."

"Perhaps. Fine. Restaurants are capital intensive, and they're investment risks. A lot of restaurants never make back their initial investments. A lot of investors won't even look at them. But Miles was a different matter."

"He had a good reputation."

"As a chef, he was unparalleled. But not exactly reliable."

I ran a fingernail over a scrap of nylon. "I've heard that."

"If he followed through, though—"

"That's what I thought. The payoff could be substantial. As could the threat. Sam Anderson, for instance. He might really care." I knew Sam had an alibi, but I didn't want Frank to think I was narrowing in on him.

Frank rose and pushed his chair into the table. "He might. He might be threatened. The bigger question is, did Miles really plan his own restaurant?"

"I think he did. At least, he wanted one someday." Avery's stories and the plans I'd seen proved that.

"It's a long shot, but maybe it's a motive." Frank headed to the back door. "In any case, I'm sure Sheriff Koppen is following up on it. He would. Let him do his job."

The sheriff is fair, let him do his job, let justice work itself out, blah-blah-blah. "Have fun golfing," I said.

A moment later, Frank's Land Rover purred to life in the driveway. I was lost in thought. Sam—or someone—might have had a deep interest in Miles's restaurant. I went to my purse and searched its pockets. Yes. I still had the key to Miles's cabin. Tonight I'd get a closer look at the plans.

I SPENT HALF AN HOUR OR SO FINISHING THE LAST SEAM and cleaning up the mess I'd made in the workshop. The comet-kite prototype was finished now, and this time it would fly. I knew it. I tied on its bridle and hoisted it to a hook in the workshop's ceiling where I could admire its wide, cuplike shape and whoosh of streamers for a tail. Maybe it looked a bit more like a jellyfish than a comet at this point, but that could be adjusted when I drew the final pattern.

Then I prepared to leave for Miles's cabin. This time I'd bring a flashlight. I checked for the spare key once again, and it was still there in my purse's side pocket.

I wasn't sure exactly what I hoped to find when I looked at Miles's restaurant plans. If I was lucky, he'd jotted down the name of his financial backers. Or maybe the location of surrounding businesses—if they were noted—would give some sort of clue as to who else had a stake in the project. Of course, maybe the plans were years old and simply inspiration.

Thanks to the dark and the clouds muffling the moonlight, I nearly missed the turnoff to the cabin. Once on the road, I slowed and circumvented potholes, the Prius bumping along. The night air was damp and cool.

From around a corner, a car without its headlights on accelerated toward me. Brakes squealing, I swerved off the road and nearly ended up in the ditch. For a moment, I idled on the shoulder, letting my frantic heart rate calm. Why was the car driving so fast? And why didn't it have on its lights? It all happened so fast that I couldn't even tell the car's make.

The car had been coming from the direction of Miles's cabin. My apprehension deepened. Steeling myself, I pulled back into the road. Dread pressed on my chest.

A minute later, I pulled up in front of the cabin. It looked normal. Its windows were dark, and yellow police tape fluttered over the front door. I got out of the car. Except for an owl hooting, the woods were dead quiet. Might as well get this over with, I thought as I approached the house.

A waft of woodsmoke drifted in the night. Someone must have a campfire burning at Myers Lake. Stella had said the lake was popular with fishermen. I imagined Miles bringing home trout for supper from time to time. I fit the key in the lock, then paused. The smell of smoke was stronger now. Trembling, my hand dropped to my side. The realization came all at once.

The cabin was on fire.

chapter twenty-six

I RAN TO THE CAR AND CALLED 9-1-1. "IT'S A FIRE. ON Myers Road."

The dispatcher took my information, but town was at least fifteen minutes away, even in a racing fire engine. As I watched, the cabin went up like it was made of balsa wood. The flames roared as they consumed the wood frame. The trailer glowed orange at its core. The fire was clearly arson—there's no other way the cabin could be so completely curtained in flames. And it explained the car that had sped past me earlier.

Who had done this? Who had killed Miles and framed Avery for it? And why?

By the time the fire engines arrived, the cabin was lost. Firemen streamed from the truck, carrying a canvas hose. The best they could hope to do was keep the fire from spreading to the woods.

A man knocked on my window. "You the one who called this in?"

Dazed, I nodded and rolled down the window, choking at the smoke. I gave him my name and phone number. He copied down my license-plate number for good measure.

"The fire marshal will be in touch, but for now you'd better leave. We'll be here for the better part of the night."

I pulled out of the driveway, my rearview mirror capturing orange flames and black smoke against the night sky. Whatever the restaurant plans had to reveal, it was now gone for good.

I DON'T KNOW WHAT I FEARED, BUT THE SIGHT OF AVERY'S house—solid, windows cheerily lit—relieved me. I pulled into the driveway next to a car I didn't recognize. My body was drained and shaky after having been amped with adrenaline.

I pushed open the front door. Where was Bear? Normally he'd leap out to greet me. "Dave?"

"In here," came Dave's voice from the living room. He stood at the window with a drill and window locks. Bear was on the couch with his head resting in Jack's lap. Of course. Dave and Jack were friends. It was only natural he'd visit. I just didn't want to deal with him now, especially after he'd refused to help me with Avery and especially in my current state of mind.

Within seconds, Dave set down the drill. "Emmy, what's wrong?"

I let it all out at once. "Someone set Miles's cabin on fire."

"What?" Dave said.

"You're joking," Jack said at the same time.

"I went to the cabin tonight, and when I turned onto Myers Road, a car drove by, fast, without its headlights on. When I got to the cabin, it was on fire. The fire crew is out there now."

"Wow," Dave said. "I can't believe it."

"It was—I can't even start to describe it. I smelled smoke, and then—whoosh!—flames were everywhere. I called 9-1-1, but it took forever for the fire engines to show up."

"I can smell it from your clothes," Dave said. Apparently so could Bear. He had jumped down from the couch and was gingerly sniffing my shoes and sweater. My stomach growled, and I put a hand to my middle.

"What were you doing out there?" Jack asked.

"Hold that thought. I'm starving, and I see you guys brought beer." I brought a bottle from the kitchen and twisted off its top. Jack pulled a slice of pizza from a box on the coffee table and slipped it onto a plate for me. Apparently the house had become a frat in the hours I'd been gone. "At the funeral today it occurred to me that someone might have killed Miles for financial reasons. And Avery had said"—a little white lie couldn't hurt anyone—"that Miles had talked about opening a restaurant. So I had the idea that he might have restaurant plans at his cabin."

"Which the sheriff would have seen," Dave said, still stunned. He'd abandoned his window-lock project altogether and sat next to Jack on the couch. "I still can't believe someone burned his place down."

"Maybe the sheriff saw them," I said. "Unless, for instance, Miles hid the plans, or the sheriff didn't know what to look for."

"Why not talk to Sheriff Koppen about it?" Jack said.

"Every time I talk to him or his deputy, they shrug me off. Besides, I wasn't sure if I even had enough real information to go off. I thought maybe the restaurant plans might give some sort of clue."

"Bad idea," Dave said. "You just don't go breaking into people's houses to look for something you don't even know is there."

I looked from Dave to Jack, both of whom stared at me. Even Bear raised his head in my direction.

"I know he had plans. I saw them," I finally said. "And I have a key to his place."

"What?" Dave said. Jack shook his head, and Bear leapt down from the couch to lay at my feet.

"I found the key." I explained about my visit with Stella the week before. "It wasn't like I crawled through a window or anything."

"It's still breaking in," Dave said. "You saw the police tape, right?"

"I'm not sure that kind of evidence would be admissible in court, either," Jack added.

"Well, what would you do?" I pushed my uneaten slice of pizza back into the box. My appetite was gone. "Leave Avery in jail while someone lines up all the pieces to frame her for good?" Take that, Jack Sullivan. Then, to Dave, "How do you know about the police tape, anyway?"

"It stands to reason," he said.

"And you," I said to Jack. I thought he didn't care about Avery. "Why are you here now?"

"He's helping with the locks," Dave said. "The frames on these windows are almost rotted out. Even with the locks, they won't be supersecure."

"That's not what I mean," I said.

Dave set down the drill again and returned to the couch.

Jack explained. "The other night Emmy asked me to help find who killed Miles. I'd heard from a couple of people that Avery was down at the docks the night Miles was killed, and I just couldn't get past that." He focused on Bear. "After talking with Dave, I know I was wrong. Obviously, it was all a mistake. And now, with the fire—it couldn't have been Avery."

"Because she's in jail," Dave said.

Embarrassment made me look away. Jack hadn't been wrong about Avery being at the dock, just wrong about what it meant. I couldn't tell him about her meeting with Miles now. Not with Dave listening.

Dave looked from Jack to me. "You guys talk? I thought you'd only just met."

"Um, sure," I said at the same time Jack mumbled "Uh-huh." I'm not sure which of us was more embarrassed.

"There's a jar of something weird on the water heater," Dave said, steering us away from the awkward moment.

My mom's kombucha. "It's a fermented beverage my mom is making for me."

"There's something floating in it. I think it's gone bad."

"It's supposed to be there. Don't worry about it—it tastes better than it smells."

"Maybe there's another way to get information about Miles's plans," Jack said. "You're right—I know he had them. He talked about the restaurant he wanted to start, about how he'd take some of the ideas he introduced at the Tidal Basin and really run with them."

"If he was going to start a new restaurant, he'd need capital," Dave said.

These guys were frustrating. "I know. That's what I

said. That's why I wanted to see the plans, see if I could figure out who else might be involved."

"I still can't believe someone burned down Miles's cabin," Jack said, fixing me with those disturbingly velvet eyes.

"I was nearly run off the road. It had to be arson."

"Did you get the car's make?" Dave asked.

"No. Too dark, and I was caught too off guard. I couldn't even tell you if it was a car or a truck."

"You left your name with the emergency dispatcher, right?" Dave said. "If so, we can expect a visit from the sheriff."

"I know." The day was starting to get to me. I hadn't gotten much sleep the night before, and that exhaustion had been chased with a funeral and arson. And the day wasn't even over. Once the sheriff arrived, undoubtedly with Deputy Goff, my biggest fan, it would get worse.

"One thing must be true, though," Jack said. "No one would go to the trouble of burning down the cabin if there wasn't something incriminating in there."

"It has to be about the restaurant," I said. "Has to be. Now we'll never know."

Jack shifted in his seat. "I know a little about it. Miles wanted to open a family-style place like they used to have at the old logging camps, where everyone shares a table and chooses from a few things he'd prepare each night, depending on what was in season and what seafood he could get."

I could imagine a place like that. It was an original idea, homey. And the food would be several steps above what any logging camp would serve, of that I was sure. "Do you know when he planned to open it, or where it would be?"

"Nope. I really don't," Jack said. "He talked about it like it was a sure thing, but I never heard anything concrete."

"What about financial backers?" I asked. "Did he mention anyone?"

"No one."

Dave and Jack sat without talking, each holding a beer bottle. Behind Dave, Avery's usual vase of flowers was gone—shattered during the break-in—and days of mail was spread over the table by the front door. I needed to get the place back to Avery's standards. Tomorrow. Tonight I had to get some sleep. Tomorrow I'd have to deal with the fire marshal, the sheriff, and heaven knew what else.

"Oh well. You guys, I'm beat. Stay up as long as you'd like, but I've got to get to bed. Could you let Bear out before you turn in for the night?"

"Wait," Dave said. "I have something to show you." He pulled a duffel bag from behind the couch and withdrew a paper roll from its depths. I immediately recognized it as Miles's restaurant plans.

I hopped to the edge of my seat. "That's them. The plans."

"You had them all along?" Jack said. "How—I mean, what—"

"Why didn't you say something earlier?" I barged in.

"You don't need any excuses to get in trouble." Dave looked to Jack, then me. "Neither of you do."

"How did you get them?" Jack asked.

"When I was at the service today, I was thinking about the murder, too. I couldn't stop thinking about how unfair it was that Miles died and Avery was set up to take the blame. So I drove out to the cabin straight from the funeral."

Dave. That sly dog. "I can't believe it." Avery had better

wake up to Dave soon. He might be quiet, but that old trope about still waters running deep could have been written about him. "How did you get in? When I left, I locked up behind me."

"Not a big deal." Dave pulled back the plans. "The plans go straight to the sheriff tomorrow morning."

"Unless he shows up here tonight," Jack pointed out.

"Well, it doesn't do us any harm to look at them now, right?" I said. "I mean, they already have your fingerprints on them." Mine, too, I thought.

Dave hesitated. Jack said, "Emmy's right. Looking won't hurt."

"All right, I guess." We cleared the pizza box from the coffee table, and Dave unfurled the plans, holding them down at opposite corners.

"This doesn't look like the whole thing," Jack said.

"You're right," I said. They were the plans I'd seen in Miles's cabin. They focused on the restaurant portion of what looked to be a larger complex. They showed an open kitchen, similar to that of the Tidal Basin, with a large fireplace in the dining room. I imagined rough-hewn walls, a wood floor, and river rock surrounding the hearth. It would have been a fabulous place.

"I can't tell where it was supposed to be," Jack said. "In Rock Point?"

"Nehalem Resort. Hopkins Management," Dave read from faded blue letters in the corner.

"Frank. That's his company." I let that sink in. He had certainly talked about building a resort, and he was one of the town's biggest boosters. The hairs on the back of my neck prickled. Miles's cabin had burned down right after I'd discussed him with Frank. "Frank was the financial backer."

Jack seemed to read my mind. "What if Frank lent Miles money, then Miles frittered it away?"

"Miles did take that culinary tour of Asia last summer," Dave said. "I liked the guy a lot, but he wasn't a solid planner."

Unlike Dave, I added silently. "Would that be a reason to kill someone? Sue him, sure, but murder?"

"Maybe it was a crime of passion. Frank got angry, and boom," Jack said.

"But framing Avery." I shook my head. "Someone thought it all out."

"Why frame Avery at all?" Dave said. "I don't get that part. Sure, a murderer might want to frame someone, but Avery?"

"There must be more to the story," I said. "We're not understanding something." Frank couldn't be a murderer. He was a nice man. Conventional. Not a killer. "I keep going back to Sam Anderson, but he has an alibi for the night." I told them about him and Deputy Goff. Dave seemed unimpressed, but Jack had me repeat the story twice, especially the "cup of Goffee" part.

Finally, he set down his beer bottle. "It wasn't public knowledge, but Sam was ready to fire Miles. He told him so just a few days before Miles died, and Miles told me. Miles was too unreliable, Sam said. He probably suspected Miles was planning on starting something up of his own. But I don't see him killing Miles, planned or otherwise."

Sam had told me as much. Deputy Goff would give him an alibi for the night of the murder, anyway. So it was back to Frank. But why? "I wish I could just ask Frank, but he's in Bandon Dunes now. Golfing. But before he left . . ."

"Before he left, what?" Jack said.

"Before he left I asked Frank about Miles and what it would take to open a new restaurant. He didn't say anything about backing Miles."

"So, either he was lying—" Dave started.

"Or . . ." Jack let the sentence hang. "The fire."

"First thing tomorrow," Dave said. "First thing, you're going to see the sheriff."

chapter twenty-seven

I'D NEVER BEFORE NOTICED HOW LOUD MY BEDSIDE CLOCK was. In my quiet bedroom, the second hand's tick as it crept around the dial was torture.

Jack had left a few hours ago, and Dave and I had turned in not long after. It had to be past midnight now. I had decided what I had to do. It was risky, but I had no alternative. I just needed to make sure Dave was sound asleep first. I'd thought about enlisting Stella in my plan, but remembering her grief at Miles's funeral, I didn't have the heart to call her. Moving as quietly as I could, I slipped from bed, already dressed in jeans and a black sweater. I tossed a black hoodie over my arm.

I tiptoed to my bedroom door and cracked it open. Out of some sort of honor, Dave had refused to sleep in Avery's room and was stretched out on the living room couch—probably not comfortably so, either. Sneaking past him wouldn't be easy. Luck was with me, and Dave's breathing was steady and slow. Asleep. Bear lifted his head, jingling his collar. Damn. I hadn't thought to remove it, and I froze, holding my breath. Bear laid his head down again, although his eyes still followed my movements. Dave slept on.

Still holding my breath, I crept out down the hall, through the living room, and past Dave. He didn't move. A sliver of moonlight through the curtains outlined his shape. Now into the kitchen and out the back door. Quietly. The new bolt Dave had installed stuck for a moment, and I held my breath as I eased it open. At last, it gave.

Outside, crisp night air filled my lungs. I walked as lightly as I could over the driveway's gravel and pulled my bicycle from the side of the house. The car would definitely awaken Dave.

Once I'd walked my bike from the gravel driveway to the asphalt road, I hopped astride, clicked on my lights, and pedaled toward town. The night was colder than I'd thought, and I shivered in my sweater and hoodie. It was unusually clear, and the moon cast shadows through the fir trees. So far, no traffic, but that wasn't unusual out here, certainly not at this time of night. When I got closer to town, I saw a few houses with lights still on and televisions flickering. The Tidal Basin's parking lot was just about empty—again, not unusual for midnight.

At last I arrived at Strings Attached. I carried my bicycle up the stairs and leaned it against the railing, where it couldn't be seen from the street. Although I could have come up with a legitimate excuse to be in my own store and workshop, I saw no need to raise suspicions. I entered the store and locked the door behind me. I padded to the workshop and turned on the tiny light above the stove.

My plan was to break into Frank's apartment using the old stairway that once connected the floors. My side of the door was simply latched shut. I undid that easily. I was less sure of what was on Frank's side. The door was an old three-paneled Victorian, probably original to the house. And like everything else in the house, it wasn't square. I shone my flashlight where the door met the frame. The crack was wide enough that I could tell Frank also had a latch on his side of the door.

I took a thin spar from my workbench and slipped it into the crack. It was a tight fit, but by sawing it gently I edged it up toward the latch and lifted. It flipped up on the first try. Man, this was turning out to be a cinch.

Carefully I pulled the door toward me and padded up the stairs. Frank had used the stairwell as a storage area, and I dodged a pair of skis and two boxes of papers before I got to the top. I'd only been up here once, to sign my lease. I remembered the trappings of a vacation bachelor pad: a nice recliner, television set, a king-sized bed through a doorway.

I'd made it in, a regular Pink Panther. Now to see if I could find where Frank kept his business files. If he had a deal with Miles, he'd have a record of it somewhere.

A scraping sound—a window opening?—yanked my pulse into overdrive. I retreated to the stairwell and crouched, my heart pounding in my ears. For a moment, then two, I heard nothing. I let out my breath and stood. Once again—but this time even more cautiously, if possible—I mounted the steps.

And came face-to-face with a man.

chapter twenty-eight

"JACK! WHAT ARE YOU DOING HERE?" I SAID.

"Shhh. Not so loud. I could ask you the same question."

He stepped back, and I climbed from the stairwell. "You know why I'm here. The same reason you are."

"You came up the connecting stairs."

"Yes." Standing so close to Jack in the dark had its appeal. Too bad I couldn't enjoy it more. "How did you get in?"

"The door. It was an easy lock to pick."

We stood, silent, for a moment. "Did you have a particular plan?" I asked.

"No. I thought I'd look around, see if I could find a contract or something showing that Miles and Frank were in business together." From the streetlight through Frank's kitchen window, I saw Jack's jaw clench.

"Same here," I said. "Well, I guess we'd better get busy."

I glanced through the small apartment. On the ocean-facing side of the apartment was a living room with a small table near the kitchen for dining. The stairwell emerged in the middle of the apartment, next to the kitchen.

"There are a couple of boxes on the stairwell. Let's go through those first," I said.

The wooden stairs creaked as we descended. I sneezed at the dust. Frank hadn't swept down here in a while. Hopefully we wouldn't leave too obvious a trail.

"Gesundheit," Jack said. He lifted the lid of one of the Bankers Boxes and trained his penlight on its contents. "Files. They're all labeled."

"At least he was tidier about records than his housekeeping." I blew a dust bunny from another box and tipped its lid aside. I pulled out one fat file and flipped through its contents. I pulled another and did the same. "Looks like he owns a miniature golf course in California. All these files are from California."

"These, too," Jack said, and replaced the box's lid. "Plus, they're at least two years old. He must keep more-recent files somewhere else. Let's try upstairs."

He lifted his penlight and led the way toward the back. As I'd hoped, a closed door led to a small bedroom with a computer desk, chair, and filing cabinet. Frank's office. "If you take the desk, I'll check out the filing cabinet," Jack said.

"All right." I twisted the blinds closed and turned on my own flashlight. On the desk was a computer mouse, but no computer. Frank must have taken the laptop with him. A dirty coffee cup and a mouse pad sat to its right. On the left were a few still-sealed envelopes—the power bill, the water bill. Underneath was my rent check. I'd wondered when he was going to deposit it. Frank must not be hurting for money. That was one point in his favor, anyway. If he'd killed Miles, it hadn't been for the cash.

"Finding anything?" Jack whispered. A drawer of files stretched in front of him.

"Not much." On a Post-it, Frank had scrawled a phone number. A boarding pass for a past trip to Palm Springs lay next to it. Nothing obviously connected to Miles or to a restaurant.

"Wait. Jackpot." Jack pulled a file from the drawer with Miles's name written in blue pen. He opened it on the desk, his hand brushing mine. "Look."

"A promissory note," I said.

Jack tapped the top of the page. "Dated almost a year ago. A hundred thousand dollars." He looked at me. "So Miles did owe Frank money."

I shook my head. "Okay, so Miles was in debt to Frank. Why would Frank kill him for it? Sure, that's a lot of money, but Frank is doing all right. His car probably cost almost that. Besides, with Miles dead, there'd be no way to repay him."

Jack replaced the promissory note but hesitated over the folder. At last he slipped it back into the drawer. "You're right."

"Nothing else in there?"

"No." Jack glanced around the room, his penlight illuminating a trail across Frank's pictureless walls, over the desk, to the closet. "I'm feeling creepy about being here. Maybe we should leave."

"There's got to be something else. Some other reason. Let's just spend another five minutes."

"I don't know. Miles owed Frank money. What else could there be?"

"Just a couple more minutes," I said.

"All right. But that's it." Jack glanced back at the door.

"Relax. Frank is out of town, golfing. We're fine." I opened the closet door and ruffled through an overcoat and two puffy jackets.

"Just coats," Jack said, clearly still nervous.

"There's more." Pinned to the wall by a long tweed coat was a portfolio standing on its end. It nearly reached to my waist. "Check it out." I pulled it from the closet.

"What is it?"

"A portfolio. Artists and architects use them for storing sketches and things like that." My gut tingled. This was it. I was sure. "If Frank has a copy of the restaurant plans, they'd be in here." I laid the portfolio on the carpet and unzipped it flat to reveal sheets of architectural sketches. *Yes.* But it was much more than plans for a restaurant. A plan for a mess of buildings and parking lots unfolded.

"It seems to be part of a whole complex." Jack knelt next to me and pointed to a building facing west, toward the ocean. "Here's Miles's restaurant."

"A resort," I said. The architect had sketched in fake trees and indicated a few landmarks in the landscape. "Isn't that Perkins Road?" I tapped a road on the east side of the complex. "And the lighthouse is up here." If the lighthouse and Perkins Road bordered it . . . "Oh, Jack." I stared at him. "It's set on Avery's land. The whole complex." I clenched my fists to stop my trembling hands.

He pulled the plans closer, then let them drop to the carpet. "You're right."

"It's red-hot evidence against him," I added. Frank had planned a resort on Avery's land, a complex including Miles's new restaurant. Avery was framed for Miles's murder. Her legal expenses could easily swallow the value of her house. We let the facts settle for a moment.

"Let's put this away and get out of here," Jack said. "We'll tell the sheriff in the morning. He can follow up there."

I agreed. We slipped the plans into the portfolio and edged it back into the closet.

"Come on, let's go," Jack repeated.

I froze. "Look." In the depths of the closet, just beyond the portfolio, was a golf caddy. Full of clubs, Frank's golf clubs. The realization hit me full in the chest. Frank wasn't in Bandon Dunes at all.

As if on cue, a key turned the front door's deadbolt.

JACK WAS AT THE WINDOW IN TWO STEPS. HE OPENED the blinds and looked down. I knew it was hopeless. We were on the second floor of a tall building. Even if we could get out the window in time, we'd break something vital on the fall down. Our only hope was to stay quiet until Frank went to bed. We could sneak out then. Jack seemed to have the same idea, because he pulled me into the corner, behind the door.

Voices came from the living room, Frank's and a woman's. I knew Frank could be a bit of a flirt, but at this time of the night? It had to be two in the morning. From his sharp inhale, I could tell Jack recognized the woman's voice seconds before I did. Annabelle.

The floorboards creaked as someone came down the hall. I held my breath. Let it be for the bathroom, I prayed.

"Make yourself a drink," Frank said.

"Do you have any wine?" Annabelle's voice came from the living room.

"Check the refrigerator. Wineglasses are in the cupboard above the sink."

My heart thumped so loud I could barely hear. Frank did this. Frank orchestrated the whole thing. He'd planned a resort on Avery's land, killed Miles, then framed Avery for the murder. Miles didn't mean anything to him anymore since he wouldn't repay his debt. With Avery in jail and on track to sell everything for legal fees, he'd be able to buy her land. He was willing to murder for the resort. For the first time, terror replaced anger. Frank was willing to murder, and Jack and I were hiding in his apartment. I glanced up at Jack, but it was too dark to read his expression.

Then I saw the office door. Shoot. It was open. It had been shut when we came in. "I can't believe you forgot our date," Annabelle said from the other room. "Good thing you called." Frank's voice was unnervingly close.

The steps in the hall hesitated, and all at once the office was flooded with light.

"I didn't—" Frank's voice said. He whirled around and saw us, his face tightening from surprise to anger. "What are you doing here?"

"Frank?" Annabelle asked from the living room. "What is it?"

Frank ignored her, his focus trained on us. "You broke in. You thought I was away and decided to break in. What do you want? Money? Maybe something to blackmail me with?"

Annabelle appeared in the doorway, clearly dressed for a night out, and not even prairie-style. "Jack? And Emmy?"

"I'm calling the sheriff." Frank reached into his pocket for his phone.

"No, Frank," Annabelle said. "They must have a reason for being here. Let's hear it."

I was too flummoxed to speak.

"We can explain," Jack said. I looked up at him. This should be good. I stepped back, and my head hit the closet's door frame. The portfolio toppled sideways.

Frank shook his head. "What's to explain? They broke in. They were probably planning on stealing something or getting into things that aren't any of their business."

"Frank." Annabelle's voice was soft, calming. "I've known Jack a long time"—she gave him a meaningful look—"and Emmy seems reasonable. They must have a good reason for being here."

My power of speech was coming back, and it was coming back angry. "Go ahead and call the sheriff. Go ahead. I'd love to tell him about your plans for Avery's land and how you framed her for Miles's murder to get it, not to mention the fact that you burned down his cabin this afternoon."

Jack shot me a warning look.

"What? You're insane. You've been going through my files. I should have known it. I should have—"

Annabelle raised her hands palms out. "Listen. Let's go to the living room and sit down. We'll start from the beginning and talk it out. See what's really going on here. I have a feeling there are a few misunderstandings at the heart of this. Frank murder Miles? No way."

For a moment, no one spoke. Jack broke the silence. "Annabelle's right. Let's sit down and start at the beginning."

Hesitantly, Frank followed Annabelle to the living room. Fear and surprise and anger—and the late hour and lack of dinner—had left me shaky. Frank and Annabelle took the couch while Jack and I sat in armchairs facing it.

"All right," Annabelle said. "Emmy, you start. Why did you and Jack break in?"

I glanced at Jack. I didn't want to speak for him. "Avery has been framed for killing Miles. I know she didn't do it. I wanted to find out who did."

"What does that have to do with me?" Frank's voice picked up volume.

"Just listen, Frank," Annabelle said.

Frank was too smart to try anything dangerous with Annabelle and Jack here. That thought gave me courage. "I knew—it was common knowledge," I corrected myself, "that Miles wanted his own restaurant. Word is that you lent him money for it. It occurred to me that Miles might have spent the money and not been able to pay it back."

"You're right. He did. So?"

"Frank's right, Emmy," Annabelle said. "Why kill someone who owes you money? Doesn't seem like a smart way to get repaid."

"I know. That's what I thought, too. But there had to be something more going on. That's why I came here. Maybe the restaurant deal was more complicated than I'd thought."

"And you?" Annabelle looked at Jack. "You came with her?"

"Sort of," Jack said. "For the same reasons, basically."

"The thing is, I was right," I said. "You planned to build a resort on Avery's land. It would probably have made you a millionaire several times over. It's awfully convenient that Avery's in jail. Maybe you figured that once it went to trial, legal fees would make her sell the house. Or worse." Worse being a life in prison. Bile rose in my throat. "That would be a reason to kill someone, wouldn't it?"

"Whoa. Careful there," Annabelle said. Good grief. She could lead group therapy sessions. "What I hear you saying is that you feared Frank killed Miles and pinned it on Avery for financial motives. Am I right?"

Now the good-little-Annabelle attitude was getting on my nerves. I wished she'd shut up so I could call the sheriff myself. "That's what I said."

"Frank?" She turned toward him on the couch.

"I'm not a murderer."

"I know that. But these are serious accusations. Maybe you can cast some light on the situation."

He fidgeted with his hands and looked toward the TV remote on the coffee table as if it were an oracle. "Emmy, you're right. To some extent. But I never killed Miles, and I would never frame Avery for his death."

I relaxed an iota. I was on the right track. How he was going to talk his way out of this, I didn't know, but I had witnesses to at least part of the confession.

"I did want Avery's land for a resort. It would have been perfect—location, geography, all of it. The house is falling down, anyway. Avery would have had money to buy a much nicer place somewhere else. And I did lend Miles money for a restaurant as part of the complex, and he wasn't able to make his payments."

"And?" Annabelle prompted.

"And—and I'm not proud of it, but I told Miles I'd forgive his debt if he convinced Avery to sell me her land."

"And that's why they started dating," Annabelle said, not without satisfaction.

Avery did tell me that Miles came to see her out of the blue. She hadn't expected he'd be interested in her. But they dated. And then he disappeared. I began to understand.

"He couldn't do it, could he?" I said. "He cared about her and couldn't convince her to sell her land when he knew it was so important to her."

Frank stared at the table. "That's what he said."

Miles had broken up with Avery in a fit of conscience. He hadn't lost interest in her at all. Poor Avery. If only she'd known. She'd been so hurt.

"That sounds like Miles," Jack said. "He did his own thing, but he had a moral code. Maybe not the societal standard, but a code of his own."

I shook my head. "I'm not convinced. Besides, why didn't you tell Sheriff Koppen about this? You have a lot stronger motive than Avery does for killing Miles. Avery might not even be in jail if you came clean." My throat was tight, and my words choked out. "Plus, what about Miles's cabin?"

"What about it?" Frank said.

"Someone burnt it down today. Someone wanted to hide something."

"You mentioned that," he murmered. "Strange." He shook his head as if cleaning an unwanted thought. "I told you," Frank said, "I'm not proud of what I did, all right? But I'm no murderer, and I don't go around burning down houses."

"Words. Just words. Go tell them to Sheriff Koppen."

A storm of anger gathered in Frank's expression. His voice was steely cold. "As it happens, the sheriff did want to know where I was the night Miles was killed."

"And where was that?" I said.

Frank rose, and I lurched back in my chair. Jack grabbed my shoulder. Frank pushed past me and went down the hall, returning a few seconds later. He tossed a piece of paper on the coffee table. It was the boarding pass I'd seen earlier. "I was in Palm Springs," he said.

chapter twenty-nine

"I CAN'T BELIEVE IT," I SAID. "I'M SUCH AN IDIOT."

After Frank had kicked us out of his apartment with the warning that he might still turn us in to the sheriff, Jack and I slumped to my workshop below. We could only hope that Annabelle's cooler head was prevailing upstairs. We sat at the little kitchen table in the dark with only the light burning over the stove.

"A real idiot," I repeated.

"That makes two of us," Jack said.

"You had the sense to keep your mouth shut. You weren't accusing him of being a money-hungry murderer."

"The money-hungry part is right, at least. He even copped to that."

"Poor Avery. I really wanted to help her, but every time I think I'm close to finding who really killed Miles, it falls apart. In this case, explodes." My chest felt heavy.

"I know. I want to find who killed Miles, too. It's not over yet."

I looked around the dim workshop, at the broad-topped worktable placed to take advantage of the afternoon sun, the windows I'd had yet to sew curtains for, the teapot and mugs resting on the stove. My dream. I'd worked so hard to pull it all together. "It looks like Sullivan's Kites will be the only kite shop in town soon."

"What's with the melodrama?" Jack said.

"How long do you think it will take me to pack up and move back to Portland?"

He leaned back. "I didn't take you for a quitter. I thought you were determined to get Avery out of jail, not to mention make a success out of Strings Attached."

"I am. It's just . . ." What could I say? "I've met with dead ends everywhere I've turned. I can't even tell you *why* Miles was killed, let alone who did it."

"You've tried."

"And left a trail of disasters. First I thought Miles was killed because he was gathering morels on someone else's territory. It turned out that the mushroom hunters couldn't have done it."

"How did that lead to disaster?"

I winced at the memory. "The morels were the family's best source of income. They have a little girl to support, too. Now that the sheriff has questioned them and word is out, no one will hire them."

"But they still have the morels," Jack said.

"Nope. They were gathering without a permit. I got them busted." My pity party's DJ was just getting started on the violin music. "And then there was Sam Anderson."

"Oh yeah. The 'sweet cup of Goffee.'" He chuckled.

"I was so sure he'd done it. Instead, when Miles was killed he had a solid alibi—with the deputy sheriff, even." I looked up at him. "She hates me, too, by the way."

"That's a tough one."

"And now I've blown it with Frank. My own landlord." I raised my eyes toward the ceiling and lowered my voice. "Do you really think he's going to want me around after I accused him of killing a man and dumping his body in the ocean?"

Jack grabbed one of my fidgeting hands and clasped it in his larger, warmer ones. "Listen. Things will look different in the morning."

"It *is* the morning," I said. At least, I think that's what I said. My heart's rat-a-tat from the warmth of Jack's fingers interfered with my brain function.

"You know what I mean. I have faith in you. And I'll help. You can count on me." He held my hand a moment longer, then placed it on the table and let go. I wanted to grab it again. Or, better yet, find a seat in his lap. I might have stared at him a bit too intensely, because he leaned forward and started to say something, then stopped.

"What?" I said.

"Nothing. I'll call you tomorrow."

"It *is* tomorrow," I repeated.

"You know what I mean. Get some sleep." His voice was low, seductive.

And with that, he was gone.

AFTER JACK LEFT, I SAT IN THE KITCHEN IN SILENCE. WHAT a debacle. Despite Jack's calming words and even more calming presence, I was mortified. There was no way

Frank could have killed Miles. He'd proven conclusively that he wasn't even in Rock Point. Worse, Sheriff Koppen knew it, too. If it weren't for Annabelle, I'd probably be locked up next to Avery right about now.

A knock at my back door got my attention. For a second my heart leapt as I thought it might be Jack again, but it was Annabelle, her long blond hair backlit like a halo from the outside light.

"I thought I'd see how you're doing," she said.

"Humiliated, but fine. Thank you for smoothing everything over up there." Why she was being so nice to me, I didn't know, but I was grateful. "I overreacted. I shouldn't have gone into his apartment. I was just so upset about Avery. I couldn't—"

"Emmy, stop. I—"

"I just can't believe what I did. It's awful. I should have—"

"Hush!" Annabelle didn't shout, but her voice cut like sharpened steel. She had my full attention. "I'm not so sure Frank's innocent."

What? I'm not sure my jaw dropped in real life, but it did metaphorically for sure. "But upstairs—"

"I know, I know. I wanted to calm him down, get him to think we didn't suspect him." Annabelle placed a hand on the chair Jack had left. "Do you mind if I sit?"

I snapped out of the shock left by her words. "Please. I was just about to make some tea. Would you like a cup?" I was exhausted, but my nerves were jangled, and half an hour with a warm mug in my hands might help.

"Please."

I busied myself with the electric teakettle. "Frank showed us his ticket stub to Palm Springs for the same night Miles died. What makes you think he might have done it?"

"Boarding passes can be faked. Easily. I mean, look at the facts. Frank wanted that land. He admitted to being willing to excuse a huge debt to get it. If he'd essentially pay a hundred thousand dollars for the chance to buy land, why wouldn't he be willing to stab someone with a filet knife to get it?"

For a huge reason, I thought. Greed is one thing, but murder is another one entirely. Then I heard Annabelle's words in my mind again. *With a filet knife.* The sheriff hadn't let out that information. Neither had I. My blood ran cold.

"How did you know it was a filet knife?" I asked.

She paused, then smiled brightly. "Well, it wouldn't be a butcher knife, would it?"

She was lying to me, I knew it. I forced a smile, but dread bubbled up in my chest. "Good point," I said. "Are you sure about Frank? I thought maybe—" I lifted my eyes toward the apartment above.

"Oh no," she said quickly. "Frank's just a mentor. We'd been out to dinner, and he wanted to show me something, that's all."

The filet knife had come from a restaurant-supply store. Avery confirmed it, and the sheriff had added it to his reasons for her guilt since she owned a coffee shop. Annabelle owned a teahouse. She would have had access to a knife like that. Ace said he saw "a blond" on the dock. Annabelle was blond. She was always talking about Rock Point's future, too. She might not have Frank's money, but her ambition doubled his.

I clenched my hand to stop its tremble. *Play along, Emmy. Play along.* "What should we do about him?" I asked.

"I need to think it over. There's a lot to consider here."

"Not really," I said without thinking.

Annabelle looked alert. "What do you mean?"

The kettle automatically clicked off. The tea water was ready. "What kind of tea would you like?" I ignored her and turned to the tea cabinet, where my fingers touched a few canisters before resting on the Lapsang souchong canister. Yes. It wouldn't hurt her badly, but it would slow her down. "How about this one?"

"Okay." Annabelle stared at me. "You didn't answer me."

"I mean, Avery's in jail. She needs to come home. Why not just go to the sheriff?" Yes, the sheriff. Right now I'd even take Deputy Goff.

"A few more nights won't hurt her."

Anger surged through my body. I spooned an extralarge helping of my mother's Lassitude Tea into the tea ball and rested it in a large mug. I fixed myself some chamomile and poured hot water into each mug. Rock Point was dead quiet tonight. Frank was upstairs, but I doubted he'd hear me through the old ceiling. Unless I yelled. Loud.

Annabelle was silent.

"Here's your tea." I pushed the mug across the table to Annabelle.

"You drink it."

I stared at her. Had I given myself away? "Oh, I already have my—"

"I said, you drink it. That's not Lapsang souchong. I run a tearoom, remember?"

Damn it. Lapsang souchong was so distinctive, too, with its smoky scent. I managed a chuckle. "I reuse these all the time. I must have put something different in it."

"Drink it."

"Why? It's just—"

She jolted to her feet and grabbed my sewing shears from the worktable. In a defensive stance, she pointed them at me. My lungs seized with fear. "Drink it."

I lifted the tea to my lips and drank, choking at its heat. "See. It's just tea." When she didn't respond, I bit my lip, then said, "Why did you do it?"

Expressionless, she looked at me a moment, then broke into nervous laughter. "Finally figured it out, did you?" The shears glinted under the kitchen light. "You should have left it alone."

My gaze swept the workshop. Fear gripped my insides, and my lungs tightened. The backup scissors were in a drawer by the sewing machine, but that was on the other side of Annabelle, as were the fabric weights and razors I used for cutting patterns.

"Look at me," Annabelle said. "I warned you to leave things the way they were, but you didn't listen."

"You were the one who broke into our house, weren't you?"

"I tried to warn you," she repeated. "It would have been best for both of us if you would have left things alone."

"I don't understand. I thought you cared about Miles." I remembered her dry-eyed sobbing at Jack's store the morning I met her.

"Of course I did. But it wasn't meant to be." Her tone was devoid of expression.

"So you murdered him?"

She let out a long breath as if I were too dense to understand. "I didn't plan anything. It just worked out that way."

"What do you mean?" In the window behind Annabelle, something moved. A face. I forced my gaze back to

Annabelle. My brain hummed double time, but a velvety wave of drowsiness lapped at my limbs. That stupid tea.

"I knew Miles had planned a restaurant as part of Frank's new resort. I'll have a part of the resort, too—a teahouse with a beautiful view of the ocean." Her face took on a dreamy look. "I'll have a special sunset tea service."

The thought of Avery's sunset view profiting Annabelle gorged my throat with bile. I glanced again at the window. No face. I must have imagined it.

"What happened?" I asked, willing my eyes to stay open.

Annabelle snapped to. "I was coming out of the Tidal Basin that night, and I saw Miles headed toward the old dock. He left like he had a date, even singing a stupid little song. It was late, and he shouldn't—"

Shouldn't have been meeting anyone but you, I finished silently. "You followed him to Avery's boat."

She nodded. The hand holding the scissors dipped. She saw me watching her hand and lifted them again. "He knew where the key to Avery's boat was kept, went into the galley. He was making her a dinner." She spit out the words. "I couldn't believe it."

While Dave and I sat by the bonfire that night, all this was happening. It wasn't enough to kill him, though. Was it? "Did he see you?"

"Yes." I thought she was finished talking, but as I forced my sleepy mouth open to reply, to keep the conversation going, she continued. "Maybe I lost my temper, but it wasn't about that. It wasn't about our relationship." She looked at me to make sure I understood. I nodded slightly. "He was ruining everything. He was going to tell Avery about Frank and my plans—I knew it."

The face appeared again. Jack. He'd come back. A queer combination of exhaustion and adrenaline had taken possession of my body. Anything could happen now. Anything at all.

"Oh no," I said. If Miles had told Avery, it might have been Avery she would have killed.

"I had to do it," she said. "And I'm going to have to kill you, too. I'm sorry, but I have no choice. That's just the way it is. Sometimes life gives you hard choices."

"No," I mumbled, my brain shorting out with energy, but my limbs heavy. Was Jack just going to stand there? Now he'd disappeared again. He wouldn't be able to see Annabelle's knife from where he stood. Maybe he thought he'd better leave since I had a guest.

Focus. Focus, I told myself. *Focus.* My latest prototype comet kite hung above Annabelle, a filmy bowl of nylon. Its line was attached.

"Maybe there's a way we can salvage this," I managed to say. "Remember? We can work together to bolster Rock Point."

She shook her head, a genuine look of sadness in her eyes. "No, Emmy. I'm sorry."

Annabelle turned just enough that the scissors flashed to the side, then raised her hand, the blades pointed at my throat. As if I were watching a movie, I heard a terrific scream rise from my guts.

All at once, the back door's window shattered. At the same time, I flung my mug at Annabelle and pulled the line suspending the comet kite from the ceiling. It worked. The kite's fluttering body—the same flaw that kept it from catching the wind—enveloped her upper body.

As she batted at the kite's nylon tail, I grabbed for her

scissors, which had clunked to the floor. I knelt and her knee struck my side, but I managed to kick the scissors under the stove, fortuitously tripping Annabelle in the process.

The back door flew open, and I heard Jack running toward us. At last. On the floor, Annabelle had swatted away the kite, now in shreds, and reached for my ankles.

"You can't do this to Annabelle Black! You can't—" she yelled.

She shrieked when I grabbed one of her flailing wrists. Jack knelt and grabbed the other, and by silent agreement we drew them behind her. I tied her wrists with a lark's-head bridle knot—thank you, kite making—while Jack dialed 9-1-1.

Within moments, Frank pushed through the back door, the sheriff behind him.

And, Lord, was I tired.

AFTER TAKING JACK'S AND MY SHORT STATEMENTS, THE sheriff took Annabelle away in handcuffs, saying he'd come out to the house tomorrow with a detective.

"We can go?" Jack said.

"I'll get my bike," I said, although I didn't know how I'd manage to pedal. The Lassitude Tea now had completely replaced my waning adrenaline. My limbs felt like tree trunks, and my mouth was full of bark.

"You don't look like you're in any condition to ride. I'll drive you." Jack led me to his car down the block. It wasn't far, but I could barely walk. I leaned against his warm, strong body. Too bad the car wasn't a little farther away.

Once in the passenger seat, I slumped against the window. It was four in the morning; I was starving, drugged, and had nearly been murdered. This girl needed a nap.

I had a question, though, that I had to ask. "Why did you come back?"

"Huh?"

"Why did you come back to Strings Attached?" As soon as I asked, I realized that it could have waited. I was too tired to make sense of anything he might say.

Jack focused on backing out of his parking spot, and the delay added to my brain's further thickening.

"I wanted to ask you—" Jack was saying something, but I couldn't make out the words.

"Hmm?"

"Something something Saturday?" At least, that's what I thought he said.

"Saturday?" I mumbled.

"Yes, do you—?"

That's the last thing I heard before I fell asleep.

chapter thirty

A WEEK LATER, I WAS DOWN ON THE BEACH WITH THE latest prototype of the comet kite. I felt good about this one. The sheriff had taken away as evidence the pieces of the last comet kite I'd made. This one was bright orange, and I hoped its tail would soar to the side against the steely sky.

Bear trotted behind me, staying close since he knew Avery had packed a sandwich in my bag. It was so nice to have her home again. She'd lost weight while away, but Mom—with my blessing this time—had come early on to stay a few days, and she'd filled the refrigerator with casseroles. We'd even finally managed to drink the bottle of champagne I'd bought for Strings Attached's opening day.

I'd introduced Stella to my mother, and now Mom was digging up excuses for rides in the Corvette. More importantly, Stella and Avery had a long lunch together and planned another date for the coming week. They had both loved Miles. They had a lot to share.

With the knife, Frank's story, and Ace's confirmation that she was on the dock when Miles was killed, Annabelle had broken down and confessed to killing Miles, burning down his cabin, and trying to kill me. She'd already been indicted, and the judge had refused to set bail.

After a restorative night's sleep and several hours of questioning by the sheriff, I'd returned to Frank to apologize again. We'd settled our landlord-tenant relationship, but I had a feeling he'd be investing outside of Rock Point in the near future. Plus, I wasn't sure I'd ever forgive him for playing with Avery's feelings like he did. His involvement would come out in Annabelle's trial. Rock Point might lose a major investor, but I didn't think we'd be the worse for it. All in all, I knew he was a good man. I guess that greed can just get the best of us.

The kite was as wide as my arms' span, so I carefully set it flat, then lifted it above my head to let it catch the wind. It lifted, and straight, too.

"Emmy. I haven't seen you for a while." Jack ambled up, Bear leaping around him. "Hey, guy. Where's your ball?" Bear dropped his tennis ball at Jack's feet, and he threw it down the beach.

"I've been around. Just enjoying things being back to normal." Dang, Jack looked fine, the wind tousling his wavy hair and rippling his fleece pullover. I absently let out a bit more line on the kite. "Have you talked to Dave lately?" I said this more to have something to say than to learn the answer. After all, Dave was at the house practically every day now.

"Saw him last night. He's really happy with the new tour guide you hooked him up with. Says he's going to be able to add some new hikes and even another kayaking trip."

So Dave had hired Ron after all. I smiled. I hoped he'd bring Hannah by the shop soon. "That's great," I said, and let out more line.

"I wondered, would you like to take a few kites up to the lighthouse someday? The wind up there is great, and the view can't be beat." Jack's gray eyes locked with mine.

Was this some kind of kite-shop-owner business meeting—or a date?

Jack quickly added, "Or we could go see a movie or get dinner, if you'd rather."

I'm afraid I was smiling like an idiot. "I'd love to."

Bear ran back and deposited the tennis ball at Jack's feet again. I felt all warm inside, and it wasn't the quinoa casserole. Jack knelt to pick up the ball and pulled back his arm to throw. Then he dropped his arm.

"Would you look at that?" he said. I followed his line of sight high above the surf.

The comet kite hung in the sky like the evening star, clear and bright enough to make a wish upon.

Connect with Berkley Publishing Online!

For sneak peeks into the newest releases, news on all your favorite authors, book giveaways, and a central place to connect with fellow fans—

"Like" and follow Berkley Publishing!

facebook.com/BerkleyPub
twitter.com/BerkleyPub
instagram.com/BerkleyPub

1844